THE PUZZLE of A TWIN PARADOX

Ein .S & Watts

iUniverse®

THE PUZZLE OF A TWIN PARADOX

iUniverse books may be ordered through booksellers or by contacting:

iUniverse
1663 Liberty Drive
Bloomington, IN 47403
www.iuniverse.com
844-349-9409

ISBN: 978-1-6632-3499-5 (sc)
ISBN: 978-1-6632-3498-8 (e)

Library of Congress Control Number: 2022901319

Print information available on the last page.

iUniverse rev. date: 01/21/2022

Synopsis

Two young men; an Artist and an Author, began The Puzzle of A Twin Paradox by introducing their talents to one another. The Artist displayed his musical talents and The Author listened, but when The Author displayed his writing talents, the two individuals were absorbed into the story he wrote, which turned out to be the same story the readers were reading.

After being absorbed into the story, the two boys woke up in an underground library having no memory of who they were or how they got there. All they knew was that they looked alike, so they named one another and from then on they addressed each other as brother.

The two brother's, Seth and Aiden, climbed to the surface together and in the midday sun they found that they were supposedly on an empty island. They thoroughly searched the island for hours and eerily found no other signs of life.

Seth became bored during the searching process and requested a little entertainment from his brother, Aiden. Seeing that both boys were starting from a blank slate, Aiden said that he couldn't recap a tale because he knew no other story but the one they were living. However, to keep his brother's spirit up, he began to foreshadow the possibility of a boy that can weild lightning to fight against monsters. He titled the boy, an Alpha and he called the monsters, the Organisms.

The narrative that Aiden had began, kept his brother focused, happy, and entertained while they search for signs of life or an exit.

After the sun sat the two decided to rest on the beach and continue the next morning. But when the moon rose, the narrative showed signs of coming to life around the brothers when they were targetted by the terrifying Organisms.

Will they remember who they are in time to escape the story that trapped them inside of it? Or is it deeper than they think and they're not inside a story at all?

The List of Doors

(1oo:

Let's suppose that you were able,

every night,

to dream any dream you wanted to dream.

-And you would,

naturally as you began on this adventure of dreams,

you would fulfill all your wishes.

-You would have EVERY kind of pleasure that you could conceive.

-And after several nights,

you would say,

"Well, that was pretty great."

But now let's um,

let's have a surprise.

Let's have a dream which isn't under control.

Where something is gonna happen to me that
I don't know what it's going to be.

Then you would get more and more adventurous,

and you would make further and further out
gambles as to what you would dream.

And finally,

you would dream,

where you are now...

9oA

Door 01&18: To Begin in a New World

Seth's (POV) -q-

Zooming through a vacant space, my awareness awakened to the pressure of a motion so speedily. My hand is clasped onto another person's hand at my side. My sight ventured onto view a boy that traveled along with me.

"What if we die up here, taking an eternity to conclude with this wandering flight? From flesh to bones and from bones to dust, our cells could forever zoom around this globe in a fixed circulation." He stated as his vision wondered toward the light glow coming from below our travel.

My eyes looked to view what he meant, and immediately they widened. My iris shook as I gazed at a world we're arcing around.

"Whoa! I'm sorry. Don't be scared. I really frightened you with that thought, didn't I?" he asks, but I couldn't find my voice.

I am simply in disbelief that we're freely streaming across the highest point above the world. The planet is dark with honey topaz lights beaming like stars on the lands, outlining their separation from the seas of darkness. Its beauty is sparkling twinkling lights on a sleeping world.

"Is something wrong, brother? Your atmosphere feels refreshed."

"Brother? Is that who you are to me?" I asked, and his eyes developed agitation.

"Please tell me that this is just for a laugh. You truly know me, right?" He lingers on this question, waiting to calm himself if I say I do.

"I'm sorry, I don't. I actually don't know myself or why I'm here if that makes you feel any better," I made clear, attempting to ease his distress.

"It doesn't. Nice try though," his voice cracked, trying to hide his unexpected growing signs of sorrow. A second passed, and gravity dawned down on my flight, causing my sudden descend. His hold onto my hand moves to my wrist and turns into a grip.

"What's happening?!" I shouted with a racing heart.

"You're—" he tightens, adding his second hand and showing a struggle to hold me up. "You're slipping! Try to come back up to me." I tried as he asked, but my body wouldn't allow it.

"I— I can't! This force down feels impossible to fight against. Am I going to perish?!" I panicked toward the boy who seemed to know more.

"No, you won't! You'll be alright. I figured that you couldn't stop this. That was just me being selfish and hoping that our journey could avoid this gap. I wish we didn't have to risk falling lifetimes apart and fall at once, but the choice really isn't ours."

His strain to keep me up placed a high tension on his arms, his eyes showing no intentions of letting go.

His continued struggle ignited a fire in me that burned for him to, "Stop this! Neither of us is budging. Why continue to strain yourself? You're in pain by keeping me up, and it's burning my heart to watch. Let me go. If I knew you before, I don't know you now."

"You've forgotten me? How ridiculous of you to say when your heart is retorting to showing me how blind it isn't. Look around, brother, we're all we've got. Even before we shared equal halves of the same soul, you've always meant-" He paused in speech then closed his eyes.

Coming down from his hand onto mine was a sudden rush of golden aura. Upon touching me, my body floated, and my energy increased beyond what I could ever imagine.

"What is this feeling?" I needed to know.

"We've each inherited two percent of a Radiant Sun. I'm giving you half of what is mine, so now you'll be at three percent, and I'll keep the last one."

"Why?"

"In magnetism, two equal forces on the same side are likely to repel one another. But two equal forces on opposite sides are likely to attract at their center point, which isn't always good. So, to avoid using half of our lives before we come face to face in Vesica Piscis, I've given you more. Making us a larger to a smaller force will draw me into you sooner, brother. You just have to recognize me when I come."

"One percent is still smaller than the eyeball; it's the pupil. What if you encounter me and my shortsightedness of you causes an omission?"

"Then I'll wait until you're far away and wave to you," he exhaled as he finished his release of energy into me. "I'm sure you'll see my point then. However, it shouldn't come to that. Our paths are now even more intertwined since you now contain my other half that will call to me. If you embrace me as you've done before, we will untwine and become two for two again, circling each other's world as equals from then."

The lightweight that had come upon me ceased, and his arms strained again.

"I'm— I'm going to let you go now, brother."

"-Wait," I kept him holding on.

"What do I call you?"

"You named me 'The Core of Midnight', but you call me Midnight for short."

"I— I named you?" I asked him in shock.

My question followed the slip of my arm from his grip.

"No!" He cried out, unprepared to let me go.

He stretched down for me, and I reached up for him. Too far apart, we ultimately separated. I fell toward the planet while he continued in travel around it.

"Don't forget, okay?! I'll land after you, somewhere in your future!" he shouted, swiftly motioning across the air as I continued in my descend. "Find me!"

"I will, I promise!" I voiced, dusking down as his swift motion becomes lost to my sight.

I'm now wondering in my thoughts of him as I zoomed into the atmosphere of the world calling to me. Our voices match, yet somehow, I was present and aware enough to name him when he was born. It felt like we were equal in existing, so how would naming him be possible for me? I faced the planet I'm fated towards, adamant on wanting to know more.

I can see a bright spot in the ocean, shining through the night sea. I'm far from the ground, but every few seconds feels like a plus one in my accelerating fall. It took no time for me to become a meteorite blaze as my motion increased to a forceful speed.

A sudden concentration of blue flames surrounded me, feeling more comforting than threatening. It grew my speed from being that of a meteorite to that of a shooting star.

Bits of pieces of land clarified to being scattered across a region in the seas below me. My vision continuously adjusted still uncertain about whether I'll impact an island in this archipelago or plunge into the ocean surrounding it.

My eyes widened, and I began to panic at the fear of not knowing. As I passed through the lowest clouds, I became astonished by the bright lights coming from an island that's aligned with my fall.

The ground continued to shoot up to me, and now I'm seconds from impacting a building. If death is the outcome of my impact, I'm sorry for providing this civilization with a new body to clean up. I raise my hands to my eyes in defense against the shock, but intangibly I passed through the roof of the building without its touch.

In an endless rush through the ceiling levels, I could not stop falling.

If I can't touch anything, will this fall ever end?

As I fell through the final story, I'm vortexed into the core of a mother, whom from her womb, brought me into life as her final one.

<u>DOB:</u> ***(o1996-o5-o17th)***

8oB

Door 02&19: To End in a New World

Twenty-Two Years Later.

(-o2o18-o4-o2nd)

Romeo's (POV) -r-

"Bei, I like this already," I said, and he abruptly paused the track.

"C'mon, at least hear it all first," he requested.

"You're right. Silence, my bad. I'll listen fully and then make comments after, okay? Continue."

"How about I run the track back, and we start again with me," he suggests, and I'm returned to the flow of his music before his familiar voice begins to go,

OB-
Back off.
My mind's been racing like a Nascar.
I tried to give em what they asked for.
Last time you did, it was the last draw.
Take that mask off,"

FYF-
Take that mask off, yo homie you ain't certified.
You ain't never pulled off, and it still ain't right.
You ain't never had to struggle every day and night.
I was out here with the gang, wasn't doing right, yeah."

OB-
Do me a favor, too many frauds, too many liars, and too many haters.
Speaking to God, pouring my heart out cause I need a savior.
Clock in at work, I'm going all out cause I need this paper, I need this paper, yeah,"

FYF-
Yeah, all I wanted was disparity.
To see where this music would carry me.
If I blow or reign now, I wonder how many girls would marry me.
Wonder why no one was hearing me,
back when I was irrelevant.
Now they show a brother rubber rings,
treat a brother like a reigning king, yah!
I've just been feeling so faaaar.
Told myself, I don't know who you are.
Always thought that I'd end up a star,
Living laarge, ooh lala."

OB-
Back off-
My mind's been racing like a Nascar.
I tried to give em what they ask for.
Last time you did, it was the last draw.
Take that mask off, take that mask off."

The music begins to fade, and I remove the ending sound from my ears with excitement in my eyes for him.

"Faraway was an awesome song. I hear a star in you, Romer."

"You think so?"

"I felt so."

"Many people hear it and claim that I'm going places, but no elite has invested in my sound yet. You identified two voices on the track, right?"

"Yeah, I did. I could hear which one was you."

"Well, the other is a long-time friend from home, FYF Aaron. 'Faraway' is his creation, and I'm simply a featuring artist on it."

"Your addition was spot-on. You synced together nicely on that track. Trust me; you two are talented, and it's only going to get better from here."

"Thank you. Your support means a lot. But you know, art has been my passion from since I can remember. My love for it developed in my touch before my voice, which is why I love it more than singing. For some reason, when I sketch an image, I'm proud to give back to the world, the beauty that my eyes intake."

"I think that sketching or singing are both capable of giving you a strong recognition. The choice is ultimately up to what you feel you want."

"Profiting from any of my art is not only up to me but up to our nation as well. If I'm not selling their taste, then I'll only flop out."

"Tell me about it," I reacted to relating. "I'm glad you understand that, so you know what you have to do. Another smart thing would be to sell your art as your album covers."

"I thought about that too," Romer's quick to agree.

"Then do it. Believe that we'll all eventually see you, and someday we will. I mean, that's how I think. From my perspective, you have everything you need to mark yourself into history. Whether it's within our country or in the lands beyond, the world is your canvas to have fun with. The best thing you could do for yourself is to make your signature matter. You can then paint a dot that will sell for a lot because it'll have your name beside it."

"Interesting,"

Curious, I asked, "Why are you wasting your time in this place? You seem very smart."

"At BTVI?"

"Not the college itself but the subject you've chosen in it. You could've majored in one of your dominant talents."

"My dad is skilled in our HVAC major, and the curiosity in it rubbed off on me, I guess. Plus, it's business. Income is essential to survival in this world. My talents would do me more justice away from here than within it. All we have here to make ends meet is general labor. Besides that, without my father's impact on my life, I doubt I'd even be at this school right now."

"It doesn't matter. I bet we'd still meet. You are who you are, and in any reality, I bet I would take to your character because I am who I am."

"You think so? Yeah, you seem cool yourself. There aren't many people I've talked to who understand and relate to my struggle in this life."

"I feel you on that. It's always good to have a trade, and it's great if that trade is your dream. But if it's not, then I suggest using it to survive until you succeed in what'll fulfill you in life. That's what I'm doing, while I work on my art. You can be anything in the world, Romer, just never settle until you've lived."

"I won't do that for sure," he confidently replied then expressed a sudden thought. "You know you haven't talked about your art to me yet, right? Are you gonna show me anything, Romeo? It's only fair, bei."

I nearly showed a questioning expression when he called me Romeo and played it off with a laugh. I nearly forgot my own alias.

"Dang, it's my turn already?" I asked, still thinking about the mistake I almost made.

I'm still adjusting to being called Romeo because it's not the correct arrangements of the letters in my last name. For my college days I've decided to take on a more extroverted character, so I came up with the alias identity of *Victor Romeo.* I'm still me but hiding behind a character is like hiding behind a mask. It helps with my confidence by anonymously communicating my truth.

"I was just getting into your world, Romer, but alright, we'll focus on me for a bit," I said. I took my bag from the side of me and rested it in front of me. Then, taking my laptop from it, I placed it onto my lap. "You'll have to take in a lot of information to understand. Time is what's needed to appreciate my work," I noted.

"I don't think I have that much time," he responded. "But whatever it is, I'll try to be quick with it,"

I looked to my closed laptop and hesitated, never showing a soul before now. "I... I'm nervous. Wow," I paused with a surprised smile. "My talents are up and down along with my confidence. Sometimes I feel like I'm the best at what I do, and then other times, I feel like I'm not good enough. By the time my confidence rises again, I'd be slightly altered from the direction I wanted to carry my skills in. This is sometimes a blessing because it comes with a new light of ideas and information. Most times, it's a curse because it feels like I'm repeatedly beginning. You'll go further than me in life because you complete your creations, and I alternate from mine after a time."

"Nah, don't downgrade yourself like that. It sounds like you're just going in circles with minimal growth. If that's the case, take advantage of it. When you finish with a scene in your life, you should try connecting it to past events in hopes that it all comes back around to connecting to sense. If you can piece together your rise and falls, I think you'll realize that those shifting scenes will have created the appearance of one big scene. You'll then know understand the shaded past and the present light. One side will be known, and the other side would be-"

"-Midnight," my voice awakens to him. "You're telling me that Midnight's in my presence right now?"

Before I molded into the reality of this world's motioning growth, a vision of a boy existed with me before my present self. At first, I didn't know who I was when I was growing up, growing into my character through the traditions and beliefs of where and when I arose. Then, when I was an adolescent, memories awakened in my dreams of a time before my first breath of life. Then was when I became a whole new person, believing in the existence of The Core of Midnight.

"It's way too early for you to think that it's midnight," he looks a little lost as I came to realize I'd paused. "Listen, I don't know where you got midnight from, but you did say the answer at the end of your last question. One side will be known, and the other side would be now."

I laughed at myself when I realized that "I thought I heard Noon. Since we were talking about my talents going up and down, I started thinking about night and day."

"Oh, I can see why your mind arrived at that analogy."

"Don't worry, I understand you now." I finally opened up my work and began explaining that "Just like you, I'm more than one kind of artist. One of my talents consists of capturing realized art and making it a reference image to your eyes. The other, however, is a put-together that you can view in sound or silence. Silence has the highest compatibility to it since it's a compilation of many parts, silently understood." I searched through my files and came up with the result of a lifetime. I clicked it and turned the page to him. "Sound has the potential to bring confusion in this story if your eyes don't view the words themselves," I stated.

"ALPHAS Book One (Chapter 2: Play with Me?)" he read.

"Wait, what?" I turned the laptop back to me and immediately smiled, remembering when I first began it. "Oh, I see. It's the correct story, but a previous title."

"That looks like a novel. So, you're an artist of the mind is what you're saying?"

"Yup," I turned the laptop back to him, presenting the present title I just wrote.

"'The Puzzle of a Twin Paradox,' inspired by ***Ein.S and Watts,"*** he read. "There's no written by or created by on it."

"It's an anonymous creation."

"And you're the anonymous author of it, Romeo?"

"In the flesh," I acknowledged, his question rippling a thought that reminded me of the past.

I'm the seventh born and the last one, making me the baby in my family. In 2012, a potential surfaced in which my mother had conceived another child at middle age. I was finally going to be an older brother.

During her pregnancy, my parents shared a little history about them with me. They'd tried having a baby together once before in 1981, but my mum miscarried. This unexpected miracle of a second chance, thirty-one years later, was a blessing to them, and so they decided to give their baby boy his original name.

I was amazed by this heartfelt story. I was also honored to have a connection to such an ancient history at only fifteen and a half years old. But not long after, tragedy struck. My mother suffered her final loss that was highly impacting on our souls.

At the center of our shared pain, I witnessed their hearts break but remain whole for one another. Their eternal love without a legacy has somehow made me complete at their core, and I've stayed everlasting to this day.

After the death of two possible timelines, I grieved, beginning to question everything about life itself. And out of curiosity, I scoured my mind and unlocked a series of patterns. Those patterns later acted as a guiding compound to formulate future existences, A Twin Paradox being one.

These patterns initially began three and a half years ago, during an epiphany event. At the age of eighteen, I had an awakening vision of a time before my breath, providing me with some of the answers I sought. However, even more questions joined the party.

In the dream, I remember fragments of myself falling from the sky but also meeting a boy in the atmosphere just before that'd happened.

To piece the vision together, I've spent all this time writing anthological scripts and giving my flashes and patterns the actions of real life. From the few fictional stories that I've written from historical concepts and mathematical imaginations, I've deduced that this dream boy I seek has most likely already descended along with me

If he's already here in this world, his landing was probably as random as mine, making this dream nearly impossible to prove true.

I know his name, but I'm sure that it has changed from what it was in the dream. If, for instance, we're born separately, and genetics made up the markers of our present-day features, he'd look different from how I last saw him, and I'd look different from how he last saw me. Because of that, my only option is to feel him out.

I do, however, have a clue to keep me from searching through all ages. If I fell first, and he fell second, then I'm older than him.

"Bei, I've never met an author whose work I've read. Especially one who writes anonymously," he's excited. "Is this why you asked about the length of my time? You want me to read all of it?"

"Yeah," I nodded.

"I don't know how much time I have before my ride decides to come for me. How long's the story?" Romer asked.

"Too long, and it's uncompleted. No one's viewed it yet to tell me how long it takes to get through the incompletion."

"Oh, well, then I'll read it when it's done," he closed the laptop.

"It's been paused for a while, but I promise you, its limited completion is enjoyable. The center of the puzzle is thought provoking."

"Wait, 'paused for a while'? If the story's that epic, then what's taking you so long to finish it?"

"I haven't experienced it yet, the ending. I'm writing from my knowledge, and I don't know the rest of what happens until it happens. The story is of two individuals but is written from one side. I can only finish 'To Begin in a New World' to 'To Begin Again in a New World', eighteen chapters that I call doors. I'll need to find the protagonist of the story to finish 'To End Again in a New World', the nineteenth door. See, my exponent belief in my work is complemented by the use of Exponents, Multiplication, Division, Addition, and Subtraction to create an apparent circulation."

"The P.E.M.D.A.S theory?" he wondered, and I confirmed. "Wow, you added all of that into it. But wait, I didn't hear you say anything about the Parenthesis."

"And that's why it's unfinished. Parentheses are parents that bracket a circle, happening at the beginning and the ending with each other. Without the end, the story is just an open bracket following a circle with an illogical conclusion."

"It sounds like you believe that the theory is completed but at the same time, not."

"Precisely. Parenthesis should happen twice. (P.E.M.D.A.S.P) is what I think. This is done so that the position of 'Division' would be a center point and not after a centered line."

"Meaning?"

"If I into it any further, I'd lose you."

"I'm not one hundred percent following all that you're saying, but you're certainly making me think. Adding such a mathematical calculation to a story of the English language sounds like a syllogistic hell to create."

"It was actually fun for me, playing with numbers and letters to get the results I got. The story's conclusion derives from a formula of deductive reasoning that I've calculated to circulate my theory of 'If A, then A.'"

"This is going to frustrate me as I read it, isn't it?"

"I think so. But the second time you read it is when the magic of understanding will come in, bei."

"I want to read it really bad now," he developed an eager expression. "Hey, if you've done all that you can and require an individual to complete what you can't, then why not just go to them?"

"I-" I paused. "I don't know who they are, but I know that they exist in the world."

"How are you planning to finish this by finding a person you believe is real if they don't know you're looking for them?"

"Well," I awkwardly smiled. "I just told you, and I was willing to show you as well," I indicated the story.

He shook his head at my reaction and said, "This method makes no sense if you plan to approach hundreds of thousands individually, showing them your story one by one to find that one. What if the lost soul you're searching for isn't even in our nation?"

"You have a better idea?"

"Yes. Publish it, Bei. I believe if you do, whom you're searching for will personally find you. Once united, you can bracket close your circular story and republish it with the ending. A remastered pieced is just as cherished as its masterpiece since it clarifies with little change, the notable original."

"That makes sense."

"Of course, it does. I'm an artist too, so I know that you can't be shy when you're talking from your heart while the rest of the world listens. The one whom the message is for will receive it, while all others will receive nothing more than a labyrinth to decipher," he turns my laptop back to him and reopens the story. "The Puzzle of a Twin Paradox, huh?" he repeated the title with excitement. "Alright, let's get into this adventure. Maybe you'll get lucky, and I'll find a way to end it for you."

"Only the protagonist can end it., remember?"

"Then let's see if I qualify." he scrolled down from the title and began to view the beginning of the story. "'*My eyes bring into vision a boy longing for happiness and fulfillment in his sight.*'" he read aloud, then looked at me, saying, "Wow, that's a deep beginning."

"Come on, at least read it all first,"

"Right," he laughs catching onto my flashback. "You're right. Silence," he says. I stood up and placed a headset over his ears to shield him from outward sound.

A sudden vibration came from his cell, so he took a time out to answer it.

"Yeah, what's up?" he asks, then listens. "It's barely noon," he voices, then listens again, "I ain't ready yet so later is fine," I heard a girl speaking from the other end of the line but made nothing out. "I'll call you before dark falls," and the call ends.

"Your ride?"

"Yeah,"

"You have to go?"

"Nah, she'll come back around later. I'm glad it wasn't one of those evening classes. I'd have to go if it was."

"I know what you mean. At least in the daytime, the jitney them still running," I added.

"Yeah, bei. For real."

Now that he's staying, I'm excited that he has a chance to start and finish all I've written so far.

"Alright, I'll pretend like I'm not here, and you do the same," I suggested. "I've collected several orchestrated tracks for you to venture through my written world and not stop along the way to ask me questions. You'll have to read it twice since the first time will seem new and the second time will be a Deja Vu. You may not have the time for two viewings, so read this one carefully. I read many scenes while listening to a sick-ass piece of art called '*Ein Sof.*' It's the name of an album and its main track that came out on March 30th.

"Three days ago?"

"Yup. It was written by a musician who titles himself Arkana. The guy is a faceless mystery, but the feelings he casted throughout that album were a spiritual inspiration for me. I doubt it's your style of music, but you'll appreciate that there are no words to distract you. I'll start you off with my personal best song from that album, *'Ein Sof'* itself."

I started the sound, and his focus gradually absorbed into the C section of the puzzle before him.

7oC

<u>Door 03&10</u>: My First Incarnation, **At2**

Hello to the Puzzle.

Aiden the Second's (POV) -f-

My eyes bring into vision a boy longing for happiness and fulfillment in his sight.

"Why do you cry?" I asked, and his eyes trembled at the sight of me. Then, without answering he rushed over to me and hugged my bare body.

"Brother!" he shouted at the side of my ear. "I thought you were dead,"

I removed him from me, and in response to his assumption, I said, "I do not know who you are, but I think it was your crying that woke me up."

I knelt down and picked up The Tesseract World, checking on my reflections from all sides. My features are indeed a twin to his facial structure.

"It is very unusual that one can be so identical to another," I added.

"No, it isn't," he opposed. I turned to his pained expression at me as he continued to voice. "That core in your hand is my brother's heart. You just rose up out of it, so in some way, you're him."

He looked around and conveniently found an outfit sitting in the dirt. He laid the lot of them in front of me and told me to clothe myself while taking my world back from me.

In the process of dressing myself in an open space surrounded by a jungle in front of a mirrored me, my mind began to question what I am and what I mean to our present reality. This boy claimed that I am not the first me, so what am I, another generation?

He's holding my world in his hand with little knowledge of the care he must continue to show it. The Tesseract's transparency indicates its potential to shatter.

"When I tossed this," he turns the shine of it to me, explaining that "There was a huge shake of some sort upon it hitting the ground. Why did it cause the whole jungle to tremble for what felt like forever?"

"I see. So that's the cause of the anomaly that brought me to life. It seems like the tesseract's impact caused an island wide vibration which awakened me to you. I came out of the darkness because of your crying and the shaking of my world."

"I was looking for a clearer answer of why you're similar to my brother, not some spin around that I don't understand."

"To understand the meaning of me, you'll need to know who I am."

"Alright, I'm Seth. Now, tell me who you are, and I'll listen."

"I have no name, but strangely I have memories. To get you to make an attachment to me, I'll explain my connections to knowing and knowing's connections to my life around you. After which, what you do not know, you'll answer yourself when I explain the origination of why I'm present."

"Wow, just tell me of yourself so that I better comprehend all that you're babbling on about," he demanded, and I stood at his request. I took my world from his hand and hovered it before me. At the core of the Tesseract, a shockwave imploded a vortex light for the willing to be absorbed into.

"It must be viewed with individual eyes and not told aloud. To hear it alone will mislead you if you do not see it yourself." I extended my arm to him. "Come into my world and let me show you what you mean to me, Seth." He was hesitant, which makes this accurate to being our first encounter. "A time like this will come again for you to pull away then. You don't know enough now to refuse or to remember that I do not forget."

He steps toward me and takes a hold of my hand with a thought no more.

"Fine, show me the truth," he wanted.

Tightly he held to me as a force began to absorb us into the heart of the Tesseract. The vortex pulled us into its minuscule shine then flashed an icy light that repaired all visions of the coming future.

6oC

Door 04&10: My Second Incarnation, **At3**

Aiden the Third's (POV) -g-

A blur in my awakening eyes gasped a breath of life into me for me to exist once more. As my vision cleared, across from me my eyes sat a focus on a celestial lining light that's piercing the sky from the ground. My head tilted down to the base of it, witnessing the speeding motion of another wrong choice.

Upon realizing my repeated descend, I screamed, "Father!" across the air to the furthest end. It has to be what makes this end. And to no surprise, he went into it again. He hears me, but he never listens to my screams no matter what I say. He always leaves me to come back around and repeatedly try again.

I struggled my body to descend faster, but my hover down was forever slow.

My feet finally touched the ground, and I sped toward the light he'd just ran into. It's thinning away faster than the force of my motion and so I jumped to reach the slimming fishing line of it. Sadly, it vanished to the near touch of me, and I landed face flat into the dirt.

I sat up on my knees and "Aaaahh!" I screamed across the air, tired of being trapped ahead of what's coming back around.

The sudden sound of a metal pearl dropped into the dirt behind me. I looked back and noticed that it landed below the line of light that had just vanished. I shook my head while looking at it and thinking of the looping cycle that this power is causing. I stood to my feet and wiped my tears, then extended my arm toward the pearl.

It hovered up from the dirt and pulled straight into my palm like a magnetic connection then liquefied to a state of mercury. From my palm, it crawled up my arms and covered the surface of my body in an armored expansion that's sleek for mobility. After it covered my neck to my toes, I stood firm anticipating the beginning of the end.

I shook my head as I looked to the ground. Then, kneeling, I began to write out a numerical value in the dirt with high meaning to me. I stood to my feet and cried down at the '82.82' I'd carved.

"If it's not too late to say," I spoke to no one. "I'm sorry for accidentally cursing the world into a loop. It's repeated over eight thousand times already. Have I not been tortured long enough for you to set me free of this?" Then, after no response, my world began to unwind to the truth of what always came next.

A loud crackling came with a swoosh across the breaking sky. An inescapable descend of glassy debris suddenly rained after it broke. In a global fall from the point of my position, large portions of shards drew nearer to my vision.

My mind tensed a flashing thought to survive, hastening an instinctive reaction from my body to drive. Dashing across space, I'm cautious not to run in vain. I jumped to a lightened area but noticed that it was thinning all around me. Above me, two shards are on a collision course as they fall, and I've lost the time to move around.

I squat down to focus a concentrated flow of energy through my legs. I looked to the moonlit night and leaped a sinking push to a successful height. The shards crashed into each other before I could pass. Instinctively, I extended the steel absorbed upon my body to cover my face. I drove through the shards so fast that I tore a hole through their blockage.

In the presence of a clear sky and the full moon, I'm at a distance in an instant. From above I watched the shards smash the island and break into smaller pieces on this land below me.

My ears twitched and bounced my eyes to the direction of a sudden whispering beginning in the distance. The sound grew in closeness and multitude producing in me an adrenal of fear.

My upwind stops and now I'm coming down. What's waiting for me on the are those things I do not wish to face. I landed upright and onto my feet, sinking a circular ripple at the base of me.

The whisperings never stopped. In fact, it's gotten louder, as though what's coming is right next to me. I kept my instincts sharp on the jungle as I waited upon this mass of broken shards. A sudden icy air exited my lungs, indicating that the temperature is dropping. A dark cloud suddenly hid my position and my vision from the moon then the whisperings abruptly stopped.

As the cloud passed and the moonlight returned, I was startled to see that one of them was fixed to my eyes and standing in front of me.

"Play with me?" It begged and smiled with its beautiful feminine face.

At first glance, its facial beauty felt so trustworthy, until my pupils dilated, and I saw its body from the neck down. The slight shift of my eyes to look at all of it caused its cheek to split and its jaws to drop.

With its tongue wagging out, it screamed, "Look at Me!" In an innocent cry out.

It then launched itself at me and swung its arm to strike my face. I ducked while stepping in with a balled fist and punching its stomach. The pressure from my force pushed it back toward the jungle as it slid on the ground to come to a stop.

Seconds after its landing, the whispers began again and brought a horde of them from the jungle. The whispers grew louder and extended to a surrounding sound they drew nearer.

At a distance, they all coordinately stopped and so did their whispering. This gave me a moment to observe them and the question mark of them existing.

Their bodies are slouched and they're crouching to walk on their knuckle. In that position their heights are six feet or more. When one of them stood straight up to attack me moments ago, it felt like a giant to me. Their bodies are slinky, and their skin are as pale as corpses.

The silence in their stop lasted only a few seconds as a rush from straight ahead commenced toward me. The pilot of a few initiated the drive of them all toward my demise.

I rewind the steel from covering my face and at the top of my lungs, I roared at those leading the horde to, "Stay away!"

A sonic boom circularly repelled an outward blast from my voice that pushed away all those in front of me, clearing a path. Those I'd missed and those from behind are still hastily coming for me. If I did something more than that it'd become a blood bath in this area.

"You just won't listen, will you?!" I shouted at their onslaught. "This is why many of you have died by my hands countless of times!" I recalled the rewinds. "You just don't know how to stay in your place and not invade my space in this ending race!" I say, then blinked quickly to the negativity that's building up in me from other timeline versions of myself. "N-no!" I shook my head, refusing to become the repeated demonstration of absolute power against them. "You will all only waste my time which means the brightest solution I'll ever have is," I knelt on a knee and boosted myself from the ground, "to completely avoid you all."

As I moved across the sky to distance myself, I watched them come together at the center of where I stood.

At a distance, I landed and made a vast sound when I impacted the ground. Immediately, I quickened my legs to beyond human speed and instinctively rushed through the jungle to further my escape.

It wasn't always like this that I'd kill them for no reason. In the first few loops I did it to wait in the same spot for my father to come back, but he never does. Eventually, after hundreds of loops had passed, I began wiping out their lives in frustration due to the annoyance of my continued circulation. The cycle would end at every sunrise and begin again with me screaming for him to stop.

After thousands of tries, I became bored and eventually started to use each of the loops to find a way to escape this world. It was only a hypothetical thought, but my search led me to finding an exit.

However, I still can't seem to stop my father from vanishing into that celestial line. I'm either useless or it's fate that we must divide, since I'm the cause of the loop. Once I leave this world, I'm hoping that time continues to grow like it used to.

As I fled through the jungle, the whispers from earlier suddenly resurfaced from behind me. They're catching up to my speed, their whispers growing louder and louder. When their whispers abruptly stopped again, one surpassed my rush and appeared directly in front of me. I halted my stop, and when I did, my eyes were already connected to the one in front of me.

"Play with me?" It asked in an innocently childish voice. This creature even has the face of a small child, but its body is the same as all the others. With my eyes locked, the crowd of them surround me.

"Why is it always a game you want from me?" I asked keeping my stare this time. Without response its body began to restructure as my soul shook in fear. It twisted its waist to shatter its spine, breaking its bones to restructure itself. The skin on its abdomen slits, spewing guts, and veining lines.

My stomach hurled at the sight of this as my vision blurred due to blood filling my eyes. If I wipe it clear, the slight second my eyes evade, this beast will come after me. However, if I don't clear them, my sight will silence to the point where I cannot see anyway. By losing my vision, they'll undoubtedly come my way. I know not their intentions, but to do nothing now means that I'd be giving my life away. I blinked by accident but reopened my eyes quickly, my pupils now viewing through a cherry red sea.

"Look at Me!!" Its body launched at my head, not accepting the sight of my eyes where they now see red.

Once more, the pilot of one led to the launch of all that stood around. With a racing heart, my steel armor rose to shield my face and again covered me in a full-body concealment. Off-balance, they shoved me, my back hitting against the ground as their jaws and claws try to puncture into my protected body.

As I'm covered in darkness because of their pile on me, a pair of glowing eyes appeared and pulled me toward a stare. The sudden sound of cracking joints revealed its body to be restructuring upon me. I shut my eyes immediately, knowing that I'm trapped, and that if I don't hurt them, I will remain as such. In an instant I reopened my eyes and stared straight into the gaze that's calling to my own.

In all my trials, keeping an eye-to-eye connection was the only choice I haven't made yet. I'd always hurt them to get what and where I wanted to but the thought of doing what they asked always evaded me.

The restructure of the being whose eyes are locked to mine continues in its sound transmutation, I felt, my vision still unable to see anything but the creature's unwavering eyes. When I suddenly felt a dizzy pull from my awareness, I abruptly shut my eyes again. In a terrifying conclusion, my eyes uncontrollably shook back open, and it forced me to continue my stare.

"Stop! Let me go! I don't want to play anymore!" I cried, feeling the essence of myself rip away. Then, a fade of my soul commenced and into the life of darkness, I'm all consumed.

The genesis of my becoming faded away with the mother of love and hate, leaving me without a care in my heart. A growing desire to destroy everything began to conquer the purity of my misguided life. Ultimately, I was transformed into a steel destroyer capable of putting an end to this world.

5oC

<u>**Door 05&17:**</u> My Third Incarnation, **At4**

Aiden The Fourth's (POV) -n-

When my spirit awakened at the touch of an icy atmosphere, my legs immediately wobbled, and my stance was lost. I fell toward an icy ground, but as it happened, I'm caught in the arms of an appearing figure.

"Catch yourself," he said, in a tone so rough his depth could not be mistaken to be anything else but a man. "Are you truly a living person? Wow, what a twist." He remarked.

While wiggling my fingers and toes to test my sudden repossession of my cerebral awareness, my eyes instantly sorrowed. Tears of life released from me as I know I'm now freed from that abyssal control.

I looked up to his eyes and in view of the first man I've ever seen through mine, "I thank you. Thank you so much for freeing me from the darkness that my nature had become."

"You're most welcome," he said, smiling down at my face. He lifted me up to stand on my own again. "I thank you as well for teaching me something," he added while stepping back.

"Me?"

"Yes. Thanks to you, I now know that tolerance determines the victor of the creature's game. I was curious about why you were and why you played, so I kept going. And now I know the truth."

"You're stronger than me to be able to hold an eye-to-eye connection with those Organisms."

"Organisms?"

"Yes, that's what they're called. I tried to keep an eye-to-eye with them once and failed by pulling away. I guess since I couldn't tolerate their being, I became one of them just the same. As an Organism, I had no control over my body, but my mind was still present, prisoned to watch the destruction I was causing out of my control.

"Wait, that's what happened? You were once a mortal consumed by the ways of those Organisms? To watch all of that must've been torture. You must know that none of what you did is your fault. You were infected by a black parasite that came out of you."

"It was quite torturous indeed, but I do not hold heavy blame on myself. However, it was not only me that was once alive before," I corrected, now more apparent. "When I shared the fate of the Organisms, it expanded me across a collective consciousness and to the minds of every human whose body is infected. A world of flames is where I resided with them, a place too hot to survive. The thick air chokes your lungs, the steam melts your flesh, and the fire cremates what remains. However, after we died, we'd come back, and it'd repeat. It was painful every time it happened, and having a mental connection enhanced our physical suffering. Even so, I would still get a glimpse of what my body was doing while my mind was being tortured," my eyes drifted to the thought.

"Wow. I can't believe that all of that is happening inside of them, and that it happened inside of you too."

"Now you're understanding why I'm giving you my full level of appreciation. You saved my whole soul."

My body suddenly lightened in weight as my feet lifted away from the touch of the icy ground. A golden aura abruptly surrounded me as the shimmering release of its unknown energy spiraled a flow of wind around me.

"What's this?" The man reacted to my sudden rise. "Where are you going? I have more questions."

"Something beyond my will to resist is doing this. I don't know what's happening or what's going to happen next. Say what you must now in case there's no later for us."

"Well, since you know yourself now, I was wondering who exactly have I saved? Let's keep it simple, so that I remember something about you. What's your name?"

I shrugged at him while saying, "I'm sorry, but I was never given one. As I was being born to my father I was given to, he was simultaneously running toward a celestial line that would loop time into a circle. When I came into life, I screamed 'father' out to him before he left, and he still left. He caused me to enter a loop that I've lived over Eight Thousand times up to now. This present scene with you and I is the first new extension of knowledge I've had in a long time."

"I'm sorry. All I really understood was that you don't have a name. See, that's not going to work for my memory," the man said then disappeared from where he stood and reappeared in my face at a lightning speed.

Dancing around him are sparks of golden lightning that's identical to the light aura around me.

He unstrapped a glass plate from around his wrist and said, "Here, give me your arm."

"What is this?" I asked, allowing him to strap it onto me.

"It calls itself an Arcana. It has a mechanical voice that read me when I first became aware of myself. It scanned me as being unknown, and I thought that maybe it was searching for an identity."

"Wait, you don't have a name either?" I asked as a light on the glass reflects my eyes, and a sharp sting punctures the inner part of my wrist.

The pain caused me to scream as my hand shook. He held my shoulders with a surprised look in his eyes.

"I'm sorry!" He panicked as I calmed down. "Are you alright?"

The reflection upon the glass started a percentage growth as a mundane automated voice appeared saying, "Now Configuring."

"I'm— I'm fine," I tried speaking smoothly as the pain passed by.

"I'm sorry, I didn't know it would hurt you like that."

"You did it with honest intentions; I can't blame you. If this short period of pain gives me a name, then I don't mind it at all."

The pain completely vanished, and when it did, an accumulation of energy rushes through me. The golden aura surrounding me begins to move up my spine and releases a burst of wind from the area of my vertebrates. In an arc apart, the golden aura grows to mimic the arms of flight.

"Whoa, you're radiant! As brilliant as you are, are you sure you're a human? If I tried to chase you now, I bet I'd fail. I'm lightning, but you're appearing to become light itself."

"That means whatever's doing this will pull me away just as quickly. I don't have many things to ask of you, but one. You have a strength in your eyes, a power of conversion that can eradicate these parasites. Free this land and gift this civilization back their minds like you've gifted me mine. If you do, some native will then reveal to you the truth behind their lost history, and maybe even the origins of the Organisms."

"That's a vast mission and I can understand why you've asked me. I'm probably the only one that knows to request an Organism's consciousness return after winning. So, I promise you, I'll do my best to save them."

"Your best is all I ask for," I smiled while opening the palm of my hand. The steel armor upon my body began to liquify and crawl toward my palm, removing itself from me and forming into a sphere ball. "I bet you didn't know that my armor was once just a pearl."

"I- I had no idea," he looked at it with widened eyes.

"You gave me a gift so I'm giving you one back. This pearl can reshape itself into anything your mind can conceive," I explained.

I split the sphere into two circles then made them thin and arc into bracelets.

"Give me your arms," I asked, and the man extended to me. I strapped the bracelets around each of his wrists and said, "Those probably have more power in them than I know. Use them to assist you in saving this world."

"Thank you. I will."

"You also claimed you have no identity as well. Since this machine on my wrist cannot read you, can I?"

"You want to give me a name too?" he asked, and I confirmed. "I would be honored, and it would make remembering you as easy as where I got my name from."

"Then it's agreed. For being the beginning of change toward making a peaceful paradise, and being the first man to my eyes, I will call you Adam."

"Adam?" he questioned while nodding and smiling. "It's simple, and I think that's great. I'm someone because of you, and you still have no identity to me. Is it fair to ask if I can give you a name too?"

"I have the arcana you gave me, remember?" I raised my wrist to remind him.

"Right, but what if it doesn't find you a name like it didn't find me one?"

"That's a fair possibility. Alright, give me a name to be called by and I'll answer to it."

"Well, you appear to be ethereal through my present eyes on you. Three precious things come to my mind as you glimmer, glow, and grow power in front of me. I see an angel, a diamond, and a rose. For those meanings, I'll remember you by the name, Andy Rose,"

I smiled at the gift he'd bestowed, loving the meaning behind my name. I honored him with one name, and he returned that honor by granting me three names appearing as two.

"The two of us can finally introduce ourselves," he said extending his hand out. I reached forward and we locked arms as he continued with, "My name is Adam."

"Nice to meet you, Adam," I grinned at how fast we've made ourselves know. "I'm—"

—an energetic thrust pulled me away from responding. This wind took me straight up into the sky and when I course shift, I pocket across the sky.

I thought I heard Adam shout something to me, so I replied, "You keep safe as well," And my journey resumed after wishing him farewell.

Adam had caring eyes, providing me a peace of mind about leaving this world behind. The story is safe in his hands. Enough has been created for any creator to leave their creation behind.

I continued to sonic above the sky of the rising sun, my energy taking me to an undetermined destination. Wherever I'm going, I wish to be at peace with the ones I love.

A tug downed on me, indicating a sudden shift in motion. From a horizontal extension to a vertical drop, below revealed my destination. Drawing toward the seas with my face against the wind, I noticed a vortex spiraling in the ocean. I was pressured down into it and right away there was a blank space of darkness all around me.

As I continued to be taken down by this force, a twinkling of stars began to sparkle in the darkness and quickly grew into a remarkable resemblance to a galaxy. With that thought, a gasp for my breath commenced as the air thinned into a vacant space.

My consciousness drifts as my temperature drops in my fight to breathe or I will die. A sudden gasp over my lungs shakes me to life inside of space. My pupils shrink at the sight of my body shining a golden light to carry me through. The energy that was acting as my flight has reformed itself around my entire body. This energy that's pulling me through this has acted as wings and now an armor. Wherever I'm being taken to, I'm wanted there alive.

Moments after being able to breathe, a black center that's outlined by a white ring appears below my fall. A white line from the ring is passing through the center and connecting to the other side, making two halves of a black core.

The white line is greatly expanding as I'm falling closer to it, and then suddenly a star appeared in my path. Flames of a small blue sun became visibly clear as I'm rushing in at a speed I can't command.

At a closer range my eyes found out a shocking truth. An individual appears to be encased within this blue sun. My attempts to try to slow myself down or change my course had all failed.

This is bad. The only thing left that I could do for a slim chance to alter this fated collision, is to shout, "Get out of the way!" I voiced my presence.

This must work. Their falling at a slower rate than me, so my collision into them will surely bring about our demise. When two pairs of eyes looked up at me, I gasped at how wrong I was and how close I am to them.

At the imminent point of our impact, I braced myself with raised arms. A tight grip on my ankles after I smashed into nothing, opened my eyes to immediate question marks.

I looked back at the feel of hands, and immediately the blue flames from one of them casted onto me and then extended to the other. As it casted onto me, my golden light vanished, and I became a part of their circle.

At my speed, I arrowhead the three of us traveling in one Sun. Since the force vanished before I got to the ring, this must be where I'm supposed to be, but why?

"I— I can't believe that worked. It all happened in the exact way you described it. How'd you know so confidently that we'd make it?" the flaming boy voiced in a familiar tone, and I couldn't help but stare at him.

"It's because it's our destiny," the other boy said, sounding like his voice was the same as the one who just spoke. I looked at him and instantly couldn't comprehend why there's a double of them.

"Midnight?" the flaming boy questions to me. I look at him, and right away, I knew that everyone here was confused. "How-"

"—That's not me. I'm right here. This is me, brother."

"Brother?" I questioned to them, having a familiar feeling behind their characters to one another. "By any chance, are either one of you called Seth?" I asked with hope.

"I am, and who exactly are you?" the flaming boy wondered, and my eyes filled with tears as I began to connect the dots.

I look to the other boy, Midnight, and asks, "And you? He calls you brother, but Seth's brother is not called Midnight."

"I gave him a new name," Seth spoke up. "How do you know this?"

"Well, if you want to know," Midnight began. "You and I are Physically one in the same. However, our minds are not on the same level of knowledge. I'm from one loop in the future but I am not you. I am your father."

"What?" I questioned at how.

"Wait, this is your incarnation? This is your son?" Seth asked him.

"Ours, yes." Midnight corrected him then turned his attention to me. "In the future loop, my soul returned to life by entering your body after you gave up on living in circles. Brother and my memory of one another are in sync with our beginning. However, your knowledge of who we are is only in sync with the moment of your creation. You may see us as your parents, but he and I see each other as kins forever."

"I—I have to process all of that," I reacted.

I'm meeting my primordial and my first father at the same time, how? Seth, my first father should be a probability to meet since he was trapped in the loop with me and still alive, but not his brother, Aiden. Aiden, my primordial father, died and I became his second incarnation so he shouldn't be here. Even if our bodies are the same with different minds, it's incomprehensible how we're both in the same reality at the same time.

"Wait, you said that you're from the future. That means that I'm the past version of you, so how are we both present?"

"I—I think that's how. The Present is the center of the Past and the Future. We can only be together right now but will have to separate soon."

"Oh, no!" Seth gasped with his view beyond me. "It looks like we'll have to postpone this topic. We're closing in!"

We're moments from passing into the white ring and to beyond not knowing what's next. Yet, I'm still baffled about what's going on right now.

"I'm afraid there's no cutting this short. Only two of us are going to make it through the blackhole," Midnight said, and I looked back at him with a racing heart.

"What do you mean 'only two'?" both Seth and I asked.

"When we enter, brother and I will pass through, but you'll have to loop around again. I remember the memories of when you did this before, and that is what happened."

"What?! No! Why?!"

"I wish there was a way to bring you along. As you are now, your mind is beautiful and pure. You feel extremely precious to existence, but I'm afraid that that's what's going to happen."

"I don't want to repeat this life, I want to come with you two. Is there a law that says I must not variate?" Tears built into my eyes as I strain left and right to look back at them both. "You're my fathers, aren't you? Save me, please."

"I'm sorry, but I don't know how. Even if I did, I don't think I'm supposed to, or I will not be made, and my brother will not be saved."

"I—I don't understand," I shook my head at his lack of consideration.

"You'll understand why when you're saying the same words that I am. We appear to be out of time."

I looked forward, and the black core appears to be gone by how close we are to it.

"Ironically, I'm fully aware of this situation, but it still stands that the three of us are clueless about what's on the other side of this black circle. All of us will now enter its darkness; one will come back around and two will move toward the unknown. This is how it always ends." He voiced behind me.

"I— I don't want to come back here! I want to come with the two of you!" I begged.

"You'll live to come again. You'll live to remember who you are and how you became me and then you will come through. Nothing can be changed, it's our fate."

Angered by his lack of care, I yelled, "You're not even trying! If me becoming you is me becoming heartless, then I never want to be you. I will change my fate and become better than you. If I become you, and I must make this choice again, I'll break fate and let my son through!"

We impacted the unknown blank and darkness engulfed us. Their grip on me vanished into smoke, and I was left all alone again. The loneliness consumed the remaining light within me, my breathing becoming impossible to keep.

As I lose consciousness, a beeping makes a sound from my hand and an automated voice echoed, *"Configuration complete. Welcome to the Arcana system, Aiden, the fourth."* I gasped to hearing my name is what I knew it could be.

After a knowledgeable reveal, my senses vanished entirely, and I'm reverted to a stillness mimicking death. In this blankness of a beginning recycle brings forward a cold reminder of a trial to live a repeating moment in life.

I don't want to relive this cycle again. I'm tired of looping around this one day, and just want a break. If anything beyond is listening to my heart, please allow me to remain gone this time or I will disrespect the gift of life by beginning to repeatedly take mine. This Eight Thousand Two Hundred Eighty-Second loop will be my last time trying. Farewell to the world.

4oC

Door 06&10: Entering My World

Third Person (Point of View) -a-

"Keep safe, Andy Rose!" The light brown eyes of a boy burst awake, and his body quickly jolted up. He abruptly sat up inside the vessel of a Slicer and found his vision directly planted onto a young man. "Wait, don't I know you?" he gained an odd expression as he suggests to the young man before him.

"Was that a dream just now?" Asked a young lady as she rushed to interrupt them. She lifted the boy to his feet by his shirt in a haste for an answer. "Well?!"

"I think it was," the boy responded, and her grip loosened with a thought. Her comrade who was facing the boy stood to his feet, and they both curiously continued to stare at him.

"He has to be lying," Another young man voiced from the front of the Slicer. "No one has dreams." he shared his opinion, sitting and wrapping up a leg wound.

The young lady looked his way and told him to, "Quickly fix yourself up and get back to navigating, Zaheem. I'll handle this." She then turned her attention to her comrade beside her and asked, "Who's this boy, Cole? He claims he knows you."

"We're meeting him at the same time, Eva. He's a stranger to us both," her comrade ends her questioning of the boy's awareness of him. "However, he's quite adamant in his surety and fixation on my features, so he must know something that I don't," he added as the belief in the boy's eyes is unchanging in his stare at him."

"I think I've seen you before, I swear." The boy continued to testify as he inched towards Cole. "You feel very familiar to me."

"Back up. I don't know you, kid."

"Alright," Eva stepped in between their tongue. "Someone's lying here." Her eyes glowed a wild nature as she looks at them both. "The truth betters do not lead to the existence of an alias, or we could have a traitor on our hands."

Eva loosened a reflective glass from her wrist and removed it, leaving behind a dotted blood stain on the skin of her inner wrist.

"You're doubting me? This is madness. Zohar, tell her!" Cole turned his focus to their comrade who's still sitting at the front and watching the scenario play out.

"Sorry, brahman. I can't help you with this one," he responded.

Eva extended her reflector to the boy and said, "Strap this arcana around your wrist."

The boy looked at her slim but athletic bodily features as he took a hold of it.

Shaking his head he responded, "I don't know how to use this."

"It'll configure itself to you. But forget about the technical use of it," Eva said, taking it back from him and strapping it around him herself. "It will tell us your name and monitor your heart rate as we ask you some questions. I only need it to work as a lie detector for right now."

After strapping the arcana around his wrist, Eva turned the face of it up and tapped an awakening button on the reflector glass while gazing into his eyes.

"I'm sorry. This is going to hurt a bit," she apologized.

"What?!" his eyes widened. A needle released from the inner wrist of the watch as it tightened itself onto the boy. "Aaaaah!" he screamed. Veins awakened on his arms and became visibly noticeable. They visually crawled up his arm and extended throughout his entire body. After completely consumed, an electrifying glow awakened beneath his veins as he continued syncing with the mystery upon his wrist. Suddenly he dropped to the floor and started wildly rolling over. His hands spasmed in unpredictable movements as the configuration tenses the muscular form of his small body.

Eva jumped onto him and pins one side of him down, containing his exaggeration of pain.

"Cole!" she called to her comrade, and his stare turns to a nod as he assisted her in pinning down the other side of the boy.

Cole's eyes are widened while looking at Eva.

"You never suspected me?" he questioned, awakened to the truth.

"Of course not. We're friends." she responded. "This boy, however, is a blank slate. He doesn't even have evidence of a mark on his wrist from the use of an Arcana. The boy also appears to be able to dream, something foreign to us. He recognizes you, yet he came out of nowhere. This whole situation is one big puzzle to me." she looked down at his eyes that are tightly shut.

The boy's eyes burst open as his brown iris sparked into a blue of the sky and formed a lightning dance around it. An abrupt release of a transparent plasma wave pushed Cole, Eva, and every object away from the boy. Cole slid along the Slicer's floor, which became unstable during the ripple of a current unseen. Eva twirled through the small space and steadied her stance on the Slicer's tilted wall as it angled to the side.

Zaheem rushed himself into his piloting seat, turned off the autopilot and quickly steered the flight under his control, restoring a leveled balance inside the Slicer's body. Both Cole and Eva looked at the boy right away and were relieved to see that he's resting again.

"He's calm now." Eva said while walking to him and kneeling to tap his cheeks. "It looks like we'll have to wait for him to wake up again to question him," she sighed.

"At this rate, we'll never get anything out of him." Zaheem shouted to his comrades he's transporting in the belly of the Slicer.

"It's okay." Cole said. "We have time to discuss what we learned from him already. He called to a name when he awakened a moment ago."

"That's right, Andy Rose," Eva repeated.

"Do you think it's his name?" Zaheem questioned.

"Not based on the tone he used it in. He doesn't seem to know his name but dreams of calling out to another."

"We don't know yet that it was a true dream or that the name can't be his. But sure enough, the mysteries of this boy are stacking up by the second. For now, we can only speculate. We'll get our answers when he wakes," Eva ended the discussion.

Cole stared down at his features with foreign eyes, still wondering what it could be that the boy thinks he knows about him.

"I swear I don't know him, this lightning boy. I felt like a scoundrel just now, holding him down to place a mystery on his wrist. I could feel his fear of us committing our violent act to know more."

"We can't be soft in this beginning stage. We have to make sure this boy's legit before bringing him onto our island."

"Eva's right, Cole. These are necessary difficult decisions," Zaheem agreed, placing the machinery on autopilot and testing the strength of his injured thigh. "We're not bad people, but while outside of the village's barrier, we must be ruthless to the unknown until we know for sure that we should show our kindness," he advised.

"I know that."

Cole moved to a stationed desk and pulled a pad from his pocket.

"I'm going to try to keep some notes on him. The bonding process with the arcana was tough on his body and I'm thinking it might be because of his recent dose of adrenaline but still unsure."

Not long ago, this group of three rescued the sleeping boy from a high rise abandoned hospital. They were salvaging for supplies when they discovered a naive young boy ignoring all signs of an infested darkness. When faced with the Organisms, he somehow managed to lock himself in the hospital's medicine room. He was lucky enough to find an adrenaline bottle he could use as an alternative solution. A Beta would hypothetically gain an energy boost from a small dose, but a natural Alpha appears to temporarily manifest their stored power. It turned out that after the boy took the adrenaline, his manifested capabilities pierced a lightning strike through the clouds from his body. It was then when he beamed bright the night sky that they learned he was an Alpha.

"Knowing that an adrenaline shot could boost us like that is valuable to the enhancements of our Alphacardia and our stance against the Organisms infestation," Eva summed up. "Way to think ahead, Cole. Keep it up." She nodded to him then turned her attention to the pilot. "How long until we return, Zaheem?" she asked.

Zaheem placed himself back into the piloting position and tracked the areal coordinates of their airborne location. "About 70 minutes," he responded. Eva walked to his side and viewed the machinery's operating system. "See, the island's northern borders are straight ahead. It's 20 minutes away, so once we make the L turn, we'll have roughly 50 minutes remaining before we see our side."

"When we're in proximity-"

"-I know, Eva," he cuts her off. "I am to turn off the automatic piloting, angle off to the southern direction, and fly along Androsia's edge. After which, I am to remain 50ft above shallow water until we enter the barrier of the village."

"Get us there safely; you know what to do." She said, preparing to leave him to focus.

"I do know, but do you?" He asked, shifting her attention back to him.

"What do you mean?"

"I think you should tie him up," Zaheem said, in concern of the unconscious young boy.

"You fear him that much?" Eva smiled at the unease in his tone. "It's okay, Zaheem. I can handle it if something happens."

"That's not my worry. That boy awakened convinced of his truth. He convinced himself so much that we couldn't believe him to know why he knew what he did. I think that you should tie him up for the drug still in his veins, the fear in his heart, and the manifestation of what he can do."

Eva squinted to Zaheem and mildly considered his words of warning. Suddenly, the sound of an arcana wildly beeped and widened Eva's eyes. The voice of Cole gripping to her name puts into play Zaheem's words foreseen.

3oC

Door 07: My Brother and Me

Aiden The First (POV) -b-

"Let me guess. The lightning boy woke up again" brother figured, and I smiled at his assumption of it all.

"Something woke up," I remarked.

"So, you're not going to tell me, Aiden?"

"I'll continue to tell the narrative later," I said while looking at the fading sky and the Sun setting on the sea's edge. "It's getting dark, brother. The first day is ending."

"Another will come again," brother said, sounding sure. "We may not know anything about this place as yet, but I'm sure that daylight happens more than once."

A few hours ago, brother and I woke up in an underground shed in the jungle. There was the first time we met each other and became aware of ourselves. Even so, we both knew somehow that we were one to one another.

We have matching tattoos on our arms, and our structures are so identical that we could be the same person. Our skin is even one in the same shade, so either I'm twice in existence or I'm his kin.

After solving that mystery of our appearance, we began to work together to rise above the ground.

Emerging into this world without knowing why and how we got here, we marked our entrance position, and began to search for an exit.

We discovered trees in this jungle that took brother and me up to seven steps to get past and more than twenty steps to get around. They're flourishing in an area that seems to have been civilized once.

The only homes we've stumbled upon are homes close to the shorelines, seeming to be ancient in creation. The stones they're made from can quickly turn to dust with a decisive blow from a storm. I'm guessing those that are still standing are the results of the overgrown jungle. For nature to grow this big, this land had to have lived undisturbed for hundreds of years.

We finally found an exit from the jungle but not from the world. The edge of the land expanded from a low sea to a deep ocean. After traveling the shorelines, we summed this place up to being an island. The smooth sands of a beach ceased in our search, leading us onto rocks so sharp that they're shredding the soles of our footwear. Brother tasted the water, and it's saltier than the air itself. The edge of the beginning is a beautiful green that I've never seen. The further the seas extend, the deeper it went into blue. Then, into the void of a star-filled space, it led out to black.

We're investigating an ancient world in hopes of finding something to set us free. Unfortunately, hope is not looking so good right now.

During our exploration, brother became bored by the silence and requested a narrative be told. Neither of us know any more than the names we've granted to one another, so I couldn't reflect on any history. While continuing our search, I thought to animate a false possibility to keep our minds occupied during this pursuit of our lives. From then to now, I've voiced to my brother a chapter-long imagination, and we've still found nothing help yet.

The semi sunlight at the edge of the world finally sunk into the ocean in a ray of reddish brilliance. After which, all signs of sight vanished until the second rising of a fluorescent globe twinkles a diamond light on the seas.

"Look, another half, but it's not as bright as the first," I said to my brother. He walked from the edge of the sea to the lining edge of the jungle and sat down.

"It's nice, unlike the first one that burns our eyes when we stare at it Maybe this second light just means that we need to rest," he said, and I nodded, walking over to where he resided.

"You're right. I also think that we need to mark a tracker of how much time passes by, or we'll get lost in it. The sooner we start, the more we'll remember the beginning of our true beginning," I said and sat down beside him.

"Okay, we'll start with what we know. We know nothing today, but if the Sun comes back tomorrow, we'll know it's a circle, and we'll call it Day Two."

"That's smart. Let's do it." I commended him by placing my hand on his shoulder.

Brother's ears twitched while smiling and saying, "Something feels off. It feels like every time you respond, I have to say something right back. Other than the waves sliding up the sand and crashing on the rocks, there's no other noise around us. There's no other sentient things but the trees, the fishes, you, and me."

"Is that your way of saying that you're already bored talking to only me, brother?"

"Of course not. I'm just wondering where the flying and crawling animals are. I've seen the swimming ones, but what about the other creatures?"

"Oh, right. Now that you mention it, this island is oddly silent. It's as though no other living thing exists on or above it."

"Except for us."

"Right, except for us. I *wish* there were more living sounds around to make this place seem livelier."

Suddenly, without warning, a bright light rose at the corner of our eyes and blasted into the sky across the seas. The power impacted nothing but clouds above, bombing apart a vivid explosion seen at miles from its location.

"Whoa," brother reacted as his attention is drawn to the light.

My heart stopped for a moment when I saw it. "N-no. It can't be," my eyes shook, thinking of the events that could be unfolding. "B-brother. I think we have to run."

"Run? Why?" He questioned with a lost look in his eyes.

Just as he asked, whispers from within the darkened jungle began. The shorelines behind us began to freeze over as blocks of lining ice suddenly washed up against the shores. I can't feel the change in temperature around us, but our surrounding displayed the signs of a thermal drop. Fresh leaves began breaking a descend from the trees of the jungle, indicating the height of an unnatural shift in nature.

The continued whispers that grew nearer and nearer, petrified brother's body to the unexpected.

"W-what's that sound? Wait, something's familiar about this," brother said, finally reminded. "It can't be. Are those the Organisms from your story?"

While gripping his arm and rushing forward, I said, "We're thinking the same thing and that's another reason not to ignore my instincts." I added, hastening us into the beginning of the jungle.

"Where are we going, Aiden?" Brother asked, panicking at the direction in which we ran.

"Right here," I said, bringing us to a tree where the branches began low, but the top ran high. "I've thought it through, and this is our best choice to avoid what's coming. Climb up fast while keeping your breathing normal, brother."

"Okay," he agreed and began to launch himself up the broad branches without further question.

As we lifted our bodies against the gravity to climb up the arms of the tree, I felt a stampede rush pass below us. It was like a horde, ripping away the grounds of the earth, bolting toward the lightning blasting the sky across the seas.

They lined off at the shorelines, one beside another and one behind the other, all whispering perspicuously toward the seas.

"Why are they whispering that? 'Look at me?'"

"I don't know, but it's the same way I described them from the narrative," I noted to brother.

"I don't get it, Aiden. Isn't the story that you're telling me something you only imagined?"

"That's what I thought but from the looks of things, I don't know what to believe right now. Please, brother, have an open mind with me and assume that everything could be real."

The bright lightning in the distance suddenly ceased, bringing the night back to its moonlight shine. The whispering from the creatures followed suit and abruptly stopped, bringing about absolute silence.

Brother and I paused, keeping our eyes on the fixed creatures. Suddenly their necks made a cracking sound as their heads turned in one hundred eighty degrees to look at us.

"Aiden, they see us!"

"Higher, brother!" I screamed and we hurried to climb higher.

In a bolting rush, they rushed in our direction off at the jungle, and swarmed the tree that we climbed. Gripping their claws into the body of the tree, they closed the distance between us in no time.

"Aiden!" My brother called, pointing at the arm of a tree that's not of the same tree. I nodded to his idea, and we both leaped across the air to another branch.

I landed behind him, but my feet caught an unstable touch. To the side, my world began to turn, and my brother grabbed me by my wrist before I noticed that I was sliding off.

"What are you doing, Aiden?" Brother asked, pulling me to a steady stance and pushing me ahead of him. "This is no time to lose your stance. We've got to keep moving."

Stabilized and back on track, I ran to the body of the tree and leaped up to another limb, grateful to have my brother at my back.

"Play with me?" voiced an innocent request from below me. I looked to the previous arm and saw that one of the creatures stared directly into my brother's eyes at a distance from him. Others had already begun climbing up the trees surrounding our location, making our escape an aerial trial.

"Let's go!" I screamed at him.

"If I look away, you know what'll happen! You've created what'll happen."

"You're far enough from it to run away. If you don't flee now, the others advancing will come at you. We need to keep jumping from tree to tree. Let's go, brother!" I begged him to move.

The gruesome form of its thin layered organic flesh began to decipher around its joints, twisting its bones and breaking its parts. More showed up and asked to play and then began in the same sequence.

I raised a hand to my mouth, vomiting a bit in my throat while observing what I've been describing aloud.

While breaking apart and restructuring their organic flesh, twisting and turning the lines of their intestines, the creatures continued to transmute their unnatural bodies. They cracked their necks to their spinal cords and their spinal cords to their chest. They busted their kneecaps and bent them back and stood upon their knuckles to support their four-legged chase.

The split of their smiles is fixed in place by the veins lining their thin layered flesh.

"Play with me?" Voices the sound of more innocent sounds from such heinous forms. They trick the ears but seeing them would make us fools not to run."

"Aiden, getaway from here. Please!" Brother cried for me to listen.

More and more of the creatures appear on the limbs of the trees singing, "Play with me," and my eyes watered at my brother surrounded.

"No!" I screamed. "I won't leave you behind. I'll never leave you behind," I voiced, thinking of our cornered position. "If we're truly a part of what I've been saying, then listen to more of this narrative, brother."

"Y-You know what's going to happen next?"

"It's all word of mouth, so only as I say it." I replied, as his eyes began to water blood as he stares at the gruesome changes in their organic forms. "I have to try this, okay? If these things are from the story, then maybe something in it can help save you. I won't idly stand by and watch you die."

"I— I don't understand what's about to happen, but whatever it is, I trust you, Aiden," his voice quivered.

"I know, brother." I replied, then carried on the narrative. "As the boy laid unconscious in the body of the Slicer, Zaheem voiced his concerns to his comrade Eva."

2oC

Door 08&10: Back into My World

Third Person (Point of View) -c-

"I think you should tie him up," Zaheem said, in concern of the unconscious young boy.

"You fear him that much?" Eva smiled at the unease in his tone. "It's okay, Zaheem. I can handle it if something happens."

"That's not my worry. That boy awakened convinced of his truth. He convinced himself so much that we couldn't believe him to know why he knew what he did. I think that you should tie him up for the drug still in his veins, the fear in his heart, and the manifestation of what he can do."

Eva squinted at Zaheem, mildly considering his words of warning. Suddenly, the sound of an arcana wildly beeping widened Eva's eyes.

"Eva!" Cole shouted for her.

"Alpha Level – 041," The automated voice of an arcana reflects in Eva's ears, her head turning to the scene as it all happened at once.

Sparks of lightning began spewing from the boy and Eva quickly shouted, "Get away from him!"

Cole backed away quickly as Eva's eyes glowed, alarmed by the boy.

"He skipped straight over his Alphacardia level and activated his Alpha Level. How is this boy so powerful?" She said while gazing at him.

A sudden glitch in the slicer's system knocked the autopilot back into Zaheem's hands.

"Eva, you have to stop him," he shouted while trying to gear a malfunctioning system.

"Alpha Level - 088," the arcana on the boy's wrist further voiced his rising level.

Eva quickly motioned toward him to do something, and lightning sparked at her when she got nearby. She raised her hand and slightly cried out when her fingers received a shock.

"Careful," Cole shouted from his position, he and Eva standing at different angles from the boy. "Are you okay?"

"I'll be fine."

A transparent plasma of circulation began to form around the boy and his body hovered up from the floor. "Eva, what if the adrenalin is still in his system?"

"Possibly. We have no way to know how much he consumed." She agreed, then showed a facial idea while looking at her arcana on the boy's wrist. "Arcana, initiate the shot!" She commanded.

The arcana upon his wrist reflected detailed lines of information then, "Error!" It spoke. "Configuration incomplete."

"I can't activate it while it's still synchronizing to him." Eva made known.

The Slicer suddenly shifted and off balanced everybody inside. Zaheem quickly shifted it back and struggled to keep the machine in the air.

"He's fighting the Slicer's system. Get him under control you two. We'll crash into the sea if you don't," Zaheem warned.

Cole's eyes widened as he rushed for a locked militant case. He unlocked it and pieced together a sidearm with a highly potent agent within its bullets.

"Cole, are you mad?" Eva shouted at him as he aimed it at the boy. "Those are tranquilizing, but they move too fast. It'll pass right through him if you fire."

"I'll aim for his leg," he targeted. "He'll be mildly injured but breathing and unconscious," he said secured fired a shot.

The bullet bounced off the plasma shielding the boy and ricocheted throughout the inside of the slicer. Eva ducked when she saw this happening and she rose when she heard it stop.

The sound of the pilot's scream behind Eva called for both her and Cole's attention.

"Oh, no!" Cole reacted to his significant error. Zaheem's right palm had been blown out and the bullet landed into the piloting station.

"Zaheem!" Eva screamed with widened eyes as the blood gushed out from his hand.

His head hit against the operating system and his eyes shut down. A sudden alarm on the monitor alerted them to an extreme situation.

Instantly, an abrupt turbulence caused the Slicer to flip upside down. Eva gained momentum in the sudden shift as her eyes glowed, and her surroundings slowed.

"Alpha Level – 001. Cheetah's Speed," She voiced an activation call. Her genes altered as she quickened her body across the Slicer to Zaheem's position. She took control of the flight that had dawned toward the ocean when it had shifted. She brought the machinery back to a leveled flight, delaying an inevitable disaster.

While looking through the windshield ahead, Eva noticed the lining of land and flashed back to a thought of when Zaheem placed himself back into the piloting position and pinpointed the areal coordinates of their airspace location.

"About 70 minutes," he responds, and she walks to his side, viewing the machinery in operation. "The island's Northern borders are roughly 20 minutes away, though."

"When we're in proximity-"

"-I know, Eva," he paused her. "I'm to turn off the automatic piloting, angle off to the southern direction, and fly along Androsia's edge. After which, I am to remain 50ft above shallow water until we see our side."

"Get us there safely; you know what to do." She said, preparing to leave him to focus.

"I do know, but do you?" He asked, shifting her attention back to him.

"What do you mean?"

"I think you should tie him up," Zaheem said, in concern of the unconscious young boy.

"You fear him that much?" Eva smiled at the unease in his tone. "It's okay, Zaheem. I can handle it if something happens."

"No, you can't!" The young boy shouted a response from behind Eva as he sat up. He quickly raised his hands to cover his lips with a questioning look on his face. "Did I just... dream that?"

Eva's head shifted to the boy's direction while Cole vigilantly cautioned himself of being near him. Tiny sparks of lightning began surging from the boy's hands and then from his entire body.

"Cole, get back!" Eva shouted, and he backed away quickly as Eva's eyes glowed, alarmed by the boy's immense energy.

"Alpha Level – o41," the Arcana upon his wrist reflects a rising Cardio Level.

"Calm yourself!" She demanded of him.

The boy looked at his palms, and stood to his feet quickly while claiming, "I'm not doing this. I promise!" he believed.

"Eva, you have to cease his power," Zaheem shouted while taking control of an operation hard to control, autopilot no longer of any use.

"Alpha Level – o88," the arcana voiced the increasing power of the boy. Eva rushes toward the boy and his widened eyes reacted a defensive rise of his hands.

"Wait, stay back!" He voiced a warning. A lightning sparked at her from his fingertips as she got near, causing her to jump back to avoid it."

"Now you're attacking me?" She accused.

"That's not what I intended to happen," he excused.

From his feet the lightning boy rose, as a mass amount of transparent energy spiraled a plasma into creation around his hovering body. He's now enveloped by a dense but thin circular forcefield.

"Get control of that kid or he'll kill us all! We're going to crash into the seas if you don't," Zaheem warned.

Cole's eyes widened as he rushed for a locked militant case. He unlocked it and pieced together a sidearm with a highly potent agent within its shots.

He pointed it at the boy, who then quickly reacted and said, "If you shoot that at me, you'll harm the pilot."

"What are you talking about?" Cole looked over at Zaheem's struggle then back to the boy's eyes.

"I have a repellent protection circling me. If you fire your bullet, it will rebound and strike the hand of the pilot."

"Why so specific when a ricochet strikes at random? You're lying."

Cole aimed for his leg and took the shot.

The bullet sparked a shield around the boy and then struck around the inside of the Slicer.

Eva, who overheard everything, sped up her vision by increasing her energy.

"Alpha Level – 001. Cheetah's Speed," she activated, visually speeding up her vision to follow the movements of the bullet in slow motion.

As the boy predicted, the shot flew straight toward the pilot's hand. Eva caught wind of this and quickly repositioned her body to protect Zaheem.

"Alphacardia increase. Alpha Level – 101. Armadillo's Shield," she added a second adaptation.

The bullet struck Eva's upper shoulder just as a layer of hardened scales had manifested on the surface of her skin. She felt no pain, nor did she receive any tissue damage when the bullet hit her and fell to the floor.

She immediately shifted her attention to the boy and asked, "You dreamt this would happen, didn't you?"

The boy nodded in reply to Eva, and she understood.

"If that had hit me, I'd be bleeding and unconscious right now. You shot that shit without even considering me, brahman." Zaheem shouted to Cole.

"You know I have to see to believe," Cole excused. "I guess he was telling the truth."

The lightning sparking around the boy grew wilder. This intense release of power caused the boy to hug his stomach, seemingly severely in pain. He screamed as the arcana on his wrist voiced,

"Alpha Level –102."

"Arcana, initiate the shot," Eva commanded her device on his wrist.

"That won't work!" the boy shouted.

"Error. Configuration incomplete." The Arcana confirmed him to be correct.

"It's still synchronizing. Neither of us can activate it until a host's body and mind are in sync with the arcana." she quickly explained. "How far ahead did you dream?"

"Until you were surprised by something you saw through the windshield," he struggled to respond.

The lightning sparking from his body surged through the pilot's system. Everything went haywire as controlling the Slicer grew impossible.

The machine flipped and tossed around everything inside. They banged to the roof of the slicer as it's now the floor.

The pilot, unstrapped, was flown from his seat, as the flight's now descending upside-down.

The boy's hovering body is unaffected by the sudden flip, but his screams of pain made him unaware of all that's happening.

Eva, whose Alphacardia is still active, rushed to pilot the controls and shifted the slicer back into its upright position. Just as she did, an engine of their transportation blew out. It shook the inside and alarmed to more danger.

"Oh no!" she shouted as she felt the difficulty in flying on a lone engine.

Then, through the windshield ahead, she noticed the lining of land and expanded her eyes in confusion. "How am I seeing land already? Did we turn around?"

Zaheem rushed to look through the windshield just as Eva had said those words. He raised his wrist and went into the operation system of his arcana to bring up a three-dimensional map

"No, we didn't turn around. Believe it or not, that's Androsia's Northern borders," he looked to her with a shocked look.

"It's only been a few minutes since we took off, not twenty. How are we seeing Androsia's island so soon after leaving The New Providing one?" Eva questioned then shifted her head back to the electrifying boy. "It's like we've time-lapsed somehow."

Zaheem noticed the smoking engine along with the instability of the slicer and moved to reobtain complete control.

"In any event, I'm thankful that the island's right there but we still won't make it on this turbine failure," he warned. She blinked quickly, pulling back to the situation at hand.

"Fly in an upward angle," she pointed.

"But that'll exhaust the remaining engine and we'll come right back down."

"I know. The plan is to parachute from the sky. Cole," Eva called to his idled body. "Prepare to air chute."

He nodded to her demands and began quickly gathering the supplies. Cole placed them into safety containments and hooked the air chutes onto the containments metal bodies.

"All done," he said and tossed two chutes over to her. "What about the boy?" Cole wondered, just as the final engine blew off.

"I'll take care of him," she assured.

The turbulence silenced, as the slicer has yet to begin its descend. In a cruising air that's lacking momentum, Eva easily lifted Zaheem up from his seat and Cole rushed the materials over to the slicer's exit during this lightweight moment.

He pushed open the door and received a greeting from an innocent upside-down question of, "Play with me?"

With widened eyes, Cole backed away from the unexpected sight of an Organism and tripped over the materials he had not yet pushed out.

His sudden movements caused it to wale, "Look at me!"

It rushed into the Slicer and reached at him with its inhuman length arms.

The shock of this left Cole with no time to react to what gruesomely came next.

1oC

Door 09&10: My Brother and Me Again

Aiden The First (POV) -d-

A breaking sound signaled my eyes to widen and my soul to come back to reality. The arm of the jungle tree I'm standing on suddenly snapped. I'm forced to scream and reach up for something to grab in this evidential drop.

"Aiden!" Brother shouted as I fell past his level.

The arm fell onto another one just below my brother's position. The impact was painful, but I'm glad I didn't fall straight to the ground. I stood up and froze at the quick realization of the dozens of Organisms gathered on this arm.

"No, stay away!" I panicked, closing my eyes, and ducking down.

A stampede shook the arm for a moment, and then there was silence around me. I opened my eyes to look around and saw that they were gone. My inner alarm triggered my attention up to my priority.

"Brother!" I exhaled when I saw the truth. The Organisms that had ran from around me were ruthlessly climbing up to my brother's fixed position.

I jumped to an arm and leaped higher and higher. I climbed a bit higher than brother's position and looked at him from an angle above. He's still struggling to keep a stare with them. "Stay focus but know that I'm here, brother."

"You're not hurt, are you?"

"I'm not."

"Well, since you're not leaving me, what should we do? My eyeballs are hurting so badly. I think they're starting to bleed because everything is turning red." I jumped from where I was and into my brother's enclosed circle. "I'm glad you're closer but is your plan to die with me?"

"I would, but no one's dying. I'll be your savior, brother."

"You sound serious. What's your plan?" he asked.

I rushed at an Organism and shoved its gory display of external guts and flesh away from my brother. The shove off balanced the humanoid creature, sending its repulsive form to the ground.

The disconnection of its eyes from brother's didn't come with the complimentary cry of 'Look at Me' that mimicked a person in agony.

"Brother, I think I can trick the creatures' game,"

"What? How? Never mind, keep going!"

I shoved the Organisms' inattentiveness of me from the trees, intervening their connections away from my brother. I began to clear a path so that he can start moving since they climb so fast.

"Look at me!" My ears twitched, gasping a breath at the sound of their attack mode.

I spun and saw my brother's eyes tightly shut.

"No!" I screamed, witnessing the danger rushing for his crimson tears.

The Organisms that stood on the jungle arms around, jittered a quick leap up from the hinds of their limbs, launching themselves to my brother's position.

"Brother, open your eyes!" I cried out. Brother's eyes burst open in a reaction too late. The rapid motion of the Organisms had already closed in on any escape routes.

"I'm sorry, Aiden," Brother quivered a response that acknowledged his doom and pained a heartache to my soul.

"I'm going to save you!" I shouted, rushing back to him.

I extended an arm, convincing myself of an impossible reach as the Organisms moved in faster than I did.

"Stay away from him!" I strained with all my might to not witness the death of the only life I know.

The desperation in my soul synapsed a stimulus between the joints of my connecting muscles, causing a sudden aerial release of a cold snap from the bones of my body. This sudden blast of an impulsive wave gushed out of me with a raging blow of wind. Its mighty release sent all in proximity spiraling away from me. The unnatural organic forms squabbled in their cries to keep a grasp onto their regenerating lives.

With the realization of my subconscious actions, my awareness brought silence to this newly discovered capability. After my power went dormant, the quietness drew my eyes toward the chaos I'd unintentionally caused.

"B-Brother!" I screamed, realizing that he was blown away along with the Organisms that had surrounded him.

In my attempt to rush again, I slipped and flipped from the icy arm of the jungle tree and began to fall. I managed to stop myself from spinning and saw the ground a second from my impact. I crossed my arms in fear. A sudden tornado of wind abruptly spiraled below me and eased my impact. Carried around a circle by the wind are sharp shards of ice, allowing me to see the motion. As fast as it came, the wind left, dropping me on the ground.

I jumped to my feet and looked to my hands wondering, "What's happening to me?"

The wind that had protected me was so thin that it formed sharp shards of ice inside of it, which allowed me to see the motion.

I looked around immediately and spotted the many frozen bodies that were devastated by my reckless and abrupt release of power. My brother's nowhere among the bodies I've seen.

"Aiden..." brother called to me, stopping my dreaded thought of the worse.

I turned to him, and my eyes immediately shook at the sight of his body leaning against a tree. Half of him was frozen, while his other half was steaming a nuclear red. He's rapidly defrosting by generating a blazing temperature from within him. I can't feel the heat that's casting from him but the leaves around us erupted into flames, so I know it's hot.

"Are you okay?" I asked.

"I'm fine," Brother gave a smile. "I thought I was done for when you sent that icy wind at me. I landed on another tree arm, not too far up. Oddly enough, the moment your ice touched me, an oven turned on in me and this is how hot I've became so far."

"It's almost as though we're a contrast of each other. Your body instinctively adjusted to a saturation that's a balance to my thermal drop."

"Yeah, but why? What are we? And that story you're telling is starting to freak me out. You first mentioned the Organisms in inside of it and now they're here, real, and trying to kill us."

"Neither of us could've imagined that some aspects of the story would come to life. Is it because I'm telling it, or is it because you're listening? Which one of us is making it real?"

"I'm not sure, and I'm also not putting aside that the entire story could be true. But all I know is they're only coming after me."

"I'm sorry, brother. I tried to catch the attention of some of them, but the Organisms wouldn't look at me. I should've told you a story of absolute purity and not one so mysterious. It's all my fault that they're attacking you."

"We're not certain whether you created the Organisms by telling a story about them or whether you simply foreshadowed them coming. All we know is that they're here," brother said while stepping to me and resting a hand on my shoulder. "And we'll make it through this together." He added.

Our talk is interrupted by the sudden whispering of the unnatural Organisms.

"They're defrosting," brother voiced with a worried look. His eyes trembled at the creatures' bodies coming back to animation.

I took a hold of one of his arms and yanked him in a direction away from death, although it was deeper into the unknown jungle.

"We have to keep running. Narrating to you doesn't seem like it can save you."

"I've noticed. You can pause a situation by telling a story, providing us time to think. But you can't change the situation itself while you're still telling the story. Since you can't do both at once, we must use this chance to get away," brother deduced.

"There's more. I tried to loop the story around itself to squeeze as much thinking time out of it for us, but an arm of the jungle tree broke and disrupted my plan. I'm not so heavy that I could so easily break a limb as large as these. Hence, I think I was intervened by time itself. It must be an error to create a loop, even if it's to save your life. If I stopped right now to further tell you the story and attempted to send it in circles again, I could get squashed by a falling tree."

"Well, that's not good," brother reacted.

"It's not. Therefore, we have to rely on ourselves to escape."

I released his hand after a distance, and we rushed away in sync. Whispering in the distance for the toys of our flesh indicated the childish pursuit of the Organisms humanoid forms.

Something I couldn't see suddenly passed through my skin as I ran. For a moment, my mind lost track of everything but now I'm back.

"What was that?"

"You felt it too?" I questioned to brother who was keeping up with me.

My eyes widened when I noticed his body shining a fiery light. Instantly, I stopped his motion with a sudden pause at the sight of his body.

"Look at yourself," I stressed. "You're still radiating."

He looked at his palms of fire and watched his temperature increase.

"Turn it off, brother," I requested.

"I..." he struggled as a wave of heat flares out with his unsure tone. "I don't know how to shut it off, Aiden!" He flung his hand around and caused sparks to fly in numerous directions.

The terrifying whispers of the Organisms echoed throughout the dark jungle, loudening with their nearing approach. Fear struck through me and all I could think was to keep moving for the sake of his life.

"Run!" I issued to him, and we did.

Loud whispering from the four primary directions indicated no escape before an encounter. One rushed forth with its mouth stretched open and I tried to react with a counteract attack. I'm shoved aside like a toddler to a beast and splatted against a jungle tree.

"Aiden!" Brother cried out.

"Play with me?" The Organism hopelessly begged of him while pinning him down with its lengthy arms.

The sound of this quickened my recovery. My eyes forwarded to my brother and from the bark of the tree, I launched myself across to them.

"Get off of him!" I shouted and powerfully kicked its abdomen. Ice released from my feet and the frostbitten Organism was send flying into a branch, cracking a few of its bones upon impact. "Get up," I extended my hand down to him. "This is no time to lose your stance. We've got to keep moving."

"You're using my words on me. I guess you're taking this savior behavior seriously," he gripped a hold of my hand and assisted me in pulling him up.

"Of course, brother."

My ears twitch to the alerting sound of an abrupt motioning of eyes on us. I turned to run and instantly froze at the four-legged sight before me. I spun back to my brother and covered his eyes with the grip of my palm.

"Keep them shut," I ordered.

An abrupt silence came with the appearance of dozens of Organisms on the ground and in the trees around.

"It must be your heated nature they're after. They seem to be unable to attack without playing, and they can't initiate the game without your eyes."

Brother raised a hand and covered his own eyes, then tightly held to my shoulder with his other. I began guiding him into a direction I felt is safe, but all directions could be compromised.

Like wildlife predators, they observed the bouncing flames of my brother from his light, longing for his eyes to slip a preying sight.

"Aiden," brother whispered as we walk along the path of their observing eyes. "Since they don't see you but clearly see me, you must be the creator of their existence. To target you would also mean to target their source of existing."

"No, that's not it." I denied then thought twice. "I mean, it can't be that which is opinionated. My power is their nature, while yours is the opposite. And so, they're attracted to the flames dancing upon your skin."

"Their nature? Aiden, what do you mean?"

"Can't you tell, brother? Our natures have adjusted from what it was when we first woke up and have adapted to align us with this world. The Organisms seem to use thermal sensory to visualize the increase in our temperatures by focusing on our cardio fluctuation. My breathing is probably undetectable to them because I'm icy like the moon. Your nature, however, seems to be growing to mimic the sun. Even if you were breathing naturally, you're heat would still draw them in."

"If our alteration has anything to do with the story you're telling me, then we could be just like the lightning boy. Aiden, what if we're Alphas too?"

A sudden ruckus from a bang in the distance boomed an explosion and caused a daunting reaction of my body. I turned to the direction of it and witnessed a thick cloud of smoke breathing a signal into the sky. A dim glow from the ember of the explosion made itself known from through the jungle trees.

The Organisms twisted their joints toward the noise in the distance. They then quickened through the jungle and toward the chaotic grounds of another scene. Their whispering began again once they were out of our sight, and it faded by the second.

"They've retreated," I said, and brother opened his eyes. After he saw that they were gone, his glowing light died along with the heat that was casting from him.

Brother exhaled in relief, indicating that a heightened emotion was the cause of his heart rate elevation and his power releasing.

"Aiden, Look up." Brother pointed to the sky at an object or two gliding down with the help of an air chute. "I think that's a person!" He rushed forward.

"Where are you going?" I asked, pausing his motion.

Brother looked back to say, "To see if I'm right," then continued motioning toward the sounds in the distance.

I pushed after his quick movements and followed him to the commotion ahead of our drive.

"And what if you are?"

"Then we'll learn what we can from them, about the creatures and this land."

"You're right, brother. My fear of losing you had blinded me to concluding that deduction. Let's go and see who else is out there."

After following the track marks of the Organisms and the smoke rising into the sky, my brother and I came to a full stop at the edge of the jungle that led out to an opening untrimmed grass. The tall grass reached as high as our waste, able to hide anything on four legs inside of it.

"We're not going in there," I refused.

"I know, but we still can't see enough details from here."

"Yes, we can," I said, grabbing onto the arm of a tree at the edge of the jungle. "Let's climb, brother."

"Right," he nodded then jumped up after me.

After reaching a certain height, brother's sudden shock of a reaction made me look out to the direction of the smoke.

With a pounding heartbeat I questioned, "What?" trying to understand what's going on and why I'm looking at, "A bridge?"

"That's not all. Look closer," brother said, and I looked.

At the near front of the bridge that's leading out into the ocean, a lightning sphere is wildly discharging power from itself. From the abutment height of the bridge, a marksman is firing a rapid release of shots toward a horde of Organisms running onto the bridge.

"Are you thinking what I'm thinking?" Brother asked.

"If you're thinking that those could be the characters from my narrative, we're both losing our minds."

"So, you're thinking it too. But I don't get it, Aiden. How did you do it? How did you bring them to life?"

"I didn't do anything, brother. I'm no creator."

"Then what's your opinion of what's going on?"

"I think I've been using a power and didn't know it. What if my narratives are stories of future events that will happen at a distance from us, but in the same world? That would mean, they've always been real, and that I can see at a distance across space and ahead of time."

"You can't be certain of that," brother argued.

"Alright, if you think I created the Organisms and those characters then I'll try to end them now. I demand that everything reverts to its original state, beginning with you and me again," I paused for a second, waiting for existence to listen to my command. "See? No change has happened, brother. We don't know for sure what is real from what is not, okay? So quit with the speculations."

"If you've already created everything to be as real as us, then why'd you think it would vanish just because you've demanded it to?"

"Alright, but there's also the fact that the characters are on the bridge and not in the slicer in the sky. When I last told you the story, the engines had blown off and I stopped telling it there before it descended. Now somehow they've gone on to do more."

"This world was a blank canvas, nature untrimmed, with fundamental laws to physically existing. Aiden, to foreshadow something falling and then looking away from it, leaves that something to act in the natural flow of continuing to fall."

"You're persistent, brother. But if I created them then why don't I know what happened leading up to now?"

"Maybe, you just have to continue telling it to me. What led to those characters fighting on that bridge?"

"Well," I tried to think, then paused at the thought of no more. "I don't know," I blinked quickly to my blank mind.

"What do you mean by, 'I don't know?'"

"I'm trying to look into the hourglass of the past, but I can only seem to think on what's ahead of time and all that is yet to happen. It feels as though my mind cannot start again in the past."

"Wait, so you can only tell me what's going to happen from here on?" Brother asked, and I nodded. "That won't help us. We'll be lost, having to use deductive reasoning to conclude why everything is happening." He looked back at the people on the bridge and blinked quickly.

I followed his eyes because of their shock but observed nothing deserving of such an alarming reaction.

"What is it, brother?" I curiously asked.

"I thought I just spotted a flashing sign of myself on that bridge," brother blinked, then shook his head in frustration. "There has to be some way for us to know what happened," he riled up. "There has to be some way to flashback!" He willed, and brother's eyes glowed to the bright lights of his dancing flames.

I took hold of his off-balancing body with a solid grip to counterbalance the sudden inanimate presence of his consciousness.

"Brother!" I screamed while holding his body that's becoming heavily close to dead weight. "What are you doing? Come back!" I begged, but his eyes only stared in blankness.

A rippling ray of heat casted from brother's flesh and erupted the tree into a blaze of flames. In my attempt to climb down with him, his weight caused me to lose my balance, and we both fell to the ground.

While picking myself up, I slid over to him. I shook his body and slapped his face for a response, but it looked like he wasn't inside of himself anymore.

The whispering of the Organisms resurfaced and grew louder by the second. The tall grass shook immensely as a horde locked onto our tails once more.

In my awareness of the creatures being attracted to my brother's blazing flames, I jumped to my feet and took his arms to drag him away while he laid on his back. His body's pressuring out a heatwave in an untamed state that's flaring up a destructive fire to the nature around us.

Just like before, the Organisms' whispers stopped after growing into an intensity. Then, an abrupt appearance of one of them faced us at a distance.

With its innocent face, it locked eyes with my brother and asked him to, "Play with me?"

I kept on my motion, refusing for him to be taken by this thing. It stood high up on its back hinds and with a splitting mouth it screamed, "Look at me!" then it rushed for my brother, whose eyes are a flaming fire in his mental absence.

"No!" I screamed as it jumped for his flesh.

The heat blasting from the radius of my brother's core incinerated the Organism when it neared our proximity.

The death of an Organism viewed up close revealed its organic flesh as being nature untamed. Its body converted into the material of a jewel then dusted into the stars of a colorful plenty.

I'm amazed by the beauty after their demise from such a terrifying prior form.

The markings of my brother's tattoo, expanding from his wrist to his shoulder began to glow. Instantly, the heat casting from him awakened array of sunlit fire.

More and more of the Organisms appeared and continued to sacrifice their bodies to grasp onto a touch of untouchable life. Like moths to a flame, their persistence to pass through my brother's offensive and defensive shield was a mindless behavior for the creatures.

I, however, feel no harm at all whiles in my brother's sunlit presence. Even in this appearance of being safe inside a fiery shield, I continued to drag him along the ground in a struggle to get him far from them.

I sat brother up and shifted from dragging him to carrying him on my back. I held his legs firmly and his head rested onto my shoulder as I continued to panic away from the Organisms.

"Brother, please wake up!" I screamed to his bobbling head as his eyes still flamed a sight of absence. His magnificent display of sunlight fire is soft to my touch but burns everything we pass by. "You have to turn this off!" I tried to get a response out of him, but his chest continued to hug my back, resting and unaware of what's going on.

Brother's ruthless in this present state of an absent mind, so the sea is what I'll need to extinguish this sun he's growing into. I curved around and began to sprint back toward the bridge that had suddenly appeared on the beach.

While running away, a physical shove caused me to lose my footing and I began to tumble down the angle of the terrain. Everything spiraled on my motion down, slipping my arms away from holding my brother. I twirled straight down and impacted a tree, which stopped my motion. I quickened to my feet and raised my head to view the apex angle of my brother's position.

From everywhere that I can see, the critter of Organisms twisted their forms and screamed out for his body. The quick motioning of their four feet shadowed the forefront of a spider's eight. They're swarming his sunlight from every direction, leveling for no escape even if brother was awake.

I stepped a stomp onto the ground and pressured my body up the angled of the hill. Splatting on top of one another, they used themselves to cover my brother's body and smothered his Sun to smog.

"No!" I yelled, impacting them with no way through to him. "Get off my brother! Leave him alone!" I screamed, clawing into the crowd of unpleasant disruptions. I pulled some off but more and more kept coming, making it impossible to reach the light of his world once more. "Look at me!" I shouted, trying to grip at their eyes that long for the light of my visionless brother. "Please! Just... Just play with me! Play with me instead!" I begged, producing a salty fall of tears from my contracting eyelids.

A beam of fire suddenly shined through all the creatures and flew up into the sky. After a few seconds of ascending, it exploded. The explosion vanquished the night as its source mimicked the brightest light of day.

Almost simultaneously an explosion from my brother casted out a solar flare that forced the Organisms and me away from his smothering body. The sudden release of it rippled through the jungle trees, blasting to all directions a touch of unwanted chaos. That circular projection manifested an inescapable cremation that ripped away the terrified flesh of the Organisms and incinerated the barks of the jungle's creation.

I was caught pointblank in the blast, but no harm came to my flesh or my life. Undamaged by the wave, I landed in a slide across a rooted-up land. I stood up slightly bruised with a spinning head and a blurry vision. Even in this state I'm shocked to see that brother has cleared the jungle from around us and left only dirt.

The bright sun in the sky, quickly faded away and the moonlit night was returned. My immediate focus went onto my brother's last known position.

"Brother!" I shouted, from the top of my lungs and pressed for him as quickly as possible. I need to get him out of here before more of those things show up.

In my rush, I passed the starry shavings in the dirt that indicated the Organisms which were burned to dust. As I neared where brother was, chills arose within me when I saw the sight of no body.

"What?" I questioned from the shakiness of my voice.

With hope in my heart, I conquered my thoughts of the worst and dropped to my knees at the center of where he'd release his explosion. I dug my fingers into the coal, and searched the ground beneath my feet, begging for a sign of his life.

"Brother, where are you?!" I cried. The sudden falling of ashes around me came with the feeling of his presence fading. I looked up quickly and shook my head at the sky. "No, you couldn't have been that sun above me," I denied, as I kept on digging and digging to search for his body below. "I refuse to believe that you blew yourself up!"

I slowed down in my digging as my hope diminished at the pointlessness of my delusion. I stood up and closed my eyes tightly, then opened them, hoping that this is only an illusion. The whispering of the Organisms hasn't restarted and all signs of them began to thin away, making it known to me that there was no more prey.

At the growing sense of my brother being gone forever, chills arise within me, snowing the slowing beat of my heart to a cold note of frozen sadness.

"Aaaaah!!" I wailed at the top of my lungs and released an icy exhalation from my breath.

While on my knees, the feeling of loss signaled a crawling release of thermal disaster from my body. Crystal ice crawled along the ground as the tattoos on my arm glowed in a contrast to that of my brother's. In my failure to keep him safe, I became unable to care for the ice age I'm currently causing.

"Please," I begged to the truth of not knowing. "I'm cold, and my scales are tipping without him. Please, let me see him again." I cried to the law of creation.

My hands began to ice over as they crystalized into a transparent glass sculpture. My emotions that are pouring out is untamed and so they began to consume me. In my tears of not being able to thrive on without him, my existence is fleeting as I follow him in death.

"Brother!" I cried to the sky one last time. The final ember of his descending ashes fell onto my cheek. At the vanishing sight of his light, I concluded, "I'm coming to you."

The beating sound of a rush indicated the heightened adrenaline of a predator or a prey approaching. In my self-destruction, I care not for the sudden movements that are coming to me.

"No need, I'm here!" voiced a familiar tone to my ears.

A grip onto the side of my shoulder followed a figure coming around to my face. This person knelt in front of me, and our eyes aligned with one another's as he panted his breath into my space.

"Aiden, stop this!" he exhaled, observing the glassy ice transfiguring my body. "What are you doing to yourself?"

I blinked at him, barely recognizing the shade he'd come back to me as. Yet, his voice still reverberates the same, and his structure is still all that it was.

"Is it really you, brother?" My eyes shook to see him again so vibrant, so light, but my form is already eighty-two percent consumed by my grievance.

I began to angle forward, and he caught my fall. While holding me in his warm arms, the futile state of my body continued to deteriorate.

"Yes, it's me. I'm here!" he said with his eye shaking down to mine, concerned about my current state. "I'm so stupid! From the moment I survived the crashing of the slicer, I should've run for you."

"Y-you..." I quivered, now uncertain about anything as my trembling body began to collapse in on itself. In his arms, I now lay as the one who's unexpectedly losing his life. "I thought you'd become ashes, brother."

He held me close and with a sobbing voice he said, "I didn't. When I asked to flashback, it really happened, and I ended up in the past of your foreshadowed story, Aiden. That Sun which exploded in the sky was only a vessel I'd left behind."

oCo

Door 10: My Brother within My World

Seth's (POV) -e-

"This world was a blank canvas, nature untrimmed, with fundamental laws to physically existing. Brother, to foreshadow something falling and then looking away from it, leaves that something to act in the natural flow of continuing to fall."

"You're persistent, Seth. But if I created them then why don't I know what happened leading up to now?"

"Maybe, you just have to continue telling it to me. What led to those characters fighting on that bridge?"

"Well," brother thought for a moment and then said, "I don't know," while rapidly blinking.

"What do you mean by, 'I don't know?'" I questioned for an elaboration.

"I'm trying to look into the hourglass of the past, but I can only seem to think on what's ahead of time and all that is yet to happen. It feels as though my mind cannot go back in time."

"Wait, so you can only tell me what's going to happen from here on?" I asked, and brother nodded. "That won't help us. We'll be lost, having to use deductive reasoning to conclude why everything is happening." I said, while looking back at the people on the bridge. My eyes widened, and I quickly blinked wondering if I imagined that.

"What is it, Seth?" Brother curiously asked.

"I thought I just spotted a flashing sign of myself on that bridge," I said, then shook my head in frustration. "There has to be some way for us to know what happened," I riled up. "There has to be some way to flashback!" I yearned for it and suddenly rippled away.

Swiftly from there to here, I'm reversed to a curse of being inside of the narrative. Thus, my recap of my brother's third perception becomes my first and only third participation of view.

"How long until we return, Zaheem?" I heard a young lady question. My heart began to race at the sound of a familiar line. A young man placed himself in front of a control panel and tracked the areal coordinates of our position. "About 70 minutes," he responded, and she walked to his side, viewing the machinery in operation. "The island's northern borders are roughly 20 minutes away, however."

"When we're in proximity-"

"-I know, Eva," Zaheem interrupted. "Remove the automatic piloting, angle off to the southern direction, and fly along Androsia's edge. After which, I am to remain 50ft above shallow water until we enter the barrier of our village."

She looked at him impressed, "Get us there safely; you know what to do," she left it to him.

A rhythmic flow of a reminder slowed my mind to think about what's right from what's wrong. I'm flying in a metal beast across the ocean, its waters so salty that the taste touches the sky.

As I visually encounter what my brother has foreshadowed, I'm reminded that I'm in a scene that will fall from the sky. How do I get out of this without dying?

"I know what to do, but do you?" Zaheem captured Eva's focus then eyed at the boy on the slicer's floor. My eyes followed his, reminded that, "I think you should tie him up," was what he said next.

"You fear him that much?" Eva chuckled a cute smile to his nerves. "It's okay, Zee. I can handle it if something happens,"

My heart nearly stopped at the silence that came after. Isn't the boy supposed to wake up screaming that she couldn't?

"That's not my worry. That boy awakened convinced of his truth. He convinced himself so much that we couldn't believe him to know why he knew what he did. I think that you should tie him up for the adrenalin still in his veins, the fear in his heart, and the manifestation of what he can do."

"He's right!" I finally voiced my presence while rushing over to them both. I reached for Eva's shoulder saying, "You don't know me but-" I paused at the sight of my hand passing through her in an intangible fog.

My whole world paused at her unseen and unfelt presence of me. I pulled my hand back and looked at it quickly as it reformed from being a fog.

A most shocking reaction rose at the sight of my arms being a shade lighter than they used to be. Why have I fallen into the past of brother's narrative? Is it because I asked to flashback? Brother was right about his story being of future events occurring at a distance. When I get back to him, I'll need to tell him that. I guess what I must do now is ride this scene straight to the end. Although I'm wondering why I can't touch or speak to them if we're all real.

An alarming beep began to sound and followed a shout to Eva from her comrade Cole.

Sparks from the sleeping boy wildly awakened a dance of lightning around him.

"Cole, get back!" She shouted to him when her eyes fixed to the scene.

He quickly retreated from his proximity as the wristwear on the boy voiced, "Alpha Level – 041."

"Eva, you have to stop that boy," Zaheem shouted, struggling to control the slicer's glitching system.

"Alpha Level – 088." The arcana voiced the boy's increasing level. Eva quickly motioned toward the lightning boy and my eyes widened.

"No, don't!" I voiced, trying to stop her but forgot that I'm beyond the plane of their existence.

Lightning sparked at her step toward him, striking her unprotected flesh. She slightly cried out in pain.

"Careful," Cole shouted to her from another position.

She looked around with a widened expression, her eyes searching for something she must've felt from me.

"Eva, the Adrenalin. What if-"

"Yeah, no doubt," she agreed, looking at a transparent plasma that's forming a circulation around the boy. His body hovered above the floor in his continuous power surge. "Arcana, initiate the shot!" She voiced to the machine on the boy's wrist. I looked at it as it reflected a failed activation.

"Error," the arcana said, "Configuration incomplete."

"It's still synchronizing to him. I can't activate it." The slicer shifted suddenly, jerking my body to an off-balanced fall.

"Eva, get him under control. He's fighting the Slicer's network. We're going to crash into the seas if you don't," Zaheem warned, and my eyes look to Cole, recalling a disaster. He's already unlocking a militant case and piecing together a mistake of a weapon.

I rose to my feet and rushed to his face, shouting, "Don't do this!" I noised and waved around to try to get his attention. "Please, hear me! You're creating a disaster waiting to happen!"

He pieced it together and pointed it at the lightning boy, completely ignorant of me.

"Cole, are you mad?" Eva shouted at him as he aimed it at the boy. "Those are tranquilizers, but they move too fast. It'll pass right through him if you shoot. He'll die."

"I'll aim for his leg," he steadied his weapon. I moved aside, watching the focus of his eyes. "He'll be mildly injured but breathing and unconscious," his index finger twitched a movement in my sight, triggering a distressing shove from me. My hands passed through his body in a storm of desperation, causing me to fall through him in a final failed attempt.

The shot echoed while my eyes were away, bouncing them back to the sight of Cole's body slightly repositioned. At the side of his foot the floor is damaged by the dent of the bullet landing into it. He stepped away quickly as his eyes shook at the weapon and a sudden transparent forcefield around the lightning boy.

"It— It rebounded," Cole looked to Eva, surprised at the closeness of it landing point.

"You're lucky no one got hurt."

"Nah, not lucky. For a moment there, something dusted the focus of my vision," he voiced to her.

"Wait, did it feel like something passed through you?" Eva asked.

"Exactly!" Cole exclaimed. "Wait, don't tell me there's a specter on board?"

"I don't know. In any event, we should first deal with the problem we can already see," She replied.

"Alpha Level - 091," Voiced an echoed update of the lightning boy's rising level. The lightning pulsing from his body surged through the operating system, causing Zaheem to struggle to keep the flight balanced.

As control grew impossible, everything went haywire and caused the slicer's body to suddenly shift. I'm slammed to the roof of the slicer when the floor flipped to the opposite direction. Zaheem had flown from his unstrapped position and Cole was also a victim of the unexpected shift. Eva, however, had adjusted her body when she'd felt the shift, allowing her to flip around to her feet. The lightning boy's hovering body was also unaffected by the repositioning.

In this instance, a sudden familiar wave passed through me. It felt just like the one that passed through brother and I when we were in the jungle. I remember that immediately right after that feeling, we saw someone floating from the sky.

I looked around for more answers but only spotted Eva rushing over to the piloting controls. I watched as she overturned the slicer and I tumbled back to the correct side of the floor.

Immediately after she resecured our flight, a motor blew out and shook one side of the aircraft.

Eva's now straining to keep a steady flight forward on a sole engine.

"What in the world? Where are we?" Eva gazed through the slicer's windshield in her continued struggle. "It can't be. That bridge..." She pinpointed, initiating a frantic reaction in Zaheem. He quickly looked through the windshield and he was seemingly puzzled as well.

"The Hour Bridge?" he voiced, and they turned their gaze to one another.

"Good, you can see it too."

"Wait, what bridge?" Cole questioned, rushing over to view too. "Whoa! How?!" He's shocked in gaze.

This situation sounded unfamiliar, so my curiosity led me to run to view it as well. Immediately, I'm astounded by what was before my eyes. A colossal bridge is lining across the emerald sea below. Its width is widely uncertain and so is its length. It mysteriously leading out into the ocean from this island they call Androsia.

"This is geographically impossible," Zaheem expressed. "The Hour Bridge extends across the Tongue of the Ocean and connects South-East Androsia island to the central of West-East Xuma island. We were flying in from The New Providing Island, and that's located North-East of Androsia the last time I checked."

"Then how are we flying in from the South-East direction now?" Eva pondered.

"That's the same question I was leading to," Zaheem replied.

"Are we sure it's really there?" Cole asked in disbelief.

"If I was the only one seeing it, that'd be my first thought, brahman. I think it's real, and if it is then the only logical thought is that we've been displaced." Zaheem gestured through the slicer's windshield at the bridge that's lining across the seas.

"Are you telling me that we've teleported?" Cole questioned.

"That's right." Zaheem nodded.

"This position is more than two hundred kilometers away from our original course. If we're truly flying in from the southeast direction then-" Eva paused, looking straight at an island through the windshield, "It's our village on South Androsia. We can see it from here." She smiled.

"You're right," They both reacted.

My eyes followed theirs, and I'm taken by surprise once more. A barrier circulating a blank space on the land is castling a haven.

That wasn't there before when brother and I searched that island through and through. We couldn't have missed such a huge place.

Wait, these people just mentioned that there's a North and a South of that island, Androsia. The two sides must be so far apart that neither side can be seen while standing on one.

When brother and I searched that land, there wasn't a bridge or a visible barrier to be seen. They all appeared, however, when a sudden wave that I felt again earlier had passed through us.

What if when these characters repositioned in the sky, brother and I also jumped positions from North to South on that island?

It's only speculations but conveniently enough, it's all connecting to saving all our lives. They needed a place to land this slicer and brother and I needed away out of being surrounded by Organisms.

My heart jolted when I remembered seeing a glimpse of myself on the Hour Bridge.

"Is this how it happened?" I asked myself.

The slicer jolted and quaked uncontrollably, the unconscious lightning boy reminding everyone of a situation ignored. Zaheem quickly placed his hands upon Eva's, who's desperately trying to keep the slicer steady. He eased her out of his seat and took complete control of his system.

"You two have bigger things to be concerned with," Zaheem said to Eva and Cole, and they quickly went into action. "By faith's grace, we're nearly home, but we still have to deal with this continuous corruption happening to the slicer," he voiced.

With her eyes, Eva scanned the inside of the slicer then looked through the windshield again.

"Flying upward will exhaust the surviving engine but should grant us the time to think as we fall," she pointed out.

"You're right," Zaheem agreed, and immediately prepared the controls. Eva then turned her attention to Cole, who's unwaveringly keeping watch over the lightning boy.

"Get the supplies ready. We'll parachute from the sky," she made known to him.

The slicer angled upward, causing me to hold on tightly in my fight to resist sliding.

Lastly, Cole placed the freed equipment into safety containments and hooked several parachutes onto their metal bodies. He and Eva are freely walking on the imbalanced floor like it's leveled ground to them.

'What exactly can someone who's an Alpha do?' I wondered to myself.

"All done. What about the boy?" he asked, just as the final engine blew off. Everyone jounced to the loss of the final one.

"I'll handle it!" Eva assured while Cole tossed her two parachutes.

What shoots up but cannot fly has a stage of its fall where it's at the point of its present level and its descending future. The lack of gravitational effort it takes to move in this small window of opportunity is a feather of a motion that causes heavy tasks to become lightly handled.

Cole rushed the containment of materials to the Slicer's exit and gripped the handle to unlock it.

"Wait," I panicked, recalling the final scene that my brother voiced. "Wait, no!" I parried in thought of the Organism on the other side.

Cole still shifted to unlock the slicer's door, so I shouted,

"Don't do it!"

My words doubled in an echo from another voice along with mine. Cole paused and looked beyond me, and so did I at the unconscious boy who's now hovering wide awake.

"If you do that, an Organism will burst into here," the lightning boy spoke of what I know is true.

Can he really be dreaming the future? It's almost like my brother's power, but my brother see's events that will happen far away, while this lightning boy dreams of events that will happen directly around him.

"You're awake?" Eva reacted. "What do you mean by what you've said?" She asked to the lightning boy whose sparkling eyes are convinced of his truth.

"I think I dreamt it to be real," the boy said, then hugged his stomach showing a sudden painful expression across his face. The lightning was tightening his muscles and fastening his veins. "Just... Just believe me!" he struggled to say as the slicer began to descend.

Cole swung back around and unlocked the door saying, "Even if you're telling the truth, this is our only way out," he pushed it open.

From the view of nothing, something of a smile greeted him with an innocent question of, "Play with me?" from the gruesome form of its humanoid body. Cole stepped in reverse and impacted his back to the materials in his way, tripping his eyes away. "Look at Me!" It cried an echoed pain of desperation from its lungs, signaling its joint cracking body to rush in.

It crawled along the floor and hastened to toy with his flesh. His lack of belief has left him too surprised to react to what gruesomely came next.

"Brahman!" Zaheem yelled out and flew to the Organism. He bulled against it and forced its body out through the exit. Just like that, the pilot and the Organism were both freely falling from the sky.

"Zaheem!" Eva rushed toward the exit, but Cole intercepted her with a parachute in his hand.

"Save the boy. This is my problem to fix." Cole said while putting on the chute. He then quickly dove through the door of the slicer with a force so strong that it offsets the fall of this vehicle. The quick jolt rose my legs from the ground and smashed my face to the ceiling.

"Ugh!" I heard the reaction of someone landing beside me.

As I caught onto the situation, my eyes connected to the lightning boy who's suddenly positioned beside me. His body is still veining out an energetic charge but his lightning's somehow passing right through me. Just like around my brother's icy capabilities, his power brings no harm to my life. While pinned to the tail of a vessel that's diving down to the seas, I noticed something shocking to my soul.

"You're not in pain anymore?" I asked, wondering if his eyes were truly on me.

"The pain of this power isn't always. It's not hurting right now," the boy responded, then he drastically exhaled. "Who are you? Why am I just seeing you?!" he stressed.

My eyes widened, confused by the truth of what's real from what is not anymore.

"I'm someone you shouldn't be able to see. Since we can see each other, I can't live on thinking that you're just a character," my reality cracked.

A sudden bright light from a celestial body overshadowed the wild dancing lightning from the sparking boy. Both of our attentions were pulled toward an array of animated auras forming around Eva. She is standing above us at the head of the slicer. The rapid dive of the craft is null to the will that's currently in her eyes. She'd already gotten the materials out of the Slicer and now her focus is on the lightning boy.

"Cheetah's speed, Armadillo's Armor, and Eelasticity," she called upon. The dancing lights began to form the animal impulses she commanded forth. "Alpha Level – 3o1," Eva voiced.

Rapidly edging over the smooth sheet of her skin are the sheaths of an overlapping armor. They extended to cover all of Eva, crowning her head with a cranium mask and through it her predatory eyes can see. In her sight, the slice of a feline pupil marked a line through the sunset iris of a wild animal's vision. Summer spots began drawing across her armadillo armor in resemblance to the wild cat she's adapted. She dropped on all fours and sparked silver electricity around her as she focused her attention on the lightning boy.

Slithering along the wall in a quick motion, she dashed from faraway to right above the lightning boy beside me. Eva struck her claws into the protected plasma of the boy and began to absorb his lightning force. She took his energy in, and as she did, she redirected it out through the slicer's walls. Eva struggled to conduct a constant outward flow in this timely fall. Finally, after dampening his forcefield enough she shattered it. She took the boy up and vanished from beside me. Seeing her hold his weakened body at the exit made me realize that I have no help.

"Wait! Save me too!" I screamed for her, and she disappeared with all my hope.

I dragged myself across the ceiling to save my soul, but a bang darkened my life that I've lost in this world so cold.

A quick gasp in, and suddenly I'm floating in the darkness of the night. An abrupt display of blazing lights from an aggressive sound pulled in my attention. Immediately, I'm confused about why I'm viewing an explosion on the bridge from the sky above it.

Wind gushed through my hair as my float became a downward fall. I screamed and panicked as I speedily fell toward the bridge of my demise. My attempt to swim across the air for an ocean impact was futile, leading me to cross my arms against the solid ground that came up at me so quickly.

I impacted the concrete, splatting my bones and blood upon its solid. Before death could come, I'm rolled over to my back with the help from someone familiar. My eyes are barely open, my body's numb, and my breathing is partial. From the blur of my sight, this person held me tightly in their arms with a saddened emotion for me.

"No, this isn't right," the person cried, as my consciousness began to fade. "It's okay. You'll become me-" his voice dimmed from my ears as my eyes laid to rest.

A drastic breath out, and I'm in the darkness once more with my feet solid on the ground.

"Stop this! What's happening to me?!" I shouted to no one, wondering why I keep dying.

A sudden bang, impacted near where I stood and casted a flaring explosion into the sky. The frightening sound pulled in my attention, following my immediate confusion of why time's rewinding to the slicer repeatedly crashing onto the bridge.

I looked up for confirmation of this being a reset and what I saw falling from the sky was a horror of an end. Upon the smashing sight of its impact, I spun away and took a breath at the image I just looked at.

I turned to the scene and rushed toward what I may have seen, jumping over rollers and evading the debris. I ran to whom I saw once I spotted the figure correctly. I rolled him over and lifted my past into my arms, his blood gushing and his life fading.

To the eyes of my eyes, I cried, "No, this isn't right," knowing the sacrifice of myself. "It's okay. You'll become me soon to come," I voiced, now acquiring the fore comfort that I'd missed.

I laid myself back down, still confused about how I'm alive after dying but I'm truly grateful. A small loop has just occurred to somehow save my life.

While walking away from myself, I gazed upon my arms and saw the answers to what just happened to me. The dark shade of my skin I once knew was no more, and neither were my tattoos. My flesh has now lightened me to a paler version of myself and I think I know why. When I first appeared in the slicer, I noticed that I looked a little brighter and now I'm lighter than tan.

"Could it be that every time I die, my shade fades away a little more? And does this mean that when I appeared in the slicer, I had died in the presence of my brother?" I wondered to myself.

A metal plate clacked onto the road of the bridge in the distance. I jolted further onto the bridge to view what's going to happen next.

It appears that the sound was of the materials landing. I looked to the sky and witnessed Cole hovering down on a parachute with Zaheem hugging his legs. Zaheem must've manage to push the Organism away from him in midair, allowing Cole to reach him in time and use the parachute to ease them both down.

A sudden pulsing energy lightened up the Hour Bridge, reminding me of an energetic situation that has come down with us. Hovering at the center of the bridge and sinking in the grounds below him is the untamed power of the lightning boy.

From wherever she was, Eva appeared in front of the plasma and clenched her fist. She sends a force forward that impacted the plasma, absorbing the strength of the boy once more.

"When it breaks this time, I'll knock you out!" She revealed to the observing boy.

Suddenly her eyes widened, and she screamed as my head turned around to the jungle.

The sudden sound of petrifying whisperings had surfaced and taken my attention.

While looking back at the scene, I saw that Eva's body was repelled away from the boy's plasma.

Then, a thump onto the bridge indicated someone landing.

I looked to the position and saw that Zaheem had let loose Cole's leg before they could both land.

Upon gaining his footing, Zaheem rushed toward Eva who's flying in reverse after being repelled from the lightning boy.

"Eva!" he flexed after her rapid motion across the air.

Eva adjusted her form in flight and twirled upright to land on her feet. She slid in reverse until she halted at the edge of the bridge, balancing her body and trying not to fall back. Her arms desperately reached forward for something to hold and clasped together was an assist from her comrade.

"Got you!" Zaheem said as he held her forearm tightly and pulled her from leaning back and into a safe stance. He then fell to a knee and hugged his bandaged thigh with both hands.

"Eva, are you okay?" Cole asked when he'd landed. He unhooked his parachute and avoided its fall on him while waiting for a response.

After a breath, she replied, "I'm alright," to Cole and "Thank you," to Zaheem.

"How about you, Zohar? Is that recent wound becoming serious?" Cole asked as Eva extended her hands down to Zaheem.

"I'm fine, brahman," he responded, "It's just a spike of pain from suddenly exerting pressure on it." He took a hold of Eva's arm and rose back up with her assistance. "I can still move, see?"

"Great, cause now there's danger on two fronts that we need to dissolve," Cole alarmed indicating the coming Organisms and the spasming lightning boy.

The three of them gathered around the materials and prepared for the inevitable encounters they'll face.

I looked toward the bridge's exit and viewed the island's edge when the sound of the whispering abruptly stopped. The tall grass in front of the jungle was suddenly torn through by an onslaught of preying cries from misleading predators. Their eyes are bouncing in a soulful glow of nature and light with their docile screams mimicking innocent living being.

A blast sounded, following a flaming flash flying toward the jungle. The continuous sound led to a rapid ray of fiery assaults that ripped and stripped at the Organisms' flesh. This force too fast for the average eye to follow, struck clean through their exoskeletal forms.

I turned to view the defensive source and witnessed a marksman letting off another ray of repetition from an upper angle above. He'd climbed up into the cross designs of the abutment built along the lines of the bridge with an assault arm to aim and rapidly snipe.

"Keep it up, Zohar," Cole spoke into the arcana upon his wrist at the man above. "This shouldn't take us long," he said, then nodded to Eva, who began to suddenly run around the lightning boy. Faster and faster and faster, she ran until her body was nothing more than a blur to my vision. A sphere began to form around the boy and in viewing it, I became mesmerized.

I shook my head and turned away, then knelt to take a breath while evaluating the situation.

"What are you doing, Seth?" I asked myself, feeling as though I'm at a cross of learning one story and forgetting my own. "I... I think I have to go." I felt a sharp pain rising in my chest.

The sound of Zaheem's aggressive firing unexpectedly ceased along with the sounds of the nearing predators that were emerging from the jungle. I looked to view the island and observed a massive number of Organisms fleeing back into the trees. Their drive for a retreat reminded me of their pugnacious chase toward a more desirable matter.

"Why did you quit shooting, Zohar?" Cole voiced, so I looked back to him. "Wait, what? Are you sure?" He asked into his arcana."

"I'm certain, brahman." the marksman's voice clearly came through Cole's arcana. *"Can't you see that the jungle tree at the front is on fire? Well, the fire's moving deeper into the jungle, and I think the Organisms are attracted to it."*

"Good for us. That should buy us the time we need to separate this boy from his power," Cole said as my eyes widened, finally connecting the dots.

I jolted around and rushed toward the jungle, tensed that I didn't realize it before.

I'm in the present that I'd left behind, and I didn't notice until now. The exact moment I left has just recently passed, and I missed it by being far away. I must get back to my brother now. I finally understand how I ended up seeing myself on the Hour Bridge. It was all because I willed to see the past.

A bright blaze rose through the jungle trees and paused my hastening body. From the ground to the sky, the transition in vision was comparable to a breaking dawn of another day. A ray of light dispersed across the air, shedding noon light upon the darkness outlined by the moonlight.

"The Sun?" I questioned then my body tensed as I recommenced my thrust forward.

My heart pounded to a silent comprehension of what I'd forgotten for too long. While bolting through the waist height grass, all imageries of understanding my situation began to process through and through my thoughts.

When I reached to the lining edge of the jungle, I met the tree brother and I last sat in and rubbed against it. The flames of it had erupted into a continuous burn that's scorching the grounds around.

My eyes altered into a concerning look when I realized that the flames still felt friendly to me, even after I've died three times to get back here.

The sunny sky dimmed back to a moonlit night, prompting me to continue moving in haste. I followed a trail of burning trees and diamond dust and as I pursued this path, the sight of ember ashes began to fall from above. Before I can question myself on what it could mean, a sudden howl from the voice of a boy caused me to move even faster.

Recognizing any tone that he can muscle, I called out "Brother!" to the pain in his voice. The closer I got, the more I could tell how disastrous the event was that's causing him to cry.

An unexpected brush of icy wind passed by my body and raised the hair fibers upon my skin. The cold shouldn't bother me, but the feeling of emptiness seeping through it is like being touched by death itself.

I arrived at a blank space in land where there's an unnatural uprooted clearance of the jungle trees. My eyes immediately spotted a figure kneeling at the center of this shaved area.

"Please," he cried, twitching my ears to the sound of my brother's longing. "I'm cold, and my scales are tipping without him. Please, let me see him again."

I pushed forward, saddened by his wail for me, but happy to be close enough to hear that I'm his relief. As I approached him from behind, my breathing became timid, and my muscles weakened at the sight of half of him being transparently inanimate.

"Seth," he called for me with a softening voice. "I'm coming to you."

"No need, I'm here!" I voiced while coming around to his face. I knelt to him and exhaled while observing his ice consuming his entire body. "Brother, stop this! What are you doing to yourself?"

"Is it really you, Seth?" he pearled his eyes at me as he fell forward.

While catching him I confessed that, "Yes, it's me. I'm here!" My eyes shook down at him, not knowing what I should do. "I'm so stupid! From the moment I survived the crashing of the slicer, I should've run for you."

"Y- you..." he trembled in my hand, and I couldn't bear the pain of watching him cold away. "I thought you'd become ashes, Seth." he revealed.

I hugged his weakening body, trying to warm his fading eyes.

"I didn't die. When I asked to flashback, it really happened, and I ended up in the past of your foreshadowed story, brother. That sun which exploded in the sky was only a vessel I'd left behind," I assumed to be accurate.

Tears drained from my eyes onto his cheeks at how close I'm keeping him.

"Now that you know I'm safe, can you please stop this?" I begged.

"I should've waited for you, but my heart's so weak that it started to die when my mind thought that you had," he whispered, as his body still converted his flesh to ice.

Half of him suddenly shattered, and my breathing intensified as he showed no facial change like everything was already numb.

"It's not on your fault alone," I strongly voiced. "My priorities became stunted when I began to focus on the story more than the storyteller behind it. I see you now, brother! Don't die, or you'll critically wound me, and I'll shortly follow after you."

"I...I don't know how to stop this from happening. I'm sorry that you're about to feel what I've been feeling, but please don't let it take your life like it's taking mine. Be better than me."

"If it brings me to you, I won't care!" I opposed his request. "I have nothing alone, brother. I am nothing alone." my voice broke to the thought of his disappearance. "Please don't do this! Please don't go!"

"I know that we're a balance, so I won't allow this circle of pain to continue on. When I die, I'll leave my heart in your hands," brother voiced a validation as his body completely glassed over.

A crack broke apart a vein of lines through his consumed body. The sculpture of my brother burst apart from within my arms and scattered across the air as snowflakes.

"Treat my heart with kindness," Brother voiced an echo of his vanishing soul all around me. "With it, I'll always be yours."

His luminous snowflakes thinned away from my sight, putting a pause to my entire being.

I screamed to the sky as the thought of any other purpose to live fades away with his absence. My entire body became numb as commanding any limb of me proved to be a difficult task. My eyes wept the liquid substance of sadness that came with an intense agony within my soul. I felt lifeless in my attempts to rise myself up from this spot.

As my feeling of touch returned to me, I felt my thumb slide against something in one of my hands. I lifted brother's clothes that he'd left behind and rested them to the side. As I viewed the object, I was unaware that I held, tears fell from my eyes onto what was left of him. A glowing transparent cube with a smaller second box within it was beautifully sitting in my palm. At the core of the two cubes a steel pearl lived, and it's mesmerizing to gaze at.

As I goggled down at the cube, I continued to shed tears upon the mystifying object not being enough to fulfil my sadness.

My sudden burst in anger brought out an energy in me to finally stand to my feet.

"I won't accept this! Don't abandon me with only an object to remember you by!" I shouted at my brother's absence. "A pearl alone will not bring me joy, as it is you that I want with me!" I threw the cube to the side in pain.

Upon the landing sound of it, the ground began to shake, and the trees rattled, bringing an instability to my stance. My legs shuffled around before I inevitably fell to my knees again.

Shortly after, the abrupt shaking to eased.

"I...I don't understand," I questioned, looking toward the cube I'd tossed. From the core of the pearl, light manifested a mystifying shape of a forming figure.

As the pearl released the last bit of mist through both cubes encasing it, the mist solidified itself into a bare person before me.

I stood to my feet and began moving closer to the figure who's facing away from me. Their masculine body became known under the highlight of the moonlight, and a boy was to be seen.

He turned to my direction and with his eyes fixed on me he questioned, "Why do you cry?" sounding like the loss of my life.

"Brother," I called, thrusting myself toward him. I embraced him tightly upon our connection. "I thought you were dead."

His arms gripped my shoulders, and he distanced himself from me.

"I do know who you are, and it wasn't your cry that woke me up. It was your tossing of my world," he said. He then knelt and picked up the plasma cube to view himself in the reflection of its shifting vision. "It is not very unusual after all, to look like your brother, since my form derives from him."

"You're right, it's not," I answered, blinking to a new light of the individual before me.

I noticed the alteration in his skin and properly examined the shade of him being a darker brown than before. He also didn't have any of the tattoos that brother had on his arm.

His visual appearance acted as my understanding of his change, if his meaning of dying is like mine.

"That core in your hand is my brother's heart. You just rose up out of it, so in some way, you're him," I expressed, while looking at the cube in his hand.

I looked around for the fabrics that my brother had shed and went to pick them up.

"Clothe yourself," I requested as I tossed them to him and took the cube from his palm to further examine the meaning behind it.

I wonder why such a disaster happened when it fell to the ground. It felt like it shook all around me and not just on the ground. I looked up and was alerted to seeing that my speculations were right. Even the cirrus clouds above were roughly disturbed by the falling of this cube.

I turned my head to the boy who's throwing on the shirt my brother wore and said, "When I tossed this, there was a huge shake of some sort upon it hitting the ground. Why did it cause the whole jungle to tremble for what felt like forever?" I asked, and he gave me a smile, seeming to know more than I thought.

"When that Tesseract landed, it caused a vibration that awakened me to you. I came out of the darkness because of the shaking of my world," he responded.

"I was looking for a clearer answer of why you're similar to my brother, not some spin around that I don't understand."

"To understand the meaning of me, you'll need to know who I am."

"Alright, tell me who you are, and I'll listen."

I begged for this to be my brother, but his eyes don't show the caring meaning of the kin I know.

"I have no name, but strangely I now have memories. To get you to make an attachment to me, I'll explain my connections to knowing and knowing's connections to my life around you. After which, what you do not know, you'll answer yourself when I explain the origination of why I'm present."

"Wow, just tell me of yourself so that I better comprehend all that you're babbling on about," I demanded, and he moved toward me with his hand extended.

From my palm he took a hold of the cube and angled it away from me. He tossed it, and my eyes widened recalling the disastrous shake from an impact, but it didn't hit the ground. Instead, the cube hovered in front of him. From within the pearl within the cube an imploding vortex tore through the fabric of reality and formed a circular expansion in the face of us.

"Whoa!" I reacted, feeling as though there's something familiar about this.

"It must be viewed with individual eyes and not told aloud. To hear it alone will mislead you if you do not see it yourself," he said, and my ears twitched to his warning as he extended his hand to me. "Come into my world and let me show you what you mean to me, Seth," he requested, and hesitantly I thought hard about what to expect. "A time like this has come again for you to pull away now like you didn't do then. You still don't seem to know enough to refuse or to remember that I do not forget."

I looked directly at him while raising my hand to hold onto his. When I realized that he'd called my name without me giving it to him, I retreated my hand with a head shaking refusal.

"No!" I voiced and stepped away from him. He tilted his head at my reaction, as my eyes began to water at the realization of what he'd done before. "Your call of my name has jogged my memory. I gave you my name in this same situation before but it's also not the same situation as before, is it? I'm so confused, but I know I must turn you down." I kept stepping back with mixed feelings about the individual before me.

"Now that you've finally remembered that we've done this before, we can move on. Have you seen enough to tell me who I am now?" he casually asked, as my mind tried to unknot this entanglement between us.

I'm trying to understand how I just lived the same course of my life twice, leading up to right now.

"I've lost energy going in a circle, and I've learned nothing new from you! I've gained nothing new from you so why did you do that?"

"Nothing new was to be grasped. You wanted to know who I was and so I showed you your life again leading up to right now. Since you've now lived your history twice, you should be able to tell me who I presently am to you."

"You pulled me into that cube, and we ended up right back here!" I still panicked, developing a feeling like my brother's death was now a lifetime ago. "We're right back where we started or…or is it where we ended? I don't know. Yet somehow, I don't recall exiting from that cube from the first time you pulled me inside of it. So, are we still inside of it or are we outside of it? Explain this to me now, before my mind collapses while overthinking on it!"

He stepped away from the second vortex loop that he'd casted and opened his palm. The vortex vanished at his command as the reappearing cube flew back into his hand.

"Carefully observe, and you will understand," he alerted to me.

His vision watered into a bridge of tears and when he blinked, a droplet fell onto the cube. A rumbling sound from the sky immediately came forth. I lifted my head up and from above, a droplet splashed into my eye following an intense downfall from the clouds thickening in the atmosphere.

With shaking eyes, I looked to him with very little understanding of the being that had emerged from my brother's remains.

Hence, I'm inclined to ask, "What in existence are you?"

The rainfall ceased, and the thick clouds dispersed for the Moon to shine down on our spot again.

"You already know the definition of me. I'm brand new, so now it's your turn to tell me the meaning of who I am." he said, stepping to me and kneeling down. "What am I to you?" He humbly asked while gazing up to my eyes.

My brows knot at the sight of his eyes imitating a resemblance to my brother's. But why won't he say that he is him? Both of us lost the original shade of our skin and our tattoos, yet he's acting as though he's also lost his mind.

"I don't get it. If your outcome is the same as mine, then why can't you kneel to yourself and become the obvious answer you are?"

"Is it that obvious if I haven't voiced it? I don't want to cling to a name that you will not accept if the answer is incorrect. So, I'm asking you to tell me to see if I am who I feel I am." He said, looking to me with the longing eyes of a fresh mind.

How he's being is not the same way my brother would, but his appearance has me taken. I began contemplating on our contrast in opposite directions to better grasp onto the truth.

"Give me a second," I requested, then turned away while I considered the details involving the previous events tremendously hard.

When my original form died, my soul had already solidified into a faraway location. I've also faded several times after, and each time, I'd blinked to a new position before my fated end.

My brother, however, shattered himself and left behind a glass cube which manifested this boy from the heart of his heart. Not only is he a darker shade than my brother but his first-person memories of me also doesn't seem to be present. His knowledge of us appears to be known only because he watched us for one loop until he was created.

"You don't know, do you, Seth?" He asked as his eyes lock onto mine.

"I think I do," I nodded, then walked up to him and asked him to stand to his feet.

"You're my brother but you're also not," I explained. "It's hard to make clear, but you're some form of a revamp of him. You and I went through similar losses, but you lost your mind in the process of your renewal, so now you're anew. You're my brother's body, but your intelligence begins from now."

"What does that mean?" he questioned.

"Since that cube seems to hold this world, and you just rose out of it," I looked to the tesseract in his palm. "You're somehow the result of my brother and our history itself," I gulped to even saying that. "If that relic is really my brother's heart, that'd make you, his successor."

"Why can't I just be your brother alone?"

"When I previously ripped away from my body to save my life, I became a subtraction of myself and now I'm lighter than I was. In this process of escaping death, my memories always remained in tack, unlike yours that are gone. This brought me to the conclusion that you can't possibly be my brother, but someone else entirely."

"You claim that I used to be him, but because I've gotten darker and lost my mind, I'm not? How does that make sense? What if our blood is still equal?" he paused, gazing at me for an answer.

"Wait. Wait..." I stopped his valid point from attaching to me on a sibling level. When I realized what this was coming to, I replied, "I don't believe you're my brother with lost memories but someone else entirely. Your mind is much younger than mine, that's why you could be my brother's son, let's say. But in that conclusion, we'd be separating who you are from who my brother is. If he's truly a person other than you, then I want to see that person again. I want to experience our memories."

My heart began to pain as I gazed at this future that my brother left me to look after. He blinked, disconnecting his eyes from mine when he noticed my growing sadness. His demeanor then altered to that of an unhappy expression.

"Again, it is not enough," he voiced to me in a differing tone than the lost boy he portrayed. "The beauty of a tesseract cube was not enough to bring you content, and the rising of your brother's renewed flesh was not enough for you to move on from his eternal rest. Even after knowing my story, you still refuse to make me real to you. If having a reminder of him back is your truest desire, then here you go," he extended the tesseract cube to me. As I took a hold of it, he continued in saying, "Shatter the boxes of the cube and let the pearl within them be exposed to the oxygen of life. Doing so will blast into creation a stream of light that, once passed through, shall take you back to everything that you once knew. You will then be united with your brother, always and forever."

"The last time I asked you who you were, you sent me into the past that led me right back here, just to explain that you had no name. How do I know that I can trust you to directly reunite me with my brother this time?"

"If you'd listen carefully, you'd know by now that I don't tell tales. Understand every word or continue to be the cause of all repeated mistakes," he said, then stepped away from me.

I turned away from him and aimed at a frosted spot on the ground. When I aggressively threw the cube, my eyes widened, remembering the aftermath of a quake. Both cubes smashed and broke into flying glass shards upon impact. The pearl within them then fell onto the ground and rolled into a spot.

"You don't tell tales, huh?" I angled to accuse him. "Why wasn't there an aftershock when it hit the ground this ti-" I paused, and instantly became tense upon looking at him.

A glossy nature began to consume his legs and is slowly crawling up the skin of his body. He's showing a hopeless expression as my eyes are lost about what's going on.

A sudden purple light shined from behind me and changed the tint of the night. I looked back at where the pearl had landed and saw a celestial light lining from the ground to the galaxy. Within it, the steel pearl hovered as its casting source.

"Are you only going to stare at your gateway exit out of here or are you going to use it?" He questioned at my paused body. I turned back to him and shook my head as I watched the glossy glass further consume him.

"What's happening to you?"

"I'm dying of course," he casually said, and more questions instantly surfaced my mind.

"Why?!"

"Those two boxes represented the duality of this world," he began to explain. "The outer box meant me before the world, and the inner box meant the world before me. If a shattering threat occurred to both cubes, one of us must be vanquished so that the other can triumph. Since no one can live in a destroyed world, a compact meaning equaling the world must act as a sacrifice for mass existence to continue," he gestured to all around him. "In order to expose the core to the world, I must give up my life."

His hands glossed into a thick stone as it continued to consume him.

"Why didn't you tell me that this would happen to you?!" My heart bled, observing his anatomy hardening into a marble.

"If I had, you would have chosen me over the memories of your brother, even though my mind is not enough for you. You would've chosen me if you knew the truth because killing me to regain your past relationship would make you feel selfish. Hence, I let you choose without telling you the consequences. I knew that if your truest desire was for him and not just the image of his skin, my premeditated downfall would be on me alone."

Anger rose in me at his deduction of my humanity, causing me to cry out, "Shut up!" at this hardening boy. "If death is the only way for me to retrieve a life once lost, then I don't want this equivalent exchange to occur!"

His eyes weren't flinching any emotion for his loss, his acceptance of death already in his being.

"The boxes are broken and everything in progress cannot be undone. For the world to live, it will take me as its own. You should go before the gate closes or you'll never see your brother again. This is what you wanted, wasn't it? Don't let my sacrifice be in vain."

Tears continued to fall from my eyes as the similarity to my brother's death produced memory flashes.

"I don't want to witness this twice and do nothing!" I voiced. "I don't want to keep making the same choices, again and again, killing you every time I do nothing. My cane heart should've been sweet to you and not so sour. If I'm able to save you, let me know how and I'll try to be better!"

There's silence before he says to me, "Your eyes have changed, Seth. I'm glad I got to see that before moving on. In the law of life, you cannot deactivate the process of death, only delay it. But as you can see, there's no way of slowing me down from being killed by my own destiny. Just as the father took himself, the land will take his son, who belongs to no one. To perish is my fate, so please do not cry, or you'll make me cry too."

It sounds like he's not okay with this, so how can he accept a foreshadowed part of his existence so easily? An aurora of loneliness empathically casted from him to me and awakened my eyes to someone who could've mean so much more to me.

"I think..." I tried to muscle out the words in my thoughts that he needs to hear, but my lungs wouldn't stop clogging my shaking breath.

All I can envision at this moment is a traumatic repeat of my brother's demise.

"Wait a minute..." My eyes widened rippling my mind back at what's happening again.

I looked from left to right and raised my feet up and down, circling like an idiot to look all around. It doesn't matter how I look; I must search for that spot fast.

"There!" I voiced at a position a few steps behind his stiffening body. After seeing the charred dirt and measuring down to the center of the ice my brother left on the ground, I'm confident that that spot is where it all happened.

I rushed to him and gently touched his body to see if he's easily shattering. After confirming his body to be as dense as marbled matter, I gripped him up quickly and quickened him toward the spot.

"What are you doing with me so hastily?" He asked as I reached the point in which I laid him down.

To both of my knees, I knelt to his face and voiced that, "I'm not entirely sure. In my thoughts, I'm creating an alignment to try to save you," I said as the growing stone petrified his right cheek.

It's hard to watch this again, but I hope I'm right about him coming again.

I looked up and revealed to him that, "Here is the center of where everything has happened. First, I exploded in this spot some levels above us, and then my brother shattered into snowflakes in this same spot on the ground directly below. He was taking his life to come to me. Since I was still alive when he vanished, he left me the legacy he began in his heart, which is you. I realized that our history was this world when I threw that core heart, and everything around trembled upon it hitting the ground. From his heart, you then rose, but you did not rise in the right spot since I'd tossed you away."

"Is that why I don't know why I am?" He difficultly voiced. "I awakened in the wrong position, so my memories were lost?"

"I believe so," I finally understood why he's genuinely who he is. "I'm sorry that I tossed you away."

"Knowing now will not change the situation. I'm already gone again."

"I know. I can't save you, but I can fulfill you before you leave. You're of my brother's heart, so you're eligible for this title I'm about to give you. I'll call you the name, At2."

"Eighty-Two?" He questioned the sound of it.

"It means, Aiden the Second," I clarified.

His only animated eye expressed a shocking look then it softened and formed a line of tears in it.

"A name is a gift, and you're giving it to me on my deathbed; why?" he asked, beginning to show his emotions.

"I'm doing it to acknowledge that you've existed once before. If you are to die here with the same name, you will die here twice in one. Maybe in an aligned miracle, we'll both get a second chance to do the right thing. If not, I'm glad you existed to teach me lesson."

"I..." his voice quivered. "I..." he desperately began to cry. "I don't want to die anymore! You've finally made me someone, and I won't even get to live as him. This isn't fair at all."

"I'm sorry that I was late, At2," I apologized while placing my hand on his chest. "Forgive me for not ensuring you a longer life."

"I'm not angry with you," he voiced. "You're slow, but you're learning and trying as you go. If your incarnation theory works, I'll die and come back as a new person all over again. And he who'll come again will not be me, so I grace you my eternal farewell." He said and his eyes showed a content expression. "Thank you for counting my short time in existence as one."

"Of course. I'll never forget you, At2."

The remainder of his flesh turned to glass and his life was completely consumed.

I stood to my feet, drenched in tears as I stared down at the stillness of him.

My brother, his second self, and I have now died as three separate one's in the same spot. If the sun or the moon was to shine down from directly above this position, their point of view would see all our deaths as zero dimensional. If that's true, then the law of life will see one from its perspective and that one in three will die. Hypothetically, the two others that can't be seen by existence should retain their lives; one being me and the other being the next incarnation of my brother that comes.

After standing in front of him for almost sixty seconds, my fists clenched and I voiced, "This has to work," as nothing happened. I stood there for quite some time waiting for something to happen, but nothing ever did.

I intended to wait for as long as it took but there was an interference that distracted my focus. A buzzing sound vibrated from behind me, so I looked around quickly. My eyes widened when I saw the celestial line that he'd casted began to thin away.

"No!" I screamed turning around to it and stepping forward. With a paused, I looked backed and immediately felt saddened by what I must do. "You yourself said that this portal is the only way I'll see my brother again. I promise you that once I've retrieved him, I'll come back for you." I turned away from him and said, "I'm sorry," then sprinted for the thinning celestial line.

Out of nowhere, an intense weight pressured down on my body, cause me to abruptly stop by its weighing force. Its growing intensity proved to be too much for me to withstand against and further brought me to a slouching fight against it. The force seemed to be coming from behind me.

I looked back and voiced, "Could it be happening now of all times?"

I can almost visibly see and feel the force coming from the marble statue of At2. Upon comprehending the source of the force, I immediately continued to put distance between he and I. As I did, the pressure eased up from me to the point where I could stand up straight again without a struggle.

The force had flattened the defrosting ice on the ground, revealing an unimaginably heightened pressure to my eyes.

A high volume of gravity pushed against the earth around At2, causing nothing but a flat surface to take shape as he began to rise from the land.

"I can't believe my life from death theory is actually working." I voiced to myself, then rapidly shifted my focus back to the light that's vanishing at an alarming speed. "He's not going to come back in time to come with me. If I stay here, I'll have my brother's double back, but I'll lose him. However, if I go into the celestial line now, I'll have my brother back, but lose his double."

Without a thought more about which choice is most important, I ran for the celestial line knowing that if I could come back for At2, I would. But I'll always choose my brother above anyone else and that's my pride. "I have to hurry!" I kept on pushing and when I was near, I reached for the celestial line, ready to pass through this gate for him.

"Brother!" A longing scream echoed across the air from behind me.

My body froze by a call I didn't see coming.

I turned around immediately and watched as the marbled statue of At2 blasted apart in midair and flamed down a shell of debris.

From that same position in the sky, the third brightest glow of light I've seen all night danced a golden fire that felt oddly familiar in my sight. The brightness began to dim as the glowing tint of a new skin floated down from the sky.

I pulled myself away from the celestial line and approached the figure, who appears to be darker than me but lighter than my brother and his double was. The aura coming from him feels like an equal balance of darkness and light.

When he'd landed on his feet, I hastened my body toward him with a further shock of his detailed features as I neared. I got closer to his face and saw that his hair was an ashy black with streaks of white and his eyes were as gray as storm clouds.

He's like a different person every time he comes back, but somehow this one feels like the closest to my brother.

He abruptly showed a longing expression and while facing me he said, "I can't believe that *brother* was all you needed to hear to stop," he voiced with tears awakening in his eyes. "Does that mean, that you really only care about me?"

"W-why are you talking like you're my brother?"

"Because I am," He confirmed. My eyes widened, and in having doubts for a split second, I hastened back toward the thinning celestial light.

I took his arm quickly and said, "Let's go! We'll talk more when we're on the other side of the gate." I pulled him toward the thinning line and unexpectedly he yanked out of my grip.

"No!" He shouted, causing me to look at his stubborn eyes with a tensed expression.

"What are you doing?!" I yelled.

"What are you?!" he yelled back.

I turned around at the light and watched as the last of it thinned away. The pearl that released the energy had completely ceased and fallen into the dirt.

"No!" I screamed, dropping to my knees, wondering how this could happen. "I've just lost my only chance to see my brother again, all because you pulled away from me."

"Wow," he voiced behind me. "You really don't believe that I'm your Aiden, brother?"

"How could you be? I was told that only by running through the gate I could have him back."

"You would've had me, yes, but not in the way you would've liked." He vaguely replied but I stayed sitting on my knees with my body turned from him. "That celestial line was a gateway to the past. It would've aloud you to live your life with me again but when reaching to this point, running into that gate another time would've just sent you into a circle once more."

I stood up and looked back at him with shaking eyes.

"What exactly are you trying to say?" I asked, feeling as though I already knew.

"The previous version of me casted a 'moving on' S.P.E.L.L for you to travel into the past. The trick of the mind to the spell was that you'd get to live in nostalgia with me. There'd be no new content, just a perpetual artificial reality of memories. What made it a curse was that you'd never begin with your present knowledge, so without any change in your way of life, you'd get stuck choosing the same path of repeatedly going back in time. Because of that, a loop was created that could only be stopped by an external intervention like me.

"Hold on a minute. Are you telling me that if I'd run into that celestial line, I would've ended up back here without the knowledge that I'd done this before?" I asked, and his eyes greenlit the answer, prompting me to proceed with a further question. "Have I gone through that portal once before?"

"No, brother." he replied, and before my relief could sink in, he added, "Not just once before." He stooped to the ground and picked up a rock to draw '82.83' on the dirt. Right now, it's the Eighty Thousand Two Hundred Eighty Third loop. "You've gone into a circle Eight Thousand Two Hundred Eighty-Two times, and this is the only time you didn't. My return has finally put an end to this active illusion of a changing time."

My body froze, never even thinking to count to that height in my life, yet I've repeated the same day over eight thousand times. If I was a baby at the start, I'd be over twenty years old right now.

"I've lost decades of life, doing the same thing over and over!" I became angered. "How could you do this to me?! How could you place a single day on repeat for me to see my brother again?! If there's a meaning behind what you've done to me, I'd call it an error in ways, sending me in circles and playing with my mind."

"Calm yourself!" He shouted back. "That wasn't my doing. Brother, I've incarnated twice, and both of their memories are intertwined with mine. First, I apologize for Aiden the Second, who intentionally created the Syllogistic Paradoxical Enneazetton Looping Labyrinth because he assumed it was what you wanted. However, after he died and you ran toward the celestial line, Aiden the Third was released from the marble shell and called out to you. He called you 'father', but you never stopped, and he ended up in the loop with you. Over eight thousand times, At3 was the one who kept coming back, and he'd remember every loop of every time he tried. Having his memories right now have shown me how torturous it was for him."

"Wait, aren't you Aiden the third?"

"I'm not. If you had responded to his call in the previous loops, you'd have met him. But this time it's me, your brother."

"How?"

"Viewing the spot where we three died from a ninety-degree angle makes it look like only one person had died."

"I know. I theorized that in hindsight two could escape death, but one still had to die," I finished.

"Well, you were the first one of us that lived, so the other to return was between me or my incarnation again. In all the previous loops it was my incarnation, At3. However, after the last loop took him to a black portal in the ocean where he met us both, he became discouraged in wanting to repeat this life again. So now, I am here in his place."

"I—I still don't believe you're my brother. If I do, I'm force to believe that you watched my struggle in an afterlife and never came back for me."

"There was only space for one to come back to life. If you had a father's mindset, brother, you'd understand my reasoning for repeatedly putting my son before me. Even if he had to consecutively try again, I wanted him to eventually break through to you. I thought that if he did, both of you could live happily and I'd rest in wait to see you two again. I had no idea how immeasurable your stubbornness would prove to be in your desire to have only me."

"I..." I choked. He paused my soul whole and sent my spirit into a spasm of disbelief.

I only ever thought that brother wanted me back just as bad as I needed him. Is this real or is he putting on a show and pretending to be him? I mean, brother died for me so how could I be wrong in thinking that this isn't like him?

"I won't believe you," I refused. "I'm just finding out that I've lived this moment over and over for ages and you knew from the start. The Aiden I remember would never allow that to happen to me."

"Unbelievable!" He strengthened his voice. "How dense are you to not realize that you're lucky to just be finding out? Aiden the third had to become the constant observer and the one to add up the loops of every time he didn't stop you. He missed you, 82.82 times so if anyone was in pain, it was him. Brother, your repeated steps went on for so long that it became difficult for him to keep up with remembering the thousands of small figures that he'd accumulated so far. It was so much so that he placed a point between it all to keep it below one hundred so that he can keep up with how fast this day would restart. If you had gone into that celestial line, it would have now been your Eight thousand two hundred eighty-third time and you would have never known that without being told. I know for a fact that remembering a loop and being unable to do anything to stop it is worse than not knowing it's happening at all."

"You're trying to project your emotion of this situation onto me, but you're right, I never knew, and it still only feels like it was a loop ago since my brother first died. You're speaking to me like I've had time to grieve and grow but it's still all too fresh to me. I'm sorry but I don't feel the same way as you do, and I'm also still unconvinced that you're my brother."

The tense expression on his face softened into a slight smile.

"That's alright if you're unconvinced, dear brother, I will keep calling you mine," he graced. "I'm alive now and I have all the time in the universe to explain. I just wish that you could've met At3 at least once before I came again. He was a lost young soul that made many mistakes in every loop except the last one. He killed no Organisms in it and because of that he eventually transcended into becoming Andy Rose."

Just as he had mentioned an unfamiliar name, a massive cracking sound broke us away from our moment. I looked up and saw huge veins lining across the sky around us—splitting the moon in half like broken glass.

"What's this?!" I reacted.

"There's a transparent global shell surrounding our location. Crap, I'm here debating with you and forgot to mention that the sky was going to fall," He voiced, looking beyond my shoulder.

He extended his arm and from behind me the steel pearl that casted the celestial line pulled to his palm. Unexpectedly, the pearl transfigured into a liquid metal and immediately absorbed to his figure in a state of thin armor that covered his feet to his neck. It solidified itself into a protective wear. In the process of this, my eyes caught an unusually familiar reflection coming from his wrist.

"An arcana?" I questioned and his eyes viewed the device then widened in a shocking loss for words.

"Wait, it can't be!"

"What can't be? Where exactly did you get one of those from?" I hastened to know, but the sudden sounds of further breakage from above took his entire focus.

"No time to explain," he said, and I looked up, shocked to see shards of the sky falling to the land. "Get ready."

"To do what? This is so sudden!" I yelled, still lost.

"That's not really the sky. A thick transparent glass dome is circling us and we're going to run to the perimeter of it. Are you ready? Let's go!" He yanked me to begin my sprint behind him.

I pulled away from his hold and caught up to running by his side. At shoulder to shoulder we synchronously pushed toward the end of this global fall. Still, I wonder how he plans to achieve the impossibility of outrunning a falling sky.

A sudden shadow appeared above me and I became tensed. I quickly looked up and was greeted by the nearness of a falling shard politely targeting my life. My surprised body is nudged out of its path before the shard splintered the earth, sinking into depths upon its impact.

I immediately got back to focusing on my run, knowing that if this boy hadn't pushed me to the side, I'd have no body left to show that I was here. His eyes caught mine and I nodded my thanks.

"Always, brother, but keep a vigilant eye," he replied. "The shards aren't falling at once so expect anything before everything comes."

Another shatter falling from above alerted my eyes at a quicker rate this time. I jumped and rolled to the side, instantly catching my balance and continuing to sprint. The shard missed me and pierced into the land, making me chuckle by how it felt to succeed on my own.

"I think I'm getting the hang of this," I voiced, as we both continued to repeat our evasive actions.

When a shard came straight at my running path, I jumped and rolled forward then stood right back up. Upon standing, my eyes froze to seeing that another shard was shadowing the first and it's a second from splintering into me.

"Brother!" a voice echoed in my ears as I'm about to come to an end. The speeding shard abruptly froze in its spot, causing me to fall to my ass at the shock. I slid back quickly, wondering why I was able to do all of that and the shard still hasn't fallen.

A mesmerizing jade glow abruptly began to grow on the edges of the glassy shard, streaming a line toward a direction. I followed the direction and immediately saw that this boy who claimed to be my brother is shimmering in the same glow. His arm is extended toward the shard with an amazed expression on his face.

"I—I didn't know that I could do this," he said, enlightening his thought and looking to my eyes. "Caring about you really does bring to surface potentials in me, you know?"

"You saved my life," I voiced while getting up and rushing over to him.

"Why so surprised, brother?" He lets down his hand and allowed the shard to fall. "I know you'd save me in a heartbeat too," he said with a large smile, and I paused feeling an immediate attachment to his genuine expression.

He's saved me twice without hesitation and if he keeps that up while I'm trying to pay him back, we'll be at a cross for life, just like my brother and me were.

In a shaky voice I wondered aloud, "Could you really be-"

Interrupted by a sudden shaking of the earth, my head rose to view the largest shards finally falling.

Abruptly I voiced, "Let's go," stepping to run.

"We won't make it," he said, gripping my wrist to keep me in place. "But that's okay," he kept his smile. "Survival is a discovery, and after my recent one, we don't need to run anymore."

Before I could question his thinking, both of his steel hands began to shimmer in a jade glow again. The shards in the ground around us and some that fell from the sky abruptly lit up at his command. He clenched both hands while hugging his chest with his arms and the shards around us immediately flew toward us.

"What are you doing?!" I questioned him about the shards speeding our way.

A few feet from me a shard struck into the ground followed by more of them landing at the same distance in a circulation of us. After the circle was made, the other shards coming at us began to stack upon one another. I realized then what he was doing.

"You're making a smaller dome to safely cocoon us? Will it work?" I questioned.

"By lapping up the same material that's falling, I'm also making a denser version of the bigger dome. When those falling shards hit against my cocoon, the thickness of it will shatter those weaker versions of itself."

"You're right," I agreed as he finished the encasing of us.

Inside of the darkness within this doom, his glow is now the only light my attention can focus on.

A loud banging collision followed the sound of larger crashes on the ground around us. The impact felt so disastrous that it even trembled the ground within the doom.

We couldn't outrun the sky, but he's somehow evolved to producing an alternative solution for us to survive its fall.

He's now saved me three times and I'm beginning to find it hard to continue stubbornly denying him. I must read him for a little longer before I'm convince.

Aiden's key element was the ability to tell the future at a distance from us. If he can show me that he can foreshadow then even consciously I could no longer reject him.

"The sky has stopped falling, brother," he said while spreading his arms. That action blasted away the dome from around us. "It's over."

Immediately after being exposed to the real world, the sound of whispering from multiple directions began to commence.

"The Organisms?" I voiced with widened eyes. "I completely forgot about them." The whispering grew louder and nearer to our location.

"Damn it, they're coming for you, brother," he voiced.

"Me? Why me?"

"You're hot and I'm cold. No matter how many times we physically change, that underlying truth will always remain as such."

He raised his hand and clenched his fist as the jade mist shrouded his body again.

A few of the crystal shards that had fallen around us lifted from the ground and in their positions, they shattered into thousands of tiny needles. At the velocity of a slicing wind, the floating pieces pulled toward him. When I saw that he and I were close enough to be one, I ducked to avoid their path to him.

While on my stomach I looked up and watched the glass needles pierce into the upper vertebrates of his steel back. The spiking needles stacked upon themselves as they formed into a sculptured pair of wings.

After they'd formed, they spread apart, and he flapped them like a bird. Wind gushed from his body as he rose from the duality of his newly developed flight.

He hovered low to me and said, "Let's go, brother," while extending his hand down.

I looked at him, puzzled by his quick adaptation to using the glass from the fallen sky. I turned my head to the direction of the whispers and thought that if I ran away from them, I could test if they'll come after me or go after him.

The whisperings suddenly stopped, indicating that we'll see them soon.

"What are you waiting for?!" He tensed up.

"Nothing," I said, taking his hand and he rose upward right away. Half a second later an Organism appeared and leaped up to try and reach us, but it missed. We were already too high, so all the others that appeared could only jump and cry in vain as their preys got away using the sky.

"Play with me?" A multiple of them asked repeatedly as more and more appeared. It took only moments for hundreds of Organisms to blacken the land below us by standing upon it.

"I'm going to swing you around to my back, brother," he said, then he did it. I held onto him after he'd let lose his hands. "There's more of them on Androsia that I thought. If I leave the Organisms to roam free, they may annoyingly follow us." He said then rose both of his hands to the sky.

A large quaking sound came from the ground below, so I looked down. When my eyes caught the larger glass splinters hovering up from the ground, I realized that his use of this newly discovered power exceeded my expectations. He guided the large glass shards to land each in a position around the mass of Organisms, circularly caging them into a single area.

"That should hold them for a long time, the walls too high for them to jump over," he said after he was done. "Alright, let's go."

"You're leaving them like that?" I questioned, realizing that he has the power to clean this place up. "Why don't you just kill them all?"

A tension entered his body, as though I'd said something of a trigger to him.

He angles his head to me and said, "I think it's time I tell you how I got this arcana," he raised his wrist to remind me that I had no clue. "One loop ago, Aiden the Third was consumed by the nature of the Organisms and he became the most dangerous one of them all, the K-Organism. It was ultimately because at the time he became one of them, he was wearing this same steel armor that I am. He was somehow saved by a man with no name but when he'd come back from being an Organism, he was a little more transcended."

"Wait, are you trying to say that those Organisms are living people like you and me?" I asked for clarification.

"Yes, brother. That is exactly what I'm saying." He replied and I immediately understood why he won't kill them. "So, what do you mean by Aiden the third had changed back from an Organism to a little more transcended?"

"Well, when he returned to himself, he also found that he had no name. So, the man strapped this arcana onto his wrist to help him discover his name. But in case it didn't, that same man named him Andy Rose. In order to remember the man's generosity, Andy gifted the man a name as well, and called him, Adam."

"Wait, they named each other?"

"Yes. It sounds like us in the beginning, doesn't it, brother?" he asked then continued. "After that, Andy Rose was taken into a vortex in the tongue of the ocean.

He was pulled down into a black ring at the base of it. Before he lost consciousness after entering, the arcana on his wrist revealed his name to be Aiden the Fourth. When he lost consciousness, the previous loop ended and then I woke up here and shouted 'brother' out to you."

"So, the moment I'm about to run into the celestial line was the start of every loop?"

"That's correct."

"I still don't understand why it took you so long to take his place and come back to save me. What's different this time? I needed to understand."

"If I didn't come back, I'd have carry the burden of watching my son take his life for not wanting to be here," he revealed. "Andy Rose remembers every loop and at the end of the last one, he vowed to become suicidal if he could not rest. After over eight thousand trials, I still ended up being the one to come back and stop you. If this was always supposed to happen then I've been putting my son through all of this for nothing," his voice struggled to conceal the pain he feels.

The sorrow in his tone alerted me to knowing that if this is my brother, he's found a bond stronger than the one we had.

"What about the arcana on your wrist? You said that Andy Rose wore it, so if you're back at the start of a different loop now, then why are you still wearing it?"

"I'm not sure. I came back at the point Aiden the third always comes back at, so I'm not supposed to have this arcana on my wrist."

"Well, do you have any idea of what's happening here?" I asked.

"I have a theory, but I don't know if you're ready for it,"

"Neither of us will I unless you tell me.

"It could be crazy to consider, but what if Andy Rose's body came back in time to Aiden the third's position, who's consciousness I've currently taken over?"

"What?" I voiced, feeling a pressure in my head. "Ow! I'm sorry but I'm not quite understanding."

"I figured you wouldn't. Well, to sum it up I'm wondering if this could be the past of the 8,282nd loop and not a new loop like I thought."

"Oh, like when I had a flashback and ended up in the past but in the past of someone else's story."

"Exactly."

"Yeah, but how would that even work in your case? If what happened in the last loop gave you that arcana, shouldn't it no longer exist since your actions have already altered from your previous ones? With me here, you won't have the same ending as last time."

"You're right. Events of the past effected by its future would normally lead to that same future coming true. On that note, this must be a different time loop or..." he paused.

"Or what?" I question.

"Or somehow the present and the past loop have merged into one. If that's true, paradoxically I presently exist in two places at once in this specific loop."

"Twice? Wow, that's a major anomaly. Do you think that your return, and claim to my brother's name is what's causing this potential twin paradox?"

"I'm not claiming to be me, I am me. And I'm not yet sure of the cause of it but I'll continue to investigate my suspicions. In the meantime, I'll fly us toward the vortex that will form in the tongue of the ocean at sunrise. I don't know if it'll give us the answers we seek, but I have a feeling that it's the exit from this world."

"Really?!" I reacted, surprised to hear that there's really an exit and that he's found it. As he began to fly us east of the Organisms that are trapped by the circulation of glass shards, I said, "Stop."

"What is it, brother?" He asked, pausing his motion forward and hovering in the air.

"If we really have a way to leave this world, you can't just leave those Organisms like that, they'll eventually get out. The characters we leave behind will then have an infestation on their hands."

"You know I can't kill them."

"I'm not asking you to, but I need you to interfere. You claim that our natures are still the same, so I'm asking you to use your ice to seal the Organisms to stillness."

"Ah, I get your point. They'll be insensate, but alive," he smiled. "Smart thinking, brother." He turned around and extended his hand down to the Organisms.

The jade glow of the mist around him transformed its hue into an icy white.

"Sleep now," he voiced, and a frosty mist began to cloud our vision of the ground inside of the circle of glass shards.

The sudden temperature drop silenced the Organisms, rewinding their lives to an ice age period. When the mist had cleared, all that remained of the Organisms were frozen problems for the future of who comes after us.

"By the time they thaw out, I hope the residence of this world are ready to save them," he thought aloud. "Shall we go now, brother?" He asked while angling his neck to look back at me.

"Y-yeah," I said, more in shock than I realized I was. As he continued to fly us in the direction of the ocean, I'm starting to believe that I can't deny him anymore.

A sudden thought came to me, so I began to execute it immediately. I concentrated my focus on the feeling I had when I first set my body on fire, trying to do it again.

"Are you cold, brother?" He asked, slowing down his flight.

I hadn't realized that I was shaking in my attempt to bring out my flames.

"I'm not cold," I said, then confessed that, "I haven't used my fire since my first flashback so I was seeing if I still could."

"Do you believe that you can?" He asked.

"Isn't seeing, believing?"

"No, you've got it in reverse, brother. You must believe for belief to show you why you're believing in it. Wait a minute. Did you ask me to use my ice only to see if I could?"

"No, I also wanted you to immobilize those Organisms, so I won in two thoughts," I confessed. "A lot has happened recently, and I've already felt how time could heal after a little distance was put between my life and my brother's death. I know nothing of the eight thousand loops that you claim already happened, but I know one loop that I'm aware of. At2 sent me into a circle in order to tell me who he was and so I feel like I've already lived twice. I'm now living like it's been a while since my brother died, even though the event first happened less than an hour ago. To go into believing that you're him right now from thousands of loops in the future will once again change how I generally behave toward you. I needed to be sure of you first before dropping my guard and letting myself go around you."

"And are you sure of me now?"

"Almost."

"Almost? Well, what must I do to make you sure that I am who I am, brother?"

"Foreshadow a story for me again. Once I see that you can still tell the future of an event that will happen at a distance from us, I'll believe that you're my brother forever."

He laughed and said, "Okay, I like the sound of that. I honestly can't wait to get back to how we once were. But I'm wondering if I could tell you the story in a different way this time."

"Different how?" I asked.

"Well, the first time I told you it, I described the characters actions and voiced their verbal dialog. This time, I want to tell the story through their eyes so that I can get a grasp on what's on their mind."

"Hmm," I unyieldingly thought about it, but didn't quite understand what he meant. "Show me what you mean," I requested.

"Okay, listen carefully, brother. I'm probably the first person to feel as though my heart is intertwined with another's. Sometimes when I close my eyes for too long, I can see lightning striking through the darkness beneath my lids. When I grasped onto those feelings having no idea where they'd lead me, my sight became shrouded by a lightning mirage, and I developed an abrupt feeling that I wasn't in my body. The next thing I heard was the arcana on my wrist beeping a signal to me, and echoing the words, *'Configuration Completed. Welcome to the Arcana System, Tyro Asher,'*"

Co1

Door 11: The Lightning Boy in My World

Asher's (POV) -h-

"Configuration completed. Welcome to the Arcana System, Tyro Asher," voiced an automated sound from my wrist.

I instantly began holding my head and screaming at an intense pain.

Memories of this world and another began to clash into a singularity within my mind.

It felt like my brain unlocked an exploding reminder of myself, and just like that, I'm reminded of my life beyond death.

'But where am I now?' I thought.

I looked down and immediately saw that I was encased in a ball of circling energy and hovering just above the floor. When I saw that, I knew that my power was still going out of control.

I decided to look around with haste and my vision caught a speeding figure repeatedly flashing from right to left in front of me. Even when I looked behind me, the figure still flickered around me in the same sequence. I sped up the quickness of my vision to slow down the motion of what's happening before me and my brows knot upon spotting the girl in motion.

"Steele?" I questioned a name to the speeding figure.

She's dashing in an anti-clockwise rotation to form a circle of energy that's a little bigger than the one containing me.

"Why did you quit shooting, Zohar?" I heard a question from a familiar voice and my heart shook as my eyes looked to the undeniable tone.

When I spotted him standing outside of the circle, my whole world stopped. Now that my memories have returned, I know why he looked so familiar to me back in the slicer.

"Gabe's alive?" I questioned at him below my breath.

"Wait, what? Are you sure?" He continued to voice into the arcana on his wrist.

"I'm certain, brahman," I heard a young man replied from Gabe's arcana, but also from above. That signaled me to look up and I saw someone brand new to me. He's eyeing a specific direction through the scope of his sniping weapon. *"Can't you see*

that the jungle trees at the front are on fire? Well, the fire's moving deeper into the jungle, and I think the Organisms are attracted to it."

"Good for us. That should buy us the time we need to separate this boy from his power," Gabe responded, looking at the circular force Steele is creating. "Eva is almost at the peak speed we need her to be," he said, then paused when he caught my eyes fixed on him.

"Oh, you're still awake? You were so quiet that I thought the pain had knocked you out again. I'm glad you're aware to witness this, because you need to." He voiced, and just as he did, a flare began to rise to the sky from behind him.

"Whoa, whoa! Something else is happening in the jungle, brahman." The sniper shouted down to us.

Gabe turned around to view the fire flying to the sky, and just as he did a bright light exploded above the island. The entirety of light had vanquished the night and brightened the eyes of the world like a sudden sunlight. This mimicking of noon made the time of the hour an illusion to our eyes.

"Is that the sun, Cole?!" Steele voiced, echoing all around me.

"It's nothing. Don't look up and keep increasing your circular haste," Gabe replied to her a bit distressed over the situation. His reply had kept Steele focally speeding around me.

He looked straight at me again and when he did, Zohar shouted at him from above, "This is insane, brahman! I can even feel its heat from here!"

Gabe rose his wrist and spoke into the arcana, "Quit shouting, we each have an arcana, remember? But I agree, this is insane," he voiced with an examining look at me. "To cast an impression of the sun is more boundless than combining the gasses to execute lightning. Whoever is releasing all that power must be an Alpha whose level exceeds even that of this lightning boy's," he said, referring to me.

As fast as the impression of daylight came, it vanished again for the moonlight night to return.

"I've never seen an alpha inside of our village with that kind of power,"

"Me neither, which is why I'm concerned about whether it's a threat or not. Either way, the others will have to handle that situation. The Organisms are going to come back if we don't see our predicament through," he said, shifting his gaze to the field that Steele has formed around me.

Gabe's arcana began to beep, and he looked at it abruptly shouting, "Stay at that exact speed, Eva! You're now moving at Two Hundred Thirty-two miles per second and spinning counterclockwise at One thousand miles per hour. If I'm right about this, his power should begin a process of self-containment."

Steele suddenly dashed away from running and stood in front of Gabe, her body smoking and her adaptations weakened. Steele's armor fell from her as her cheetah spots vanished and her eelasticity died. As she fell to the side, highly out of breath, Gabe caught her in his arms and lowered her safely down.

"While I'm asleep you betters protect my body, Cole," Steele said as a sharp remark.

"Don't worry, Eva, we've got you. You did well, so rest up and leave the end of this to us. It's my turn to be the Alpha for our squad."

As he said those words the lightning field around me thinned away, following the descend of my feet to the ground. I stepped forward, now able to freely move about this circle they've created. In my approach toward the edge, Steele lost consciousness as Gabe's attention abruptly lifted to view me. I walked to the edge of the thin plasma and continued to quietly observe.

He raised his wrist to his mouth and spoked, "Zohar, get down here," into his arcana.

A pair of feet landed firmly onto their box of materials as Zohar jumped down from them and ran to Gabe.

"Is she alright?" Zohar stressed his mind upon seeing Steele.

"Eva will be fine. Hold her while I get the lightning boy out of there," Gabe told him, and Zohar rested his weapon aside while switching places with him.

After Gabe stood up, he walked toward me then stopped a few inches away.

"Alphacardia Increase. Alpha Level – 001" he said, as his darkened iris began to glow in a neon green shade. His veins throughout the skin of his body began to highlight in the same color as he added, "Circulatory Configuration," to his activation call.

The transparency of the plasma abruptly became shrouded by sapphire lightning, thickening by the second. I lost my vision of him as the blue sparks become all that I can see.

I stepped back when I noticed that this widening circle was continuously being soaked by an uninterrupted flow of the raw lightning that vanished from me.

In short, this entire space will become nothing but an internal energy source.

Since this is my power, will it kill me if I touch it? I don't want to test that theory just yet, so I'll continue to step back.

As I kept moving away, the floor beneath me began to make a drilling sound. I hastily looked down as tiny green lines shot up from the floor before my eyes.

After they pulled back into the ground I stared down and saw that they'd dotted a perfect circle on the floor around me.

A sudden crack followed the floor sinking in and pulling me down with the rubbles from it.

I screamed as I fell below the floor. I couldn't think fast, knowing that I was falling to my death.

Suddenly the green vines appeared again and wrapped itself around me like a cage. After catching me, I watched the rubbles splash into the dark water below me.

The birdcage encasing me moved me from beneath the bridge, and into the moonlight. The shine of it upon the sparking ocean opened my eyes to all that had happened so fast.

As I'm lifted by the green vines toward the topside of the bridge, I kept my eyes vigilant to see where this power was coming from.

Upon reaching the top, the birdcage separated, and I'm dropped to the floor of a bridge.

The green vines had started to rewind back into their rightful place, and I was most surprised to see that their place was beneath the skin of Gabe's hand.

After realizing that the vines were his veins and they'd returned to him, his eyes stopped their neon glow.

"How long are you going to lie there? Look at what's happening," he said to me while pointing to the lightning within the circling plasma.

I stood up, walking toward him while watching it compact around itself. It grew into a hovering ball of energy that smoothened to a soft glow of fluorescent light.

"Whoa," I reacted, keeping my focus on the energy.

"Watch where you're going," Gabe said, as I got near to them. I stopped, noticing that he was concerned about Steele's unconscious body that Zohar is holding low to the floor.

Gabe stepped to me and took my arm, tapping a few positions on the glass face of the arcana around my wrist. "Looks like we can finally stop calling you 'the lightning boy'," he says, looking in an angle down at me.

"Wait, why are you so tall?" I asked, remembering that we were close to the same height when I first met him.

"Obviously, you're not finished growing. You're about Fifteen or Sixteen, right?" Gabe guessed while looking closely at me. "Well, I'm nineteen," he said, and my eyes widened as I'm finally realizing that this is not the same reality I knew. There's no way I should still be this young.

"What's his name, brahman?" Zohar asked.

"Tyro Asher," Gabe voiced then looked at me and asked, "Do you remember that?"

"Yes, everything came back to me when the arcana voiced my name."

"Great. We have a lot to talk about, but we'll do that after our comrade awakens," Gabe said, then turned to them. "I'm Cole, that's Zohar, and the girl who's asleep in his arms is Eva."

"Wait, didn't she call you Zaheem before?" I spoke directly to Zohar.

"Yeah, that's my first name."

"Oh, that makes sense. So why did you two introduce yourselves using your last names and called Eva by her first?" I asked.

"Because she doesn't like to be called Steele," Gabe responded then his eyes widened. "How did you know that Cole wasn't my first name?" He quickly developed a defensive expression.

I was shocked as well to know that I was right about her last name, so even if her first name is different, she must be the same person. If she is, then so is he. This is a different reality but it's very similar to the one I'm from.

To quickly kill Gabe's suspicion, I said, "It's the first thing that came to mind when I heard your name. Is it wrong for my first guess to be right?"

"Nah, just very intuitive to even think it. I may tell you my first name later, if I ever come to trust you enough." Gabe replied, calming his expression, not knowing that I already know it. "We'll call you Asher, got that?"

"Yeah, okay," I understood.

"Oh, and who's Andy Rose?" Gabe questioned, and I shrugged.

"I remember screaming out that name when I woke up in the slicer, but I don't recall dreaming a thing about it."

"Even so, I've already seen that you can dream of future events that will happen directly around you. You predicted that an Organism was outside of the slicer's door before I opened it and when I did, I learned that you were right. I won't shrug off the name Andy Rose so quickly, it may come up again in the future. Also, you claim to know me, yet your name and face bring no familiarity to my senses. I've never met you in my life, are we clear on that?"

"Yeah, loud and clear." I responded, knowing that I may know too much.

It's best to keep his guard to the ground and just observe for now or my potential friend might kill me before we get the chance to be. I'll start calling him by his preferred name until he gives me the other one to use. And if Eva doesn't like being called Steele, I won't call her it. For now, I'll move at the level of knowledge they think I know.

"Good," Cole said. "Now initiate the shot," he demanded of me.

"The shot? Eva asked this arcana to give me a shot before, but it didn't work. What's in it that's so crucial for me to have to take it?"

"Anesthesia," he replied, and my eyes widened.

"Are you mad?! That'll knock me out!"

"Are you new? It's to tame your Alphacardia. When our heartrates step onto one hundred beats per minute, the Organisms can see us using their thermal detection and commence their game with us. You're on their radar the minute your heart rate fluctuates too high. Beta's get lucky by only averaging around Seventy beats per minute. An Alpha, however, can rise to hundreds in a second, depending on their level of mastery. An Organism will change its course of pursuit depending on the highest point of energy they feel. To get that energy down quickly, you'll have to release it all from you or initiate the shot to become serene."

"That's interesting. But what use is it for me now if you've already separated me from my power?"

"If you're still alive and able to reach the manifestation level of your heartrate, then something will manifest in the place of your missing abilities. Alphas are genetic so your cells will recycle and eventually reignite the beginning stage of your power."

"Wow, really? It's good to know that I don't have to reobtain my power to still be an Alpha. So, if I take the shot it'll only keep me calm?"

"No, it'll knock you out this time. I can't be certain that you won't flare up again, which is why you're taking it in this already calmed state of mind."

"In a situation like this, you're choosing to have two unconscious people on your hands. Wouldn't I be much more use to you staying awake?"

"He's right, brahman," Zohar agreed with me. "Listen. Can you hear them?" He asked, and we all went silent.

It was faint and distant, but we both heard the whispering of the Organisms clear enough for him to understand the situation at hand.

"Fine," Cole settled. "We'll make use of your conscious body for now, but the second you hear your arcana beep a warning of your Cardio Level nearing one hundred beats per minute, initiate the shot." He then turned his focus to Zohar and said, "If he doesn't initiate the shot, knock him out, Z. And if he tries to run, paralyze him."

"Alright, brahman."

"A little brutal, isn't it?" I said.

"A lot necessary, I would say." Cole replied. "Let's get ready to move."

Right away, Cole and Zohar discussed a setup that implied me carrying the ammunition pack, Zohar carrying two to four weapons, and Cole bringing Steele onto his back.

They're going to leave the rest of the supplies behind and return for it later. The main priorities seem to be getting me, the package, and Eva, their comrade, into the village barrier safely.

Zohar and I helped to secure Eva onto Cole's back tightly as her safety was their topmost priority. Her adaptations have fallen off with a reduction of power in her state of unconsciousness. When Eva was falling asleep, she acted like she knew it would happen. This must be her drawback from excessive usage of her Alpha abilities.

Cole synchronized my Arcana to his and Zohar's then brought up a three-dimensional map to display our location.

"This is us here, and that is the position of the village's barrier there. The distance between these two places is roughly Eleven kilometers. I'll set our coordinates to a specific path so that we'll keep pushing forward to align to this route if we're ever separated.

"That's quite far to run without our cardio levels changing from our tired breaths," I voiced.

"The village is far, yes, but a secured surrounding it is about midway from here to there," Zohar explained. "If we stay invisible the entire time, five point five kilometers will be all we have to walk."

"So, no wall jumping I'm assuming?" I asked.

"There's a barrier around the wall, kid. Only at the gates will it allow us passage through," Zohar clarified.

"This village we're traveling to wouldn't happen to be called Syracuse University, would it?" I asked.

"What's a Syracuse?"

"What's a university?" They both began to question.

"Hmmm, I guess not." I concluded by their reaction. "Either way, it sounds super secured and I'm curious about it now.

"I'd tell you the name of our village, but it's against our law to say it anywhere but inside of it," Cole said. "Hence, we must make it to it in order for you to know more."

"You're using my curiosity against me but know that I was never planning to run away. Now, lead the way," I gestured, and Cole laughed while beginning our motion toward the exit of this bridge.

While we walked, I found that my mind still wondered about the technique or formula he used to seal my lightning the way he did.

Because of this I asked, "What did you have Eva do to take away my power, Cole?"

He glanced to his side at me then looked forward while keeping his pace.

With a slight smirk Cole then responded, "I contained it within a miniaturization of a perfect circle. Imagine that you were the equivalent of an unstable core that needed to be abruptly tamed, and that Eva was the meaning of a motion that sped and spun around in an anti-clockwise rotation. She would then become the meaning of two life cycles circling one life, the core. In theory, ten hundred is said to be the speeding milage rate of our planet's rotation around its own axis per hour. In addition, our planets motion around its Sun is said to be two hundred thirty-two miles per second. I simply had Eva perform the meaning of a world circling around the meaning of a sun, you."

"Wow! How did you even think to do something like that so quickly?"

"It's always been natural for me to do. I'm fascinated by the combination of Alpha abilities and some math. A lot of what I come up with would be of no use if Alphas didn't exist."

"Nah, you seem to be naturally smart." I replied.

"With his liberated power just chilling right here, you'd think they'd come our way right away, brahman," Zohar mentioned.

"Asher's lightning is currently tamed with no living matter or host to exercise it," Cole enlightened. "Without disturbance, it'll remain in a perpetual state of peace until forever ends," He added. Being secured by that answer, we kept on walking toward the island.

Even in this reality, Cole is mentally advanced. I'm scared of what to expect after I reach their village. This is a different world but the similarities of Eva and Cole to the ones I remember, are like seeing paradoxical versions of them.

We finally exit the bridge and entered a tall grass that grew between the jungle and the sand before the sea. It reached up to my waste, indicating that anything on four legs can hide beneath our eyes. Slowly and soundlessly, we walk to stay hidden from the creatures' chattering in the bushes around us. Their whisperings are quite terrifying and nothing like I've ever heard. While fully observing the ambiguous body parts of the ones that stood tall above the grass, their facial structures resembling innocent human beings shook my heart. They're far different that the Shredders that once took over my world. A beep sounded from my wrist, and they both focused on me quickly. "Lower it before they see us!"

"Cardio Level - o96," the Arcana echoes with a red-light indication.

"Want me to knock him out now, brahman?" Zohar raised the butt of his weapon to my face.

"Wait, wait!" I raised my hands in defense as my thoughts cleared. After I'd quit acting brand new, the beeping stopped. My CL went down to seventy-seven beats per minute, indicated by a yellow orange glow. "See? It's all good."

This place is different, but the danger in existence is like what I already know. I also have the power I've always known, so my confidence should be unshaken at the slight differences in my reality.

"We haven't even made it to the jungle as yet, and he's already threatening the Organisms on us," Zohar said, lowering his weapon.

"If there's a second time, don't bother asking, Zohar," Cole said to his marksman. "Let me remind you that getting Eva home is our utmost priority."

"That was never forgotten," Zohar replied, then slightly gasped, appearing to sense a sudden danger.

Zohar quickly turned to the jungle and raised his weapon to scope through its eye for a target.

My body shivered the hair upon my skin to spike up as though a threat I've yet to sense is already lurking around.

Cole swiftly turned his face to the jungle and takes a step back while tightly holding Steele's unconscious body.

"We're not alone, brahman."

"I know. Something's out there watching us," Cole said, beginning to shiver.

"I'm frozen," I voiced. "If the three of us are this frightened, two to one, shouldn't we run?"

"Over there!" Zohar indicated with the point of his weapon.

A slight silver shine appeared in my sight at the edge of the jungle's beginning. As it further exits into the open, I came to see the metal lifeform standing before our eyes.

"N-No..." Zohar reacted with a shake in the tone of his voice. He then quickly turned my way and gauges the side of his weapon, saying, "I'm sorry but this has to happen," while pulling the trigger. He let off a bang at me, that signaled my unforeseen end.

Co2

Door 12: My Brother Adapting to My Return

Midnight's (POV) -i-

"You died?!" brother panicked.

"How could I be dead if I'm right here talking to you? Let's not forget that this is the story you asked me to tell," I reminded. "Don't get caught up in exaggerating it into reality."

"I really can't help it this time," he made an excuse with a slight laughter at my back. "It's just that you've never told it from through your own eyes before, only ever overhead."

"That statement you made gave me two verifications from you; One, you believe that I'm your brother, and two, that I'm also telling the same story."

"I recognize the names of the characters you just mentioned so it has to be the same story. However, the way you're telling it now is like how I see my life through my eyes. You gave the lightning boy a name and allowed me to hear what he was thinking. This upgrade in the way you define the story is so interesting that I'm drawn in, but I can't be certain of everything yet. I mean, nothing has come true so far so it's not a problem, can you keep going?" he humbly requested.

The difference in his tone has adjusted to more of a respectful one than his demanding one earlier. Can he not see that he already sees me as his kin?

"Brother, if only the end will make you quit denying in what you already believe, I may run out of time while telling the story to you."

"Out of time to do what?"

"During the sunrise, a portal will open for a short period. If we miss that exit, there's a chance I'll loop around again. The next time may be different as well and possibly won't run as smooth as this one is going. The only way to break the spell on us is to get out of it. We have to leave this world behind, or we could get trapped in its small cycle forever."

"You're always dropping new information on me, and I was finding it so hard to casually go along with them at first but now it's becoming easier."

"If you trust me, you'll believe me without seeing that what I say to you is always true. It looks like you're almost ready to see me for who I am again. Alright, I'll continue, but when we reach our destination, no more of the story. You'll have to deduce your thoughts of me from there."

"If enough of it is told by then, that should be easy," he voiced, almost excited to hear more. "Tell me what happened after Zohar shot Asher in the face."

I laughed at his fondness of me already being a reward as big as him accepting me.

"Well, after Zohar made the shot, a loud ringing in Asher's ears revealed to him that he was still alive."

Co3

Door 13: Entering the Lightning Bubble in My World

Asher's (POV) -j-

It happened suddenly, Cole swiftly intervening by shifting Zohar's target to the sky. As Cole tightly held the firearm in that angle, he tensely gazed into his comrade's eyes.

The weapon trembled with a smoking release from its tips, indicating a hasty reaction without thought.

"You're shaking, Zohar. I thought I told you to knock him out in a situation like this," Cole reminded him.

"This situation is different, Brahman!"

"I hope so! You almost killed me," I finally reacted to their stance before me.

Cole looked back toward the silver shine that's gradually approaching us and said, "I can sense that thing from here. What is it that you saw through your scope?"

"I saw a K-Organism."

"What?!" Cole reacted, looking back at Zohar with widened eyes. "Impossible!"

The silver shine from the jungle suddenly vanished from my sole sight on it, and I tensed to interrupt their reaction at one another.

"It's gone!" I voiced, and they both abruptly turned to review the spot where nothing was anymore. "Bring me up to speed on what the hell a K-Organism is." I requested.

"P-Prepare yourselves," Cole reacted in the same nervousness to his comrade Zohar. As Zohar placed his focus on trying to breathe naturally, Cole voiced to me, "Asher. A K-Organism is standardly known as a Know Organism," he quickly began to describe. "Know Organisms are advanced aberrant versions of the common kind of Organism, history has described. They were dangerous and said to be wiped out by the Prime Alphas in the first war for Androsia island. Where the average ones use thermal sensory alone to detect your whereabouts, a Know Organism can also use its eyesight. With sensory and visualization, they're not mindless enough to ever lose any prey they lock on to."

"Wait, why are you speaking like they don't exist anymore?"

"Because they shouldn't. Well, at least not on Androsia. No one presently alive has faced one before, but we still learn about them in the village, just encase. But who knew that the case would be on our island? First you, then that sun, and now this in less than twenty-four hours. What is going on today?"

"Aah!" Zohar slightly yelled, alerting Cole and me to the closeness of the humanoid silver before our eyes. It vanished, but somehow, I kept sight of its movement around us. I turned around first as its mirage became whole, confirming that it's incredibly swift but not teleporting.

"Cardio Level- o83." The arcana upon Zohar's wrist reflected his rising heart rate.

"It's behind us," I said as calmly as I could as to no longer startle their hearts.

This humanoid Organism is wholly covered by a silver steel plate from head to toe. The mouth of it doesn't exist, while the eyes of it focus its threatening icy glow in our direction. From afar to my face, it dashed, and I stepped back, terrified by what it my do.

"Oh!" Cole reacted as the arcana on our wrists sounded off our raising heart rates.

"Cardio Level - o88," His read.

"Cardio Level - o81," Mine read.

"Don't let your CL go beyond one hundred! I don't know the reason behind it, but the K-Organism can't start the game unless our rates are on the right level, just like the regular ones. Since this is the case but it still sees us, the K-Organism will try to disrupt our hearts natural pace by frightening us into participating."

"Cardio Level - o99," Zohar's arcana echoed, and we both turned to him to calm down.

"I'm trying, brahman," his breathing worsened to a pant. "Sorry for attempting to take you out, kid. I thought you'd perform worse than me in this situation. Karma, right?" he apologized.

"Cardio Level - 1oo, Alphacardia Level - oo1." The arcana switched over on the next level beyond one hundred.

The Organisms in the vicinity immediately began cracking their joints in our direction, as their abrupt whispers from all around commenced a close in on us.

Zohar shuts his eyes tightly then shouted, "Get from around me. I'm the fault, not the two of you." He looked to his comrade and said, "Get her home safely, Cole."

"Get a hold of yourself, you fool. You're not the only one frightened in this situation. I know my Cardio Level will rise to the Alphacardia too, so It'd be selfish of me to buy time by using you."

"In another scenario I'd fight you if you'd used me, but right now you and I are both trying to save her," I looked to his indication of Eva's unconscious rest. "Don't let me be the reason she dies, brahman," he begged.

It was abrupt and sudden when the figure appeared at Zohar's back. At that moment I realized that we'd stopped paying attention to it for too long. Its hand rose and rested onto Zohar's shoulder immediately, causing him to turn toward it.

"No, Zohar!"

"Don't look!" We both warned, but a pause came right after his slight sight of it. That eye-to-eye connection was all it took for he and the K-Organism to link. Beneath its nose a zigzag slice split its mouth open from ear to ear.

From its lipless steel mouth it voiced, "Play with me?" wearing the drawn-on smile of a slaughterer.

My heart shook at the sound of its voice sounding like a living boy.

This K-Organism seems to be much more of a mystery than what his light history has told me. First, it frightens its prey up to an Alphacardia heart rate level, then it asks you to play a game. Its most genuine intentions are not for our fun, it appears. The game competes between who looks away first and not who can stare the longest. Against these creatures, can any side win or is it bias to them?

"There's no way we'll all survive this," Zohar said as the creature's neck began to extend upward like a snake while keeping its gaze locked onto him. "Let me do this," he begged as the other Organisms around us still drew near with all their focus on the highest Cardio Level.

My CL went up to Alphacardia Level - 003, and Cole's own went up to Alphacardia Level -011. But with Zohar's own slightly beyond ours at Alphacardia Level – 019, their attention on him is unwavering.

"Alphacardia Max." The arcana beside me echoed, and the K-Organism's eyes shifted to the sound right away. *"Alpha Level - 011,"* Cole's arcana reflected as I look to his eyes, suddenly glowing in the neon shade of green from earlier.

"Circulatory Configuration," he activated. Beneath his skin, the neon glow of his veins awakened their lining presence throughout his body.

The creature vanished and abruptly appeared before Cole's eyes, and asked him to, "Play with me?"

"Why did you do that?!" Zohar shouted, looking back at what Cole had done. Zohar's eyes were already red as though they'd started to bleed from within.

I'm starting to understand the differences in Cardio levels, and if I'm right, Cole just increased his heartrate by ninety-nine beats per minute. He just went from Cardio Level 111 to Cardio Level 211 in the blink of a thought.

Cole loosened Eva from his back and said, “Catch her,” while letting her freely fall. I reached out quickly, but Zohar rushed in and acted as her net. “Now take Eva and Asher away from here,” he ordered Zohar.

“I won’t just abandon you, brahman!”

“You’ll only get in my way,” Cole replied to him. “You haven’t trained your Alphacardia enough as yet to reach your power manifestation level, and Eva just helped me to temporarily dispel his by using hers,” Cole indicated my way without shifting his eyes. “If either of you were a scapegoat, you’d die in seconds, and they’d come right after the rest of us that remained. It would be a waste of a sacrifice, don’t you think? The strongest is usually sacrificed for the masses when he or she can buy more time than anything less.”

Cole looked away from the K-Organism and dashed from his position with the turning of his head. He left a vanishing shimmer of green energy trailing behind his motioning away.

The K-Organism’s head followed his direction and its silver body vanished from our eyes.

“Look at me!” It waled while pursuing Cole’s sudden flee.

The regular organisms around also followed them at a much more average speed than Cole and the K-Organism are moving.

The K-Organism appeared in front of Cole’s dashing body and reached its silver claws for his face. He barely dodged the creature and kept on leading it to a distance from us. It’s a bit faster than him, so it’s only a matter of time before it gets a hold of his distraction.

“Let’s go,” Zohar said, pulling onto my shirt. “We have to make some grounds while we can,” he took me away from observing and guided us through the Organisms ignorantly rushing by us. The closer I got to the jungle, the more I looked back at the figures speeding through the fields toward him.

“I’m not abandoning him just because he asked it of us. That thing seems to be way too much to be taken on alone. Without support, he’s fighting a losing battle.”

“I’m sure he’s aware, but what can I do with a life on my hands?” he angled his head to Eva’s resting body. “My Cardio Level is untrained. I’ve never maxed it up to the Alpha Levels, so I’m powerless. On top of that, your Alphacardia is drained since we had to dispel your lightning madness. Which is also why we’re handicapped with a man down for the time.”

“I’m sorry that Eva had to exhaust her energy for me. But believe me, I can save Cole. I can save us all!” I turned back to the scene, and a clicking sound immediately sounded. Is he absurdly pointing his weapon at me for caring to save his brahman?

I can't take this guy lightly; he's already tried to kill me once. "Why are you doing this?" I asked.

"There's a chance of brahman surviving, but not with you. I don't trust you. You were brand new a minute ago, and now you're acting all familiar with the world. And even if I did trust you to go, he's protective of those he trusts, not knowing how to stand idly by and watch a potential development die."

"You think he trusts me?" I asked.

"He saved you from me, didn't he?" Zohar asked. "When it comes to Cole, that's enough trust to throw his life away for you."

"I won't put him in that position. I won't be dead weight to him, so let me go!" I begged.

My heart triggered a quick beat that sets my arcana off. I felt electric lines flow through my veins as the speed of my eyes heightened to an electrically quick dance.

"Alphacardia Max - Alpha Level - o10," my arcana voiced.

I quickened from in front of his weapon at my back and reenergized behind him.

"This is great, isn't it?" I voiced, causing him to jolt around to me. His hold onto Eva became a slip, causing him to lose a grip of his firearm to hold her tightly. "You have your hands full, but not me. I'm beginning to grasp onto what it means to be an Alpha in this world."

"You still have so much power after we've ripped it from you? How is electricity already surging through your body again? At this rate, you'll produce lightning once more in no time," he reacted surprised.

"I'm listening, learning, and feeling the changes within me as my Cardio Level changes. I just thought to try out what I know, and it came to me at such an intuitive speed. With this newfound control over how much power I release, you can trust me to stay below Gabe's Alpha level and support him unseen by the Organisms," I proposed. Zohar's eyes suddenly widened then tensed at me.

"Where did you hear brahman's first name from?!"

"Shit," I reacted to saying it before I should've.

"Shit? Speak!" he demanded, reaching for a side arm.

"Are we doing this again? Listen, I'll tell you who I am after I save our comrade, but you won't believe a word of it anyway. Get Eva to safety," I said. As he pointed the weapon at where I was, I'd already flickered away from him and sped in Cole's direction.

In my original awakening, Cole and Eva were the first two humans that I'd met when I learned about the mutation of the world, but they were called Gabe and Emma in the world I know. I recall Gabe telling me that there was a pilot I'd never met because he'd died just before Gabe and Emma found me. Now in some beginning again, they've found me once more but this time with a pilot I've never met. If Zaheem Zohar is that pilot whose story I never learned, then this place could mean another possibility of the beginning I once knew. I'm hardly troubled by being lost in an alternative dimension of the universe because my bond is somehow alive and well here. That's a significant gift to have even if I'm new to him once more. He died in the world I came from so now I can't help but to keep that from happening again. This time we will grow to be bonds again, and this time I will save his life.

At a swift speed, my impetus motion electrics me through the high grass of the area. As I ran toward Gabe's location, the grass got lower and lower. When it was calf height, I noticed a horde of Organisms piled up in an area they circled around. I quickened in as close as possible, then pulsed an energetic leap from my feet and boosted higher up by using the head of an Organism. Upside-down, I twisted through the air and spun upright before landing at the center of the gazing Organisms.

"You idiot! You came back for me?" Cole asked when I'd landed.

I'm standing behind the K-Organism so Cole's panorama vision of me can see both the K-Organism and a blur of me in the background of it. The creature had taken on a four-legged figure form with an extended neck and concentrated eyes. Just like Zaheem, Cole's eyes are beginning to cry blood.

"If you can sacrifice yourself for me, a stranger, then I can do it back for you. Enough chitchat!" I panicked at the sight of him. "How can I save you? How do we take this thing out?"

"You think because you've manifested a small percent of your lightning again that you can be of any use to my situation? You should've run while you had the chance, now we're both going to die," he unwaveringly believed. "We'd normally disconnect the Organism's mental circuits by destroying the mind or severing its head. But in this case, I don't have the kind of power to punctures through or divide the matter of steel. A power like that is necessary right now because this K-Organism is armored in that substance."

"It's difficult to think up but it sounded like you said there's a way to stop it. What about the stare? What does that lead toward?"

"Unfortunately, usually death. This Organism will continue to shift into grotesque forms until my vision is lost from blood or I cringe away from the pain of watching. After my eyes lose sight of it in any way, it'll assault me and rip me into five or more pieces before leaving me behind for some other predator to eat."

"Wait, they kill to kill and not kill to feed?"

"Wow, you really are new, aren't you? The Organisms only exist to cause pain, Asher." Cole explained. "They're harbingers of death."

"And is that a proven fact or only what's been observed so far? They play with us so there must be a way to win their game. The victor can't always be one-sided, or the game isn't a game but a pending execution for all participants."

"You're quite perceptive and wonder onto the right questions, Asher. There's a history book in our village called 'Olivia and the Organism.' The synopses of the tale revolved around a girl who'd won their game once. In the end, the Organism she'd triumph against said, 'You've won. I've blinked my eyes, and now I must abide by a single request from the champion I'll never play with again. Look into my eyes and state what you desire from me.' The girl exhaled that she wanted to be left alone. The Organism then began to rip apart all its kind from around her. After all life from around the girl had died, that Organism vanished from her eyes. It then reappeared when the girl had encountered other Organisms in another area, proving that she was being followed by it. She knew it was the same one because after it killed its kind, it vanished in the same way as it did before.

"Was that its meaning of keeping her alone? She basically had a protector now if you ask me," I assumed.

"No, she had an oppressor that knew no law. When the girl encountered a human group, the Organism didn't hesitate to make a move, attacking and ripping apart all it encountered without asking any of them to play a game. The girl was shocked by this, realizing the sadness of her new life. That Organism aberrantly followed a determination to keep her alive and all alone as she'd wished of it. Since the creature would bring no harm to the girl, she felt like it was in her duty to rid it from the world. She eventually did just that, and it did not resist its life being ended by her. The story of 'Olivia and the Organism' ended there."

"Great, so it's winnable. Like an affair with a Jinn, just be careful what you ask them for in the end."

"That's your conclusion of that story, Asher? You're either a diehard daredevil or extremely suicidal to accept miraculous odds so easily. Since we'll die in short, Gabriel Cole is my full name," he finally gave me the title that's familiar to me. "Don't call me G-man, Gaby, Gabe, or anything else. Just call me Gabriel or Cole," he added

"Nah. Gabe's already stuck in my head so you're going to have to live with hearing that from me."

"Luckily I won't be hearing it for long," he grinned then gained a serious and saddened expression.

"You've got to have more optimism than that, Gabe." I said with an idea coming to my mind as I looked around. "The other Organisms around us aren't interrupting your stare with the K-Organism, why?" I wondered, trying to see if I'm right on what I'm thinking up.

"I'm not sure. Usually, a multitude of them would try to catch your eyes at once, but not this time. Maybe it's because this K-Organism is as advanced as an Alpha or kingly to the others so they're not getting in its way."

"You should've said that sooner."

I dashed to a side angle while remaining at a distance from their stare. While rising my palm toward the creature, I formulated the highest flow of my energy at Alpha Level - o10 into a concealed ball of electricity. Releasing it was a vicious assault across the air as an untamed power wildly bounced through its spherical form. It smashed into the K-Organism, blasting it away from sharing a stare with Gabe. The K-Organism impacted the crowd of Organisms circling us, and in a sizzle, they all danced to my shocking electrical continuity.

"That'll distract them for a bit!" I quickly shouted to Gabe. "Let's get out of here!"

"Asher, you're a naive fool! You can't electrocute a conduit," his voice trembled back at me. "We're dead," he said, as claws gripped his neck from behind in a sudden silver flash. Holding onto his leg as well, the K-Organism raised Gabe above its body and began to stretch him apart. "Aaaaaaahhh!" Gabe screamed.

"No!" I raised my hand and reached from afar, causing the K-Organism to suddenly be pushed back. Gabe was released from its grip, so I sparked to him and took him up. "Run!" I shouted, and his eyes glowed a neon green before we both sped away.

"What did you do, Asher? How did you release me?" Gabe asked as we rushed through the grass. When I looked to him to respond, a hand gripped the back of his head and smashed his face into the ground.

"Gabe!" I stopped to view the K-Organism sitting on his back and gripping his head with both hands.

It attempted to rip Gabe's brain from his body, so I impulsively raised my hand at it again. The electricity in me died as a force to hold it in place surfaced in me. I rose my hand slightly and the K-Organism lifted off Gabe and the ground. When its weight released from him, he flickers to me then looked back it.

"How are you holding it in place like that?" Gabe asked.

"I'm not sure," I replied, and he looked onto my arcana.

"Your Alpha level is still on ten but you're not displaying any electrical output. Is this even the same power?" He asked and my eyes widened.

I suddenly remembered that I was possessed by an Alpha assassin in the world I knew. This assassin was one of twelve that called themselves the Zodiacs. Every zodiac assassin has two abilities and if I'm one of them in this world too, then so would I.

"Either way, we should run before the others come," Gabe concluded.

"Wait a minute. Check on the skin of my back for me and tell me if you see anything."

He raised my shirt up and said, "There's a tattoo of two large vertical parallel dashes. Wait, an eleven? Why is eleven tattooed on you?" He asked and my eyes widened at the possibly that this new ability could also mean that Scorpio is still in me.

"Yes, and I'm sorry but I can't run at the speed of electricity because this is a second power."

The whispering of the other Organisms echoed their approach toward us and at the same time the K-Organism began to move and struggle through my hold. It forced me to exert more power, which ultimately rose my cardio level.

"Alpha level - o51." My arcana voiced, indicating that the Organisms that will soon appear will surely attack me.

"Alpha Level – o49," Gabe's arcana read his new level close to mine.

From a side pocket, he pulled out a knife and sliced both palms before putting it away. From his palms, the flow of a red lake extended with a kept connection to his hand. Three feet down, the point was revealed as the liquid animated into a sharpened duality.

"Dromograph Configuration. Twin blades of blood," he labeled as his iris glowed in a crimson rose.

He dashed at the oncoming crowd and spun a slicing sever through and through their ignorance of him.

"I'll keep these minor ones off you while you keep that major thing off us! I don't care how average you run right now, so long as you're moving, Asher."

"You finally have some faith that we can make it through this," I smiled, turning away and rushing forward while keeping my hand extended back at the creature.

I kept it in place as Gabe and I fled. Gabe kept close to me and warded off the Organisms' incursions from behind and in front of me.

After witnessing his manipulation of his blood into a sharp weapon, I can't help but ask, "Do you have another power too?" while we still ran.

"This is the same power, Asher," He responded while slicing through two Organisms and flipping into the air.

While above, his bloody weapons shattered before he landed to his feet with his eyes closed. He'd landed at a distance in front of my running path, and when his eyes opened, his iris were an icy gray that camouflaged with his eyeball.

"Osseous Configuration. Spinal strike." A crackling sound came from him as a white spike came up from behind him and rapidly speared toward me. Beside my face, it flashed passed my eyes and punctured into an Organism I didn't see beside me. As I looked at what speared it, I was shocked to see that it was Gabe's bones. They pulled out of the Organism and sucked back into his back as he jumped out of my way.

"My Alpha ability is the gift of all senses," he said while we ran side by side. "I can sense and manipulate under my control down to the smallest cell within my body."

"Wow," I reacted, surprised by how intricately impressive that is. A second after we'd moved a slight distance closer to the jungle, the remote grip I had on the K-Organism suddenly vanish. "Uh-Oh!" I stopped and looked back.

"Uh-oh? Why uh-oh?" Gabe questioned, and I lowered my palm.

"I can't control the K-Organism from too far away. My grip has slipped, and I can't make a new one until it's up close again."

"That's bad. It could end up following us straight to the village."

"There's another problem before that. How far are we from the village's gate?"

"Still over four kilometers. We haven't even entered the jungle yet."

"Then your worry should be on whether you're able to use your Alphacardia for four kilometers of average running or not."

Before he could respond, a silver flash dashed at us, and to my eyes the K-Organism cried, "Play with me?" in the innocent voice of a young boy.

I quickly raised my hand to it, remotely gripping a hold of its steel body and keeping it in place of its closeness to us.

"We can't keep doing this. I have an idea, but you've got to trust me for it to work," I voiced to Gabe.

"What is it?"

"Electricity may not be able to shock steel, but lightning can burn right through it. Let me retrieve my power and defeat the K-Organism. I feel like I can control it now."

"After everything I've seen, that's hard for me to blatantly believe."

"That's fine because I'm willing to bargain my life. If my lightning goes berserk again, don't hesitate to kill me," he was surprised by my assurance.

"Fine, let's try your idea," he gave in.

"First, I need to know whether you can share a stare with the K-Organism again?"

"I can't. The game can only happen twice in a day. All other encounters against the same Organism today will mark me to be attacked. After today ends the K-Organism should allow me to play two more times before the same law is applied."

"Oh wow. They really take their game seriously, huh? The minute your Alpha Level grows beyond mine, the K-Organism will target and dismember you with no questions asked."

"That's right," Gabe confirmed.

"Then let's hope that you can outrun it for a while," I said then strengthened every bit of my power to my palms and muscle out a bursting rise of the K-Organism to the sky.

"Alpha Level – o40." My arcana voiced the reduction of my cardio level.

"Wait, what are you planning, Asher? Why did you drop your Alpha level below mine?" Gabe asked, as the K-Organism flew upward.

"I need you to be bait for a hot minute. Before it lands, begin to run toward your village as fast as you can. I'll run too, but in that direction," I pointed at The Hour Bridge while reigniting my electrical output. "Once I reabsorb my lightning my Alpha level will surely shoot up beyond yours, shifting their focus to me, okay?"

"The plan's already in motion so how can I say no? Become the lightning boy again and show me I'm no fool for trusting you," he said, then dashed into the jungle. I looked up and saw that the K-Organism was already falling.

"Don't worry, Gabe. I won't let you die," I voiced, then electrized away as well.

I rushed onto the bridge and sizzled passed the vehicles toward my stationed power. While passing by the slicer's crash, I came to a sudden pause when I spotted a body at the corner of my eye.

After pausing my motion, I hesitantly but quickly moved toward the individual that I see. The breaking dawn of a sunrise on the sea helped me to identify the face of the individual. Right away, my eyes began to water as I've discovered the eternal rest of a boy I'd forgotten. I knelt and unsurely rested my hand on his chest to see if I can feel him. I wasn't feeling for his life that is gone, but to see if he was real and he was. Our first and last encounter is but a memory and a dream, in which he spoke to me and asked,

"You're not in pain anymore?" He wondered for an answer about this out-of-control lightning around me.

"The pain of this power isn't always. It's not hurting right now," I responded, then I drastically exhaled. "Who are you? Why am I just seeing you?!" I couldn't understand his sudden appearance. He wasn't here when Eva was strapping the arcana on my wrist but now, he suddenly is. Somehow, he's also unharmed and showing immunity to my lightning outburst.

With an equally surprised expression, he answered, "I'm someone you shouldn't be able to see. Since we can see each other, I can't live on thinking that you're just a character."

After that, Eva shattered my forcefield and pulled me to the exit of the slicer.

I focused on the boy, now dead before me, and said, "I've done you an injustice by not telling Eva to save you too, but I don't think she saw you, or she would've. I don't think anyone saw you but me which is why I thought you weren't real at first. I couldn't believe my sole eyes on you and because of that, you've died. I'm so sorry."

The sight of this made me shed tears for forgiveness that I don't even know his name. I placed a hand on his shoulder to bear my peace, then turned back to my ongoing mission, having no time to bury him.

A second thought made me look back to notice that his death was from impacting the bridge. That could only mean that he'd escape the slicer, but no one was around to catch him, so he died in the fall. I shook my head trying to stop myself from thinking about his tragic end.

"How are we looking, Asher?" I heard Gabe cautiously voice through my projector watch. *"I don't know how long I can keep this up."*

"You're alive, brahman?" I heard Zohar's voice come through as well.

"Not for long. The K-Organism is on my tail and I'm not even close to the village's gate."

"I'm not either. Don't tell me you're coming this way? I wondered Why I began to hear so many whisperings nearing me."

"I am. I'm baiting them to buy time for Asher."

"Don't trust him," Zohar voiced.

I closed my eyes when I heard them panicking and concentrated on my cardio level.

"Alpha Level – o75." My arcana voiced my risen level.

"Wait, it sounds like their retreating."

"They are," I finally joined their conversation. "They're coming to me," I revealed.

"Zohar, why did you say not to trust him?"

"Because he knows your first name, Brahman."

"I know. I told it to him," Gabe voiced, not knowing that I knew it before he did.

"That's right," I went along with it. "Now let's back to the plan."

"Is sacrificing yourself the plan, kid?" Zohar wondered.

"You must be confused. They're the ones that are coming to die." I said as a horde of Organism emerged from the jungle in and rushed through the grass and across the sandy beach. "Do me a favor and keep your distance guys. I'm not going to hold anything back," I warned.

The quickness of the Organisms led them onto the bridge in a short time. Dominating the foremost pursuit of their drive was the most antagonistic looking one of them all, the K-Organism. There's no doubt that the grand finale will be a clash between this creature and me.

As they neared, I electric toward the spot where it all happened, and it only took me a second to get there. I arrived expecting to find a lightning circulation and was stunned by the star that had formed instead. Like a ring of a planet, the lightning took on a golden tint that shined like a compact version of the sun.

"You can look different all you want as long as you're still compatible with me," I said then nervously and hesitantly stepped toward it.

Even if my power is not compatible with me anymore, this is my stalemate option.

At the edge of reaching for it, I became annoyed at my hesitation as a lot of Organisms closed in.

I looked toward the bridge's exit and saw the K-Organisms moments from me.

"Just do it!" I willed myself in frustration.

I abruptly dove straight into my power without another thought.

I'm then rapidly taken around the inside perimeter of it at a tremendous speed. The speed was nothing faster than a continuous light of motion to my eyes. As I got closer and closer to the center of this altering illumination, I'm slowed with every passing second.

The continuity of my inward pull motioned me around until I'm centered enough to be stationed in my moderated spin. I was nearly dizzy, slowing to the point where I'm now at a standstill. Here, in this central position, I've visually became the constant observer of all around me. Upon the walls of the inside of my power, the sapphire lightning I'm familiar with still danced all around.

Knowing that I'm successfully inside of my power and feeling like it's safe to move on, I attempted a step forward. After succeeding, I started to run as fast as possible. I arrived at the inner face of this lightning shell containing me, and with both hands, I tried to grip a hold of my power. As I easily connected, a light shined from my palms and awakened the veins upon my forearms as an absorption initiated.

A sudden forceful pull at my back disconnects me from my becoming and sped me away in reverse, bouncing and dragging my body along the way. I have no control or free will to slow down this force that feels like a gravitational strength in measurement. Beyond the center, I'm sent, slowing down halfway between the outer shell and my center. Afterwards, I'm flung back beyond the center and slowed down halfway between it and the halfway point. I'm then pulled back for the final time, and I landed at the center position that stationed my stance once more.

It took me a moment to catch myself before asking, "What?" to the apparent whiplash that just occurred. "I don't have time for this!" I turned around and impulse an electric flow through my feet that flickered me in the opposite direction. Upon arriving at the inner wall, I pressed my palms against it and began absorbing the lightning force once more. A few seconds passed, and a forceful tug onto my body caused my eyes to widen as I'm elastic back toward the center again. Just like before, it sent me back and forward multiple times again before pulling me to a stationed standstill.

My realization of this stopping force caused me to place even more aggression toward the wanting of my power's return. I don't just want it; I need it to save my friend.

Again and again, my attempts were foiled by a force I can't physically fight against. My body grew tired with every continuous attempt, and strangely, the amount of time I could remain at the shell extended as well. With the extension of time equaling my growing exhaustion, the amount of lightning I'm able to absorb before being pulled back is remaining the same.

Jogging with barely any electricity around me, I began to slow down until I stopped at the shell again. With my palms rested onto it, tears built into my eyes, lacking the energy to try and absorb once again. In my belief that I've failed by taking too long to retrieve my lightning, my ambition began to be stampede upon by my doubt.

I raised my arcana to my wrist and said, "Hello? Can you guys hear me?" The only thing that came through was static. It could be because I'm encased in here, but my mind is thinking the worse has happened out there. "I've been at this for way too long," I muttered to myself. "In my lateness, the Organisms have probably begun to pursue Gabe again. If the K-Organism catches him, he's dead."

A forceful pull against my back began to take me to the center again. I didn't struggle, remaining stationed even after my central arrival. Sitting with my knees up for my arms to cross, I laid my head on myself, disappointed in my failure.

I stayed this way until my vanishing consciousness drifted my thoughts deep into the world of REM sleep.

"So, this is how he dies," I heard an echoed imitation of me.

This caused my senses to gasp me back to myself. My head rose to a familiar feeling, and I quickly realized that I'd dozed off.

I looked ahead at the lightning arcing around and knew that I'm still stuck at the center of my power.

It's been some time now since my imprisonment, and I'm hoping that there was a miracle that saved them out there. With faith being all, I can have in my lateness, I stood to my feet with the intent of still getting myself out of this.

Electricity burst out from around me as my hands dropped to the ground to grip it for a boosting start. I set my focus toward the outer circle, convinced that I'd tame its power this time.

"Here we go!" I shouted as I launched myself forward.

"To fail again?" I heard myself ask. My lack of confidence slipped my focus and tripped my step for me to fall onto the ground.

My eyes shook up when I doubted that the voice came from within me. I got up and looked around quickly, immediately becoming frighteningly surprised to see a materialized double of me standing where I was.

"No way," I reacted.

His facial structure and body type is everything of mine, but his hair was white like that of a elder, and his eyes were a foggy gray shade. His skin is paler than mine and when he speaks his voice echoes.

"Why so shocked? I thought when you confirmed the Eleven tattooed on your back, you know I was here."

"Yes, I know. But you're supposed to be in my head!" I tapped my temple to indicate his escape. "How did you get out?!" My eyes shook, thinking about this new reality I've awakened inside. "Wait, who am I to you?" I asked to make sure it's truly him.

Just as I did, a force lifts me from my feet, and I'm taken back to the center once again. Now standing closer to him, I'm angered in his presence but also confused at not knowing whether I should be.

"You're still a pain in my side, is who you are," he said, taking a step away from me and beginning to circle my fixed position. "Even so, it seems like we've both come to realize that this world is unfamiliar."

"So, you are the Scorpio from my reality?" I turned to him with confirmation.

"I am."

"H-how did we get here?"

"Before I answer, I needs to know how much you remember of the world before this one."

"I remember that a pink mist devoured the school and disguised within it was a Syracuse siege led by the Tridarcity Empire. While incarcerated in the new colonization, some of us had our memories while others, like Snow, had forgotten who they were. Tridarcity wiped the minds of some of us altogether and rearranged others into new characters, ultimately killing the people we used to know. If my father wasn't one of three kings of Tridarcity, I doubt either of us would be here right now. But ultimately, the last thing I remember was when Emily brought me to a bar, and out of nowhere, I met my childhood friend again. Everything went blank after that, and I woke up here, in this world.

"So, seeing your childhood friend, Kohl is your last memory?" he pondered. I'm in shock to having confirmation that this isn't imagined. This entire time watched everything through my eyes, so our memories are dually synced. "I was present when you met him again, and sadly more happened after that." He stopped circling me and looked directly into my eyes. "I regret giving up my fight to take dominance over your body since your actions led us to our death."

"What? I-I'm not dead. We're not dead!" I refused to believe him.

"Yes, we are, and here's what happened. The barrier Emperor of Tridarcity revealed himself to us as a war for dominancy over the empire broke out on that same night. We were the ones who staged the coup against that place which enslaved us."

"I don't trust listening to this from you. You're a villain, so I'll take all your words into consideration."

"A villain is one who deviates from what another believes, so I guess we're villain to villain. Villain or not, you have no choice but willingly listen to your only source of information, me. And if you hear me now, you'll believe me in the end whether you want to or not. Don't worry yourself because helping you is me and I'm selfish enough to do just that. So, sit back and hear what happened," he said to me. "The war was basically the final battle to determine the legacy of Tridarcity. You'd given me control because you didn't have the wrath within you to succeed in our duel for supremacy. I'd won against their Emperor, but you stopped me from making the final blow to end his reign. You took back your body and preached to me about how killing each other was wrong. Your attempt to come to an understanding with his majesty failed when he blew a hole through our chest. That's the last thing I remember before seeing this lightning around you here and hearing that thing on your wrist call out your name."

"I-I could really be dead? If I'm dead, where am I now?" I wanted to know.

"For most of my time alive, I assumed that death meant not knowing anything afterward. Somehow, we're still aware, and I think it means life to me. But where we're alive now could either be paradise or purgatory."

"It's infested with these creatures that they call The Organisms. This place is no paradise."

"An island is not a continent. Eradicating these mindless monsters from here should be an easy task for an alpha veteran like myself. I see a potential paradise.

I balled my fist whilst staring at this falsified image of me. I don't know what took over me, but an urge to swing my arm planted my fist across his face. He was knocked back, and my eyes widened at how real he felt. He abruptly jumped to his feet and viciously launched at me. His movements toward me were so swift that I felt it in my stomach before I saw it from my eyes.

"Are you dumb or suicidal?!" he asked as I'm leaning over his fist that's pressuring into my abdomen. He removed his hand while stepping back with a sigh. I dropped to my knees while tightly gripping my stomach and coughing for air. "A hit for a hit, but mine was just a little harder, I'm sorry. I didn't come out of you to fight so you should be grateful that I didn't rip out your heart. What on earth were you trying to prove by making such a carefree action toward me, Asher?"

"I wanted to-" I choked, still catching my breath while getting to my feet. "I wanted to see whether you were real or just a mirage."

"A touch would've been sufficient."

"Nah, Scorpio. You deserve more than a punch for killing Gabe!"

"Ah, so that's what this is about. You're angry at me for assassinating the traitor that was Mother's puppet when you should be thanking me."

"Thanking you?!" I questioned at his soulless tone. "He was your brother and my bond!".

"And he watched me die!" He enraged back at me. "What kind of brother does that?! We were going to run away from Mother together because I was done with killing humans for her. He ratted out our plans then stood at her side as she showcased my execution to the organization. She beheaded me in front of the world but not before I managed to slip out of my body in the form of a soul. My original Alpha abilities were astral projection, so I used it to save my existence from dying along with my flesh. After exiting, I had no physical form to return to, so my soul was pulled toward the nearest vacant space, into you. Because you were comatose and classified as brain dead, I was able to take over your life from then on. With the promise of vengeance against my brother, I destroyed more than just Shredders without a care in the world in the way of my goal. However, as time passed by, I began to feel your conscience rising to the surface the longer I gave your brain activities," Scorpio said then laughed in an ironic tone. "Your anger should be directed toward him since even in the afterlife, we're stuck together because of his initial betrayal of me."

When he just said what he said, he instantly reminded me that the Organisms of this world are called Shredders where I'm from. He knows the same world I did, and that's a great help to my present reality, but I still disagree on his thoughts revolving Gabe.

"I can't be mad at him, or I'll be a hypocrite. How could I show hate when you just said that your appearance gave me life again? I could've been thankful to you both, but I was there, trapped in my own head as I watched you use my body to take his life. You never even asked him any questions when 'redemption' is a word that exists. From our time together, I learned for a fact that Gabe was a very kind soul. Your brother could never be as wicked as your stories of him depict. With all these undiscovered Alpha abilities in the world, how do you know that Mother, the compiler of power, didn't deceive you?" His eyes widened at the thought, then softened in frustration.

"Upsetting me on topics of an old world that we can never return to is pointless. We're gone from that past, and the Gabe of this present is probably long dead by now. You've been in this lightning bubble for forever, trying to regain your lightning force."

"Ridicule me all you like," I turned away from him with his reminder of my pending task. "You will not squash my hope that a miracle has happened outside of this lightning bubble." I prepared my stance and readied myself to run from the center point to the outer crust. "If the Gabriel of this world is still alive, I'll be his tutelary against your hunting stance. You won't get past me now that I know the nature of the Scorpio in my head."

Electricity erupted from around me, and I sped toward the outer circle. I pressed my palms against it and began absorbing the mass of lightning as quickly as I could. My frustration grew when a gripping force dragged me from my task once again. I elastic back and forth as usual, then spotted at the center like all the times before. Angered, I dropped to my knees, shaking my head down at myself and wanting to shout.

"Are you done making a fool of yourself, Asher? You despise me so much that you didn't even care to ask why I'm outside of you and suddenly so talkative today. Obviously, I don't like you too, but if you're stuck in here, then I'm stuck in here with you. I have an idea on how to get us out, but I don't have the body to execute it."

I looked up at him with a lost expression and asked, "What do you mean you don't have the body to do it? I just hit you, so aren't you real now?"

"I'm astral projecting from your mind. If another human was around, they could not see me, only you. You were able to bruise me, and I was able to bruise you because you and I are real to one another. To someone else you and I would be seen as one person."

"Wait a minute," I reacted when I noticed how long he's been standing there. "Now it makes sense how you're freelancing around the iris of this lightning, while I'm stuck being dragged back at the center."

"Yes. When you were still asleep a while ago, I manifested from your mind and went to touch the lightning spinning around us. I tried to absorb it myself, but it didn't respond to me, nor did it strike me down."

"I'm not even going to ask about what you had planned if it had allowed you to take it," I laughed at him. While standing to my feet I continued by saying, "I understand now. You need my help."

"You need mine just as much!" he roared then calmed down. "Raw power without order's understanding is repeated chaos. I have no problem with watching you make a fool of yourself for a while longer. Eventually, you'll sire to me for my help because repetition gets you nowhere."

"Don't speak as though I'm always wrong, alright? Just tell me your idea, and let's see if you're right."

"Alright, but you're going to have to perform it as I'm saying it."

"What?" I argued, but eventually agreed.

Agreeing to that was a horrible idea because what it led to, was the slowest motion of my life. Over three hundred steps into this madness that he's counting me toward, and I start to have my doubts.

"It's legit if you're wondering," Scorpio said, as I step after step toward the end.

He thinks that from the point I stop moving, a shadow of steps follows behind me to take me back to the beginning again. When I rushed to the inner shell at electric speed, I took twenty footsteps, the most.

Of course, I argued against this, but then he included the moment I became tired. The number of steps I began to take were extended, so the time I was able to remain at the end was also longer. The problem then was that I lacked the energy to absorb at a productive speed. I was taken back to the center and lost all hope in how much time I'd wasted. In the end, I rested my head on my knees and fell asleep from my saddened failure.

"I am wondering if it's legit. Why do you think so when I'm not even at the end yet?" I asked Scorpio.

"You've taken three hundred, seventeen steps. If each step was seen as a second, it's been about five minutes and seventeen seconds. This is the longest time you've been gone from the center, and you're still going. I'd say that's evidence enough to call this a legit plan," he proudly said.

I looked down at my feet as I stepped one after another with no space in between them. This is the moment I realized that even If I'm going slow, the fact that I'm going at all remains true. I suppose that for now I can believe that he's on my side.

At the mark of the millennia, I couldn't help but exclaim, "One thousand."

"The end is right there, Asher. Don't stop," Scorpio said as I continued my step by step. "This is still only a theory, so it's best to do it right on the first try and not rush the end. When you get in hands' reach, continue forward until your feet touches the end."

I walked as he counted, ten seventeen, ten eighteen, ten nineteen, and then ten twenty became my final step. He told me to set my arcana to seventeen minutes from now, and I asked it to.

The reflected glass on my wrist lit up and responded, *"Countdown commenced. T-minus 16 minutes, 59 seconds,"* the automated voice responded.

"Start absorbing now!" He shouted.

"I know!" I shouted back.

I took a standard step in reverse and pushed forth my arms. I pressed my palms onto the lightning force and my spirit enlightened at the endless flow of power entering my body.

"It... it feels so alive," I gasped, mesmerized by the feeling of its reconnection to me.

This is the longest I've been drawing energy from it, and I'm still going. This moment is so intense that my body's lightning a brilliant display that's brightening through all of my veins. Like the flip of a switch, the power surge abruptly stopped its output into me. The sapphire lightning I've obtained ceased its display as it once again became one with me.

"Whoa," I blinked quickly at the sudden transparency before my eyes. "Why's there suddenly a glass dome in front of us?"

"Asher, turn around now," Scorpio said, and I quickly looked back at his alarming sound.

My eyes widened in seeing that, "I've only absorbed half of it?"

"Not just that," he replied, and I began to see it happening before my eyes. From the edge of the other end, the hue of the lightning began changing from its natural aura into something other. The sapphire tone is progressing the lightning beyond a violet and toward a crimson display of wild energy.

"Red? That's quite far from blue, isn't it?"

"It's one of the exact opposites of the three primaries colors," he stated while looking around.

I turned my attention back to the outside again. From the scattered debris to the abandoned motor vehicles, The Hour Bridge of this side of the circle could finally be seen. It looks to be the side that leads to its broken edge.

What we've gathered so far is that the entire lightning bubble remains present, but each side of it now has a semicircle difference. This end is transparent, while the other end is shielding our view with a new developed crimson display of natural lightning. However, I could feel that this lightning has a different vibe coming from it.

The next big shocker was a relief that I could suddenly roam around like I was free and not fixed on that tug back to the center again. Scorpio's a little skeptical about my sudden case of free will, so he's allowing my arcana to continue the count down.

We headed to the other side but was stopped at the semicircle transparent wall of the circling halves. I placed my hand on it to feel if it genuinely was solid, and it was.

Lightning from the other side fiercely struck where my palm pressed. Aggressively, more and more of the red lightning struck in an outrage. I pulled away quickly, refusing to test it any further.

"Aw, it really misses you."

"No, it doesn't!" I denied. I looked back at Scorpio's remark and saw a humored expression across his face. "Oh, a joke."

"Just like that mental delay of yours. The lightning on the other side was really at your throat just now, wasn't it? Did its taunt really scare you away, Asher?" I turned to look at it again, still not understanding what I felt and still feel.

"It's not going to be kind to me, is it?" I asked myself.

A swift grip of my throat from behind followed the tripping of my legs into the air. Before I could gasp the suddenness of what was happening, my back was slammed to the ground.

"Ugh!" I sounded on impact. I became angered by his smile over me. "Quit playing with me, Scorpio, or I'll get serious," I warned.

"Your reaction time and lack of awareness is unanticipated and disappointing, Asher. You've absorbed exactly half of the lightning, yet you're frightened by the other side, which is now equal to you. If the crimson lightning doesn't let you absorb it, you should be powerful enough to not let it absorb you. Fight back and don't cower away." He coached.

I threw him off me and stood to my feet while brushing myself off.

"You lack confidence when it comes to displaying your current level of supremacy and that is your weakness. If guarded by me, your power would be seen as godlike," he bragged. I smiled, now understanding his unaltered nature.

"That's just like you, willing to rain down lightning from the sky if it'll make heads turn. I'm not the flashy type, so I'm glad I possess the lightning, and not you. I'm only upset that I must remain possessed by you too. But as fate requires, the prisoner and the key forever remain beside each other, guarded by me," I smiled and stepped away from him.

"Let's play a game, Asher," he asked, and my eyes tensed, reminded of his historically violent impressions of gaming. Sapphire Lightning flared up around me at an intensity unlike before.

"Alphacardia Max. Alpha Level - 0998," my arcana voiced as I turned to face him.

I rose my hand to the side, and the sight of a lightning rod rooted up from the ground. The sapphire lightning spiraled along a straight line until it impacted the clear plasma on the other side.

My power calmed down to a dormant state, lowering my Cardio Level as I glanced back at him.

With eyes of fascination he wondered, “How did you cast a creation of lightning from somewhere other than your body?”

“No clue.”

“Wow. I mean, you didn’t even create clouds to do it.”

“Ever since I absorbed the Sapphire lighting, it’s been adjusting to me and clarifying in my mind all I can do with it. The space on this side now feels like it’s all mine, so manifesting from any position around is now but a thought.”

“That’s unbelievable. I wonder what it’ll be like after you’ve reacquired all of it.”

“That’s what I have to find out. No more games, Scorpio; we have to keep patterning what comes next,” I said, starting our walk toward the center of the circle, now divided by two.

Scorpio revealed that his attempt to rile me up came with him wanting to see my power. He wanted to know if I was strong enough to break the plasma, so he called the example a win-win since I attacked it while showing him.

Scorpio theorized that by obtaining the full power, I’ll be able to break the plasma globe that’s containing us in the end. I’m honestly thinking that it’ll disappear on its own once I take everything.

Arriving at the center, we noticed that an oval pathway is the lone entrance into the other side.

“When you absorb the crimson lightning, the entire globe should become transparent. You’ll then have the power to shatter your exit from it.”

“Yeah, yeah, you said that.” I looked ahead and gulped to myself, sensing the rage of the lightning from the other side.

This could end badly for me, but still I walked to the face of the entrance and prepared myself for my next step into the red zone.

As a test, I pushed an arm into it and immediately screamed to an intense pain unlike anything I’ve felt before. I tried to pull away, but I feel it pulling me in further. Crimson lightning danced through my arm, shocking bursts of blood from my separating veins.

“It’s killing me!” I screamed for his help. “Get me away from this!”

“You have to fight it back, Asher!” Scorpio reminded.

I surged forth an intense release of lightning from my arm that’s inside the other side. The impact of the two forces clashed into shining a violet light. The shine intensified as a tingly feeling ran through my trapped arm. The build-up of energy brightened to an explosive force that pushed me far away. I was launched across the air and upon impacting the ground, I was knocked out of my senses.

I sat up in a quick gasp, holding my left arm as I stared at the burnt tissue all around it. The feeling of extreme pain is still vibrating from it, enough for me to cry instead of scream.

"I don't get it," Scorpio said while standing over me.

"Then let me spell it out for you. That lightning is vicious, and no one should have it!" I shouted, pointing a finger.

"I can see that, but why?" he extended a hand to help me to my feet.

After pulling myself up with my one good arm, I muttered that "I don't know why. When it was hurting me just now, it also felt like it was exterminating the lightning that I already have."

"It had no intentions of bonding or taking it back?" He asked. I shook my head, and his eyes widened as though he had an enlightening thought.

A sudden beep began to sound, and my eyes reflected the glass of the arcana on my wrist. They shook as the timer read, *"T-minus, 10 seconds."*

"The seventeen minutes countdown. I'd totally forgot about it," Scorpio reacted.

Three... two... one... counted down to completion. A loud ringing sound waled from the reflector as I'm lifted from my feet by a force.

"Asher"

"It's going to pull me in!!" I shouted, and he unexpectedly grabbed my arms. I screamed as one of them is badly burnt. He loosened his grip on it, and I said, "No! Don't let go of me! I'd rather be in pain than to be let go." he tightened to me again when I cried, and I muscled through the pain.

I'm being pulled toward the center, where the line between this side and the side of the red lightning is nonexistent. If I'm dragged to there, I'll surely die.

"This... isn't working!" he struggled to hold still his sliding stance. His hold is slowing down the pull of the force, but it's not stopping it at all.

"We can't stop this; you're only being dragged along with me. You were right about the steps equaling the amount of free time I'd have. I should've listened sooner," I apologized. "I'm a hinderance on you so you can let me go, okay?"

"Not okay! I want to live and you're my physical body, you idiot!" He shouted. "I'm a soul tied to yours, so any suicide of yours is a murder of me. You're killing us both by giving up so easily!"

"Fine, continue to hold on, and we'll die at once so that no one's to blame."

"That's not going to happen either. You need to think more, Asher," he fought me with surety. "Based on your experience, that lightning on the other side seems to be attacking your lightning and not you, right?"

"Tell that to my third degree you're pulling on."

"This only happened because your lightning is a part of you too. Purge your power from your body, and I'm positive that you'll be okay when you're pulled into the other side."

I looked at our positions and immediately knew that "I can't electrically output to thin air, only in through something."

"I'm holding onto you and keeping my stance on the ground, am I not?" He rhetorically asked, showing awareness of the conduit he'll become. "Just do it! I won't die unless you do, so use me to send your lightning through!"

I gripped his wrists tightly, commanding forth the lightning within me. From my arms, I focused a continuous release of concentrated energy into Scorpio. His hold onto me clenched as his body is being consumed by the jolts of raw power passing through him. When his resistance to the force that's pulling me ceased, we're both yanked across the air as I still cast every inch of my lightning into him. When I ran dry, his hands loosen, and so did mine to let him go.

Just as I'm to impact the core, his unresponsive body smashed to the ground. The feeling of all power within me faded as my back impacted the crimson lightning force.

Seamlessly, all residues of the supreme force vanished along with the conscious reminder of an unconscious state.

Co4

Door 14: Exiting the Lightning Bubble in My World

Scorpio's (POV) -k-

I pushed up from the ground and rose to a stance, surprised that I'm still physically here. A bright cherry glow brightened my eyes in that direction. On the other side of the plasma, the crimson lightning is blasting from a single object within its force. I strengthened my eyes to view this object closely, and it looked to be a crystal shell. It's attracting the lightning's attention as it moved toward the center point of that side.

"Asher," I voiced, realizing what had just transcended between us. I looked at the entrance point, and suddenly I was here, a distance in a second. I turned to view where I was quickly, and immediately I saw a mirage of myself, vanishing a trail of yellow lightning to my position. "What's this?" I looked at my palms and realized that I'm not as pale as I was moments ago. "I feel a foreign but familiar feeling," I muttered to myself, unable to explain it, and then it hits me like a muscle memory. "This is how I felt when I took control of his body and how I felt when I used to have my own. I... I feel alive again." My eyes water, still gasping a breath toward the enlightening feeling of life again.

The lightning behind me sparked a brilliant dance, causing me to look around at it again. My eyes widen as I viewed the crimson lightning drawing to the shell on the other side. I stepped back, smiling at the understanding of what's going on.

"He's doing it. That punk is actually absorbing the crimson lightning," I voiced in excitement.

All the red lightning absorbed into the crystal shell, causing it to crack. It broke free a blinding light that shattered the dividing plasma. The plasma fell from the air and flaked away to nothing before reaching the ground. In an instant, the semicircle expanded to a whole one.

When the light dimmed, Asher was shown hovering down from the air. The only trace of the crimson lightning remained dancing around his lowering body.

I rushed for the other side and just as his feet touched the floor, I abruptly appeared a few steps from him. I looked back and again a lightning mirage of me disperses from my path to here. I'm extremely fast now, but how? I turn back to him just as his eyes are to fix on me, and I took a shocking inhalation. The sudden breath from me skipped my heartbeat at his rosy iris connected a glowing stare to my sight.

He grinned while taking a step forward and voicing that, "I've never seen you so on edge, Scorpio." His eyes calmed down to their natural state before he reached close to me. "It almost looked like you were afraid of me."

"Keep dreaming, Asher. My only concern was that I'd have to waste time and energy killing your corrupted ass. Still, good to see that the lightning didn't change your personality." I raised my brows, noticing that both of his arms are in excellent condition. "You're healed?!"

He reached his right hand to his left arm to massage its previous burn. With a smile, he said, "I guess I am. This lightning has an amazing feeling to it. It may seem a bit frightening because of its hue, but it feels like a balance to the sapphire one I had. However, this one gives me a sense of incompletion that the last one did not."

"Incompletion?" I questioned.

"You know, lacking the feeling of a wholesome power. I do feel mighty at least," he gestured his hands for his crimson lightning to moderately awaken around it. "Wait," he focused on me.

He stepped back then rushed in and circled around to all of me.

When he'd gotten too close for comfort, I asked, "What's your problem, Asher?" while shoving his prying eyes away.

"It appears that I'm not the only one who's changed. Your hair is no longer snow-white, and your eyes don't have a foggy glow anymore. Your skin isn't so pale, and your voice no longer echoes to me. Scorpio, you seem different, yet somehow you still look exactly like me."

"A curse, I know,"

"Are you trying to call me unattractive?" he asked.

"A trial isn't necessary. But besides appearances, check out what this body can do," I extended my arms, sparking up the dancing yellow lightning around my palms to show that, "My appearance isn't the only thing that has adjusted. When you released your lightning through me, I felt it passing into the ground at first. But when I lost consciousness, and we were being pulled across the air, I sensed it flowing into me. Upon awakening, I realized immediately that your previous power had somehow became my own."

"Your eyes glow yellow when you're releasing that lightning from you, you know? It's a dead giveaway."

"So is yours, mister red eyes."

He laughed then said, "Well, in any event, this is great news. The last step in getting out of this bubble is to break through it," he gestured to the plasma concealing us here. "We know that half of the power wasn't strong enough to break through, but now that I have both getting out of here should be easy," he walked past me and said, "Let's head to the center of this place, I have an idea."

I walked after him with an immediate want for an elaboration on, "Now that I have both? What do you mean by that?"

"And you preach about being a wise guy," Asher remarked.

"You're a physical manifestation from my subconscious. If I stored my lightning into you then ventured out to absorb more from another source, wouldn't your power mean mine as mine is mine? Let's not forget that my body is real, and yours is nothing more than an illusion of me."

"Mind how you speak to me. Leashes don't last forever, and neither does the state of my serenity."

"And apparently, neither does this cooperation," he sighed, stopping to stare back at me.

"Nah, don't stop," I walked by him. "I'm dying to see this bright idea of yours come to life," I said in a relaxed tone.

"Is that so?" he continued after me.

Sarcastic is what he thinks me to be, but I am truly serious. If this plan doesn't involve me re-entering his mind, I'll flee from this bridge the second the plasma containing us is destroyed.

"Isn't this lovely?" Asher asked as we enter the center. "I can freely roam around now without any worries of ever being pulled back to here again,"

"And why exactly are we here again? What's the plan?"

"When I first entered this bubble, this was the point where I landed, and this was the position that kept pulling me back to it. It must be special, so this is where I want us to blast through from," he points to the sky. "Up there is where we'll simultaneously release the strongest lightning shot that we could muscle."

"Oh, right, the original plan," I'm reminded.

The plasma remained even after we've claimed both sides of the lightning. Assuming this would happen, I told Asher beforehand that all the power is needed to break our way out of this. We've obtained all of the lightning, but the outcome is far different than I thought it would be. Instead of one of us having one hundred percent of All, we're in two divisions holding one hundred percent of each half, fifty-fifty.

We readied ourselves with one another to synchronize our release. My left arm is raised to the sky alongside his right. Our lightning within manifested around each of our arms. The difference in our lightning's shade caused a clashing build-up between us.

"Now!" I said to him as I took notice of what was happening. We both casted a bursting line of lightning to the sky, his from his palm and mine from my fingers. The two blasts collided as they dually impact the plasma above. The strike exploded a thundering sound while displaying a brilliant shine of sizzling lightning. After stopping, I looked left and right and all around while Asher still looked up. "It didn't break," I sighed. "We're still trapped in here."

"The top is still too foggy to see."

"A circle ripples, Asher. One large crack and the entirety of it will crumble. Look around, nothing's happened," I frustratingly said. He looked at me then looked toward the exit of the bridge.

Folding his arms, Asher confessed that, "This was the only plan I had," He thought then got excited. His eyes glowed red and a burst of lightning of the same color generated around him. "I'll come up with another one; just wait there," he sparked away from me, and I saw every step he took as he distanced himself.

I sighed voicing, "It looks like it's up to me," I turned to head in the opposite direction. "That kid only knows brute force, and he's a copycat whose only plan was an old one of mine. His thought processing would be useless without me."

"Yo, are you mumbling to yourself?" I paused quickly with a blinking stare at him suddenly in my face. "In other news, I cracked the plasma. Come check it out," he excitingly said, lightning away again.

"Wait," I reacted and spun toward his flee. "You did what?!"

It took mere seconds to get from my previous position to where I am now. The plasma has a striking mark that's glowing lava through its cracks as though it's continuously damaging.

"After marking it, I tried to strike it some more, but nothing more was happening. I thought that if you struck it with your fancy yellow lightning, you could probably make it worse."

"Fancy? Really? Fine, let's try it," I easily agreed. I surged a flowing force of energy through my arm and casted forward the sizzling lightning. It fiercely impacted the exact spot that he'd struck but didn't cause any further damage. A second after I'd blasted it, I noticed the plasma healing itself from the mark of the red lightning.

"What are you doing? I thought we agreed that you'd make it worse, not make it better!" He looked at me in annoyance.

"That's what I intended to do. I didn't think it would heal itself." Embarrassed by my performance, I struck at it again, and a crack roots into the plasma from my lightning strike. "See, I did it."

"Yeah, you took us back to square one," he said, flaring up the lightning around him. "Let me show you how it's done," he produced a lightning whip in his hand and lashed it at the plasma. He struck the same spot that I did, and a second later, the damages started to rewind until it was healed again. "Wait, what?! Why?!"

"Wait a minute, Asher," I thought as I watched it happen. "What if nothing happened when we simultaneously sent a blast up at the center because we neutralize one another's lightning?"

"You mean like the Libra scale or a karma balance or something?"

"Yeah, exactly that. We are of two separate ends of the same power, so using it together causes nothing more than a nullified circle between us."

"That can't be right," he denied. "We know that one power isn't strong enough to break out of this; that's why we needed to retrieve both. We have both now but can only cause damage one at a time, making this entire plan pointless."

I stepped away from his misery to gather up a clearer conscience on my own. I visually studied the plasma, wondering if there's more than meets the eyes. I looked up beyond the barrier, and my eyes caught the sleeping clouds that still await the rising sun.

"Hmm?" I thoroughly wondered, as my eyes widened. "Asher, have you noticed that the sun hasn't risen as yet after all this time?" I questioned him away from mumbling to himself. "Come to think of it, the shade of the morning hasn't changed at all since you've entered here."

"Are you certain?" he asked as he viewed the reflector upon his wrist. "Arcana, what time is it?"

"I'm sorry, that feature is currently unavailable," the device echoed a response.

"You've got to be joking. It's everything but a clock?" he reacted.

"Just look at the tint of the sky, Asher. Or look at something that should be moving but is not," I set his focus to the mystery of outside. "I'm certain that beyond this plasma, time has stopped." "You're right," his voice projected from above me.

"When did you...?" I reacted to his hover above. My eyes following his stream of lightning as he's gradually floating back down.

"Leap up. You have to see what I saw," he rushed me when he landed. "With your lightning sight, you should be able to scan the bridge as quickly as I did."

I crouched to send a force of energy through my calves. From the ground, I pushed myself up high as yellow lightning danced around me.

My eyes fix on the high grass between a jungle and a beach. Within it, I saw the tainted forms of this world, stunned in the way their bodies are paused. They're in confrontation mode, and their masses are stopped like statues toward our direction. Their numbers reduced from a horde to a single leading one as my eyes followed their placements onto the bridge. The leading one at the foremost reach of the lightning bubble is the K-Organism, petrified by the stillness of time.

I glided down using the heated lightning dancing around me. When I touched the ground, I looked to Asher, whose eyes are now hopefully fixed on outside of this bubble. His body seemed tense, and I can understand why. What we saw out there just then is the exact moment he entered here, unchanged after all this time.

"He's alive," Asher softly voiced.

"You can't be sure of that," I said.

"Really?" he sarcastically asked, looking my way. "When the K-Organism didn't pursue me after I entered here, I assumed that it turned around and went back after Gabe. This is why I was so impulsive to get out of here at the start. Now..." he looked back to the outside. "Now, I can see that the world stood still right after I'd left it. I asked for a miracle, and it was answered. Gabriel's still alive, and now I must believe in what I can see," a bright smile developed across his face.

"I don't think it's completely stopped," I voiced.

"Are you blind or ignorant, Scorpio?" he gestured.

"Intellectually speaking, something and nothing can't happen at the same time, only something and something else. If we're able to observe out there as being paused, then inside this plasma is like a world of its own, and out there is like the space around it."

"I don't understand that analogy."

"It means that time could be extremely slowed to our eyes, and not paused. One second out there could just mean a very long time in here."

"If out there is slowed enough to appear to be stopped, then that's great. I can take forever in here, and I still won't be late."

"You're foolish to think that you'll be a victim of old age before Gabe's killed. Look around us, Asher. You have nothing to consume in here. If anything, you'll die from the lack of resources to keep your body functioning first."

In frustration, he shouted, "the point is that I have more time than I originally thought! Wait." he faced me with a sudden smile. "I'm such a fool for not doing this sooner," he said, gesturing his hand to me. "Return to your cage," he commanded.

I stepped back with shaking eyes knowing that this was coming sooner or later. I'm not afraid of him at all, just apprehensive in wanting him to learn so quickly that I may already be liberated from him.

"Return to your cage?" I rhetorically asked. "You know that when I manifested from you, my body never left the mental prison you keep me in."

His eyes shut for a mere second, then opened as he dashed to my sight. His sudden flash of crimson lightning danced in my face as the feeling of his knee pressured into my stomach. I'm forced back at high speed and impacted the plasma wall of this bubble. I began to fall forward and was assisted down by a kick against my spine from above. My body slammed to the ground and while laying on my stomach, my arms were forcefully held behind me in his grip.

"At least ask me questions first," I grunted to suggest.

"Shut up.," his voice shook. "How did you get out of my head, Scorpio?! Is this another trick of yours?!" He asked, confirming that he can no longer find me within him.

"Now you ask the prominent question after you've sent me flying with your toddler fists. Sorry, but none of that hurt just now."

"Quit taunting me and tell me."

"It was a while ago when I thought I could be free, but now I believe it. I'm truly alive again, Asher."

"You're not," he released my arms and turned me over. "You can't be..." he placed his hand on my chest and his eyes widened while quickly saying, "No heartbeat, you liar!"

His eyes darken as his lightning went wild around him.

"Come back to your cage, Scorpio!" he held my arms to my side, and like an exhalation of breath, my power and my life began to pull away from me.

I riled up, releasing a furious blast of lightning from my arms. He's pushed into the plasma and attentively landed firmly on his feet. I adjusted up to his leveled stance as I caught my breath.

My heart's racing, but still he's saying that I have none. When I felt it for myself, my heart skipped a beat as I understood why he'd felt nothing just then.

He flashed at me from his position, his motion at a speed that my eyes tracked clearly. I caught his arms at a challenging pace, clashing a treacherous force between the two of us.

"My heart is mirrored to yours. Feel it again," I demanded.

His eyes seemed to give in, so I loosened one of his hands. His palm rested on my right chest and his lightning immediately died when he felt it beating.

"W-What does this mean?" He questioned.

"I told you, I'm alive."

"Your heart is beating as you say, but it shouldn't be on the opposite side of your chest." He stepped back, adding that, "Moments ago, I tried to reabsorb you and it felt as though I could. To you, doesn't that mean I should?"

"Kill me? Just for power? You must've lost your mind."

"Not only for power but for my way out and not yours, Scorpio. After finding out that the Gabriel of this world is still alive, it's changed how I feel toward you. I can't let you retake his life, so I won't let you get out."

A flash of ember lightning flared up his untamed force of power. If felt like Asher's hatred and anger toward me cannot be tamed by any voice of reasoning.

"You're itching at every spot in your heart to throw a blow at me, huh? Your frustration dwells on what I've done in the past, thinking I'll do it again in this present opportunity of my homicide being undone. You obviously don't know me well enough, so release your frustration if you have to. I'll tell you the truth when you're done with your tantrum."

"Sorry, but you'll miss the chance to taunt me like that again. The dead don't speak, and I wouldn't want to hear it."

He raised his fist and clenched an awakening shake of the ground. My eyes bounced all around, unsurprised by the burst of a lightning rooting up from the ground around.

I escaped to the air, and like a shadow, a lightning string followed me up. It latched around my ankle and whiplashed my back to the ground.

A press against my chest came with his presence over me and the gaze of his red eyes.

I smiled up at him, and he's triggered to ask, "Are you that happy to die?"

"No, I'm just surprised by your speed. You're extremely fast in general," I remarked then and pointed to the sky beyond him. "But sadly, you're terribly slow to me."

He hastily looked up when he heard the synchronized sentences from my voices present and above. His head rushed back down at where I am not and witnessed only the disappearance of yellow lightning.

"Interesting," he voiced, then looked up at me and raised an arm to the air. He clenched his hand and from behind, a beam of red lightning bolted through my stomach.

While observing from the ground, I witnessed more bolts striking through where I am not, killing the mirage of where I was.

"You can't reabsorb the dead," I said, and he hastily looked to my standing position and cynically smiled. "What's with the murderous intent behind your strikes at me?" I wondered.

"Those were fatal, yes, but none an instantaneous death. My main objective is to keep you still for a short period of time, fatally wounded or not. How else will I catch hold of your tricks and absorb you?" he gestured an arm, and from another perspective, I witnessed a lightning beam shoot into the arms, legs, and heart of my mirage.

"Those look pretty instant to me," I said. He angled to view the new position of my voice came from. "Your lightning's remarkably wide-ranging. You can bring it up from the ground and manifest it from the gases in the air, besides already being able to produce it from within you."

"And your speed is unfathomable, no doubt. Let me guess," he smiled in my direction. "You're not where you are right now, are you?"

I grinned, surprised by his quick study.

"You're right, I'm not," my voice tripled, displaying my odd number of positions around him. "I'm neither there nor here in your seeing and hearing of me. Every time I voice anew, I'm furthermore, acting as the flow of time alongside history."

"To fool me with this even as I'm aware would require you to have speed far beyond my own."

"If you can't leave a destined thought in a mirage that green lights after you're gone in an instant, "A version of me slipped away as I continued with, "yes, my speed far exceeds even yours." He looked to my new stance with haste. "The ideas I embed into my mirages as I slip away can be one of speech or one of action. For example," A multiple of me in five positions surrounded Asher. "The order is to subdue you," we rushed at him, and in a point of a second, we all held him down. "Are you ready to talk now?" the five of us asked.

Lightning spiraled out of him, forcing back all of me except for myself that I'm still within. The others fell and disappear as I'm kept in the range of his rage due to his tightened grip on me.

To my eyes, he wickedly gazed and said, "You should've kept your distance well, being much safer avoiding from me. Your speed is to flee from my chase and not to attack back. You've gotten too close and now I can take you back into me."

His force shifted from an external push to an internal pull. Abruptly my skin began to convert to the electric energy I'm made of and absorb into his hands on me.

"Welcome back to me," he graced as I'm reverted into lightning energy and completely absorbed for his bodily nutrition.

The mental link I had with my mirage vanished as I watched him pull that piece of me into him. The aura surrounding his body grew to some extent, threatening even the ground surrounding his feet. He laughed historically as his appearance of lightning also strengthened in its destructive potential.

His head turned directly to where I truly am and in an instant, he's in my face.

"Look how much I've just grown and that was only a taste," he smiled.

I miraged myself back with widened eyes, surprised his rapidness. I watched as he kicked my head to the ground and stepped onto my face. How did he nearly catch me?

He looked to my true self as his feet absorb my past into him.

"I almost had you. If you keep leaving behind your residues for me to absorb piece by piece, I'll grip a hold of your true self in no time," he explained.

It makes sense. If he's already absorbed twenty percent of me, then he's at seventy percent and I'm at thirty. He's getting faster and equally I'm becoming slower.

He turned to me, showing his crimson eyes that are striking raw energy through them. "Let's play a game, Scorpio."

I froze with widened eyes at his request.

"Now it all makes sense," I voiced, understanding my sudden reluctance to want to kill him and his sudden change over to a cruel nature. "You're not acting like yourself, Asher." I shouted, figuring us out. "And neither am-"

"-I?" he gripped my shoulders and questioned in my face. "I know we're not ourselves because I'm much stronger now." Instantly my being began to be vortexed into his hands on me. "The gaming rules are simple. In this circle, the last one alive is the winner," he reached for my soul as I gulped, patiently resisting and gradually shifting the tides of the pull. He's taken by surprise, feeling my forceful pull back. He gripped my throat with both hands, so I clenched onto his wrists to prevent him from squeezing. "Stop trying to take mine and give up yours!"

"No! Why don't you try asking yourself how I'm even able to pull back, huh?"

"I don't care how. Just become one with me now and leave me alone!"

"Think about it, moron. When you transferred your sapphire lightning into me, I must've also gained your heart because ever since then, I started to feel life. I couldn't think of killing anyone anymore. What if when you absorbed that red lightning, you gained living energy while having no heart, so you're now like this. What if we're like this now because we've switched perspectives?"

"Stop talking! You're not making any sense! And even if you were, there's always an ulterior motive to your suggestions, Scorpio."

His aggression grew to wrath as he shifted his hands to snatch my wrists. In an unexpected force, he reattempted the depletion of my energy into him. I resisted, withstanding his pull in an equal tug back.

Our contradiction of one another echoed a spark that followed a ray of light which erupted an explosion between us. The pressure blew me back at a sonic speed, impacted my back to the ground and slid me toward the edge of the plasma bubble. I rolled up onto my feet and stumbled in reverse to slow my motion until my back ultimately hit against the end.

As I leaned against it to catch my breath, casual steps toward me raised my eyes to Asher's approach.

"This has become quite annoying," he voiced. "It seems we're blown apart when we synchronously try to take power from one another."

"Now we know what not to do to cause our own self-destruction," I warned, stepping from against the transparent wall and facing his approach.

"Of course, I know what to do. I'll weaken you and then begin the absorption process," he concluded.

Lightning erupted around his body as his ferocity focused on me.

His anger toward me is untamed even after learning the truth about why we're acting like the negative and positive ones.

As he made a move for me, I voiced, "Wait a second," while thinking about our dilemma. "I think I get it now. It's hard to trust information from someone who's operating under a codename. If getting rid of 'Scorpio' is the only way you'll agree to unite in our escape from here, then I'll tell you who I truly am.

"At this point, no name you confess to me can stop your pending execution."

"People are selfish, and you're no exception, Asher. If the name is important to you, you'll let me live to hear me out."

"Then let's test your theory, shall we? Who are you?!"

He accelerated a vanishing rush toward me, and so quick I said, "My name is Michael Grey."

In the blink of an eye, he's paused in the face of me, holding a raging ball of lightning in his palm. His muscles are tensed and frozen, along with his petrified eyes on me.

After a second more, he muttered, "I don't believe you," to my face.

"Then why am I still alive and talking?" I asked.

"Because you brought up a reminder of pain from my past that only I should know about."

"Then let's talk some more about it," I suggested, then rewind in my head what he just said. "Wait, you never told anyone what happened? I guess we were both remorseful then because I never said anything to anyone either."

"Quit it! You've lived in my head. You could be using my memories against me to try and gain my trust."

"Our minds live alongside one another, not within each other. I can't go into your past just as you cannot go into mine. From the moment we became one, we shared the same history, but any time before that our memories are individually divided."

"Alright, if you know so much, then tell me how Michael and I began. Let's see how far back you claim to remember."

"We met in high school, four years before the Shredder infestation. At the time, some bullies were disrupting my focus at lunch in the gymnasium, so I put an end to their ruckus when I kicked their asses from the bleachers. It turned out that they were bullying you, so you thanked me, even though I'd done it to save my own concentration. Either way, you quickly became fond of me afterward. And as the new kid, I stuck around you to gather information from someone seasoned who seemed to hold me in high esteem." His lightning died when I described the scene in detail.

"Wow, that's what you thought of me?"

"I'm just being honest."

"Okay, then how did Michael and I end? He hesitantly asked while stepping back from me.

"We ended with you on the ground and my knuckles rosy from smashing in your face," I recalled as my heart began to race. "You and I went to a Thanksgiving carnival held in the park nearly three months after we'd met. Sometime that evening, we distanced ourselves from the loudness and ended up watching the carnival on a bridge from afar. New York was a pass-through for me, so I never learned the title of the bridge we stood on."

"Bow."

"To whom?"

"Nothing, keep going."

"It was on that bridge that you found the comfortability in our friendship to tell me about your preference toward the male figure," I said, and a sudden pressure against my jaw came from his fist striking me. My body stumbled back as the back of my head hit against the plasma and I fell onto my ass.

"Do you remember that?" he attempted to calmly ask as he stepped back into the spot he stood.

I laughed, tasting the blood on my lip and saying, "How could I forget?. I deserved that."

I got back onto my feet and spat out blood from the first real bruise I've allowed him to land on me.

"I like the little bit of emotion you're throwing into it, but you're not fooling anyone, Scorpio. I remember that Michael's older brother used a wheelchair to get around. If you're somehow both Scorpio and Michael at once, then your older brother that I've never met before would have to be Gabriel. Do you see how that doesn't add up, since Gabe can use his legs perfectly fine?"

"You already know why he can walk. He ratted me out to Mother because if he loses her 'gift of all senses', he loses his legs. My brother's first power was angel wings that granted him the freedom to soar across the sky. He could fly then, but he still couldn't walk, and so Mother gifted that power to him. This power healed him from the disease that took his legs and was later aiming for his life. Heck, it didn't just heal him but granted him a divine manipulation over every cell within his body. He could manipulate his veins, blood, bones, vision, and much more. Since Mother is connected to every power she grants, this allowed her to strip them away with the snap of her finger whenever she wants. Gabe owed Mother everything after she saved him and powered him up, so to pay her back he became her puppet to keep her gift of All senses."

Asher's eyes shows that he's lost in thought, thinking on everything I'm saying.

"If you're pondering this hard before answering, then you're already at a contradiction of what you used to believe." I stated.

"I know Gabe brought out black wings once before and revealed himself to be Mother's black angel. I just never knew that his 'gift of all senses' abilities was from her. But now that the Gabriel of this world uses that ability so freely, that aspect of what you said could be considered true. However, I'm still searching for an error in what you've said."

"And if you don't fine one? Wouldn't this mean that ultimately, you've known me for four years before knowing my big brother."

"You don't deserve to call Gabriel, big brother, Michael! Even if I knew you from the start of my life, I'd never let you kill him again."

"I've lived that story once before, and I have no desire to live it again. Unlike you, I completely understand that where we are now isn't the dimension or reality we once knew. I no longer have a need for vengeance, and your grudge against me is minuscule compared to the story we've just fallen into."

"Wait a minute, your last is Gray, right? Well, that's not Gabe's last name."

"We have different fathers."

"What a convenient excuse."

"Will nothing I say be convincing enough for you to consider that everything could be real? We're wasting time in here, Asher!"

"Outside seems to be motionless to the eyes, so we've got a lifetime in here to come to terms. But still, I'll trouble you with a conclusive question to end it all."

"Yeah? What's the question?" I asked, wanting to finally end this.

"What pulsed you to assault me when I came out to you that evening?"

"Oh," I reacted, as those heavy thoughts reemerged. "That story is a novel to tell, beginning as far back as my childhood, Asher. The mental scars built up from then to now has made my memory extensive. I'll tell you all about it when we're not in this bubble."

"Nah, summarize that shit right now, and then tell me the long story later. I just need you to share something about why your reaction was so hostile toward someone you called a friend. I just... I need to understand."

"So, it's like that?" I asked, and he didn't say anymore. "Fine, if that is your final request before we can exit, then I'll tell you the point of how I felt at that moment. But after I answer this, no more questions asked, agreed?"

"If the answer is your honest truth, I'll concede."

My eyes looked away from his as I thought back and voiced that, "I've never lied in general, only ever withdrawn information. When you came out to me that evening, my eyes opened and saw a window of opportunity that terrified me. Over the months after meeting you, I'd began to bond with you on a level where my heart looked to yours more than anyone else in that city. This bottled-up feeling was easy to express through brotherhood but then immediately became difficult when you revealed that we had an equal attraction to one another. It caused a haunting flashback of my father to appear as if he was present. The aggression I showed you that evening was of a boy cowering over what a dead man thought about him. If not for that traumatic intervention, I'm sure that I would've shown you love."

I looked to his eyes, and they uncomfortably evaded mine. With a numb expression, he turned away and placed a hand on his chest. After removing it, he immediately walked off.

After about a dozen steps, he paused and turned to me saying, "I'm not waiting on you to catch up."

"To come where with you?" I asked.

"To the exit, of course. As you've demanded, no more questions asked," He continued forward while acting a bit peculiar to me now.

His lightning has calmed to the point where I cannot even sense that he has power. I'm skeptical about following him, yet I feel as though this may be the end. He stopped walking after a long while and remained fixed in his current position until I caught up to him.

Looking around, I asked, "What's your plan this time? Why are we at the center again?"

"You and I cause a blast apart when we try to take power from one another at the same time. I think that if we stand here and mutually try to give our power to each other-"

"-we could internally collapse into nothing. An implosion is no better than an explosion, Asher."

"The collapse would not happen in the case of compatibility. Do you recall who Marcus and Lucas are?"

I thought for a moment, then quickly remembered, "The British twins?"

"Yes, those ones. Those geniuses managed to pull together and fuse into a single entity. They ultimately doubled their power and released it at a monstrous level from their singular form."

"Their succession was more than likely based on their biological compatibility," I reminded.

"Aren't we two minds with the same separate body now? Beyond that there was another aspect to their compatibility. It was ultimately up to their love, trust, and transparency."

"Transparency? Alright, then let's make this fusion work. Tell me what you thought about what I said earlier," I requested.

"Honestly, I just wanted the truth. You've waited until your physical body was gone, your spiritual body to get trapped in my own, and your manifested body to resurface looking like my doppelgänger before you told me all of that. If my emotions were sentient, they'd debate each other in confusion right now."

"You don't know what's the right reaction to have, and that's understandable. Well, I apologize for taking forever to say I'm sorry. And about my brother," he fixed to me as I mentioned Gabe. "If you're right about Mother deceiving me, then I'm an imbecile for executing my blood without interrogation. My problem is that I refuse to address what bothers me when I'm bothered. But now, I think I'll express my feelings more and maybe try to learn about this version of my brother. I'll try to make up for all that pain I caused the both of you in this second chance of an alternative universe. However, I'll only do it, if you're right about him being a good man."

"That's a great start, Michael." he smiled, finally accepting that I am who I am.

"So, no more, Scorpio?"

"As long as you don't kill anyone anymore."

"Deal." I nodded. "At least you didn't say that I couldn't hurt them pretty badly."

He laughed while shaking his head. He then took up my hand and as he placed it on his chest he said, "Do you feel that?" My eyes widened as my hand clenched for an answer, so he continued. "Even with the proof of your heart being on the wrong side of your chest, I questioned whether you were alive or not. After you tried to absorb me earlier and we blew apart, I wondered how it could be that you were equal to me. Then when you told me the truth, and I saw myself in you, I realized the answer." I moved my hand to the other side of his chest and verified for myself as he said, "I no longer have my heart because you do."

I lifted my hand from his chest and placed it on mine. While wondering how there's only one heart beating between the two of us, I asked, "How? Is this really your heart I have?"

"I'm not sure myself, but yours is not on the correct side, and the change does mirror along with our personalities. I transferred my previous power into you and absorbed the red lightning. From then, I was coming to reason with only my mental understanding. I didn't know until recently, that I wasn't using my heart to make any decisions."

While thinking about it, I replied, "I had a feeling that this reluctance to hurt you came from a change in me. I just thought that this change was from me, but it was from your heart alone."

"In this fusion, that heart will be ours, but our minds will be of two separate souls. You have a potential to be a great man, Michael, and my heart has helped you to see that. I accept that all you say is true because it's all from my heart that I know so well."

"Hmm," I thought. "This makes me want to know one more thing, but I fear asking it to someone without his heart."

"I may be heartless right now, but with enough information my deductive reasoning should bring me to the point of correction. Haven't you noticed that my anger is all but gone? It's easier to tame now that confusion has been stripped from the equation. What would you like to know? I'll answer it directly."

"If I was transparent back then and told you everything that I am telling you now, what would the rookie version of you have responded to me?"

Asher smiled as he suddenly took up one of my hands and placed it back onto his hollow chest.

"Here," he said. "Let me show how it's done."

Lightning flared up around Asher, but this time his eyes remained natural as he began to output his energy into me. The immensity of the force widened my eyes to him already starting the exiting process.

I reacted by tightening my hands onto his chest and releasing an equal flow of power back into him. The dual output and intake from us both caused an unusual spiral between us. From him to me, our lightning energies altered in circulation with the feeling of his heart pulsation moving back and forward between us.

Our power acted in the same wavy motion as the lightning quickly trading between us began to become one tone. This constant continuity that sped up with every cycle caused a ball golden lightning to form in the space between us. That lightning passed through us, and it grow into a tiny sphere that contained us.

"Wow," I reacted at the golden universe we're inside of. "Now that's a sight, huh?"

"Michael, look at me," he called my focus to his eyes. With a genuine smile at me, he revealed that, "If you had shown me love, the rookie version of me would've felt like it was in my right to express more to you. I also planned to tell you that evening, if things went well, that I had a crush on you."

He voiced and took my breath away as I thought about a past that can't be changed.

"A timeline where we could've had the best year of our lives together is a dream to imagine, wouldn't you say?" He asked. "Maybe with you, I could've lived a less lonely life before the old world was killed by the Shredder pandemic. But alas, because of my impatience and your resolution at the time, we ruined a happy ending for us."

All I could do was stare, feeling like it was mostly my fault. And if it wasn't, then was this outcome always meant to be?

Striking through the surface of his skin, sudden veins split apart his flesh and exposed a glorious light coming from within him. The slip of his touch on my chest became the feeling of wind motioning into nothing upon and around me. I looked for his hands that had completely vanished, then back to his eyes that are moderately calm.

"I guess it's about that time we become one," he said.

"Since I'm not entirely sure who our minds will become once we're one entity, I'll say this," I voiced quickly. "As Scorpio, I never hated you. I agitated you most times for you to focus on me because I still liked your attention. I also acted out once and ripped a good person's heart out because I was jealous of him gaining your attention. Those actions showed my interest in you, but my weak ass couldn't even find the courage to declare that I had a crush on you too." I conveyed, focusing on his eyes that are shocked to hear any of that.

From his shock, a smile surfaced while shaking his head at our heart to heart.

"You know what? If possible, let's become someone else entirely, forgetting our past and starting over as a man with a blank slate."

"That'd wipe away both of our consciousness. We'd die, Asher."

"I know, and I'm actually okay with that. If we become someone new, Gabe's fate to die by my body controlled by you would never come true."

"And it won't now. I've changed."

"I know. But I was thinking that maybe we were never meant to live in this world, just pass through it. If we do this, we'd break into existence, a whole new timeline. So, what do you say? Will you fuse with me and create a new character to become our legacy?"

After thinking for a minute, I said,

"Okay," agreeing to exit my life with him. "If this character we'll create can become more than just a protagonist but also a hero, then this is the ultimate sacrifice, and my chance to repay all of my wrong doings."

After I voiced that, the two of us gradually lost our physical forms and in our transcendence, we vanished, ultimately becoming nothing more than perpetual energy.

Our vision, hearing, and all other senses were consumed by the split-brain fastening of our unifying power.

Farewell, to the separate existences we once knew, for our dual mentality and our single heart is now under the control of a primordial man made of us.

Co5

Door 15: My Brother's Acceptance of My Return

Midnight's (POV) -1-

The sound of a snore twitches in my ears as I'm voicing an ending scene of my narrative. While I questioned if I heard correctly, I hear it again.

"Brother?" I called in disbelief that his quietness upon me meant that he's asleep.

"Huh?! What? Where?" His movements on my back hastily agitated as his grip onto me tightened.

"Were you napping?" I asked.

"No!" He quickly answered. "Well, maybe for a second," he honestly disclosed.

"I'm very disappointed. I'd be okay with you falling asleep on a regular basis, but not right now. I'm telling you this story to show you the proof you requested of me. Is this your way of saying that you don't want to hear it?"

"No, of course not. It was a very mixed-up night that came with a lot of information and thinking about it made me a bit dizzy. I just need to slap myself a tad some," he said as I heard his cheek smacked from left to right. "And keep going, you know?"

I couldn't help but laugh at how carefree he's still being around me. He just casually fell asleep upon someone he denies having a meaning to. His actions appear to lack premeditation, making me believe that this is my brother's genuine self again. Was it something I said that's causing him to gradually come back to me?

I angled upright, and he held onto my neck tightly as I started to bring us down to our destination.

"We're landing?" he reacted, attempting to look around while we lowered. "Wait, we're at The Hour Bridge."

"This is Androsia's broken end of it a few miles out into the ocean. You were sleeping for a minute, yet you missed us leaving land?" I wondered.

I landed us onto the road, and he loosened his arms and stepped back.

As I stood in the direction of the ocean, I noticed a flaring peak of daylight rising at the edge of the globe. In this, I know, it's almost time for the end.

"Look, it's about to rain," brother called to my attention. I looked up, and the dark clouds forming above us began dancing in a theme of golden lightning.

"Those don't look like rain clouds, brother," I said, and almost right away, a loud thunder sparked a single lightning strike down to the seas. My eyes followed it quickly, but I lost vision of it, and an impact did not sound.

Brother and I ran to the side of the bridge for a better view of the sudden scene. Brother's expression was astounded when he saw a man of immense golden lightning, hovering above the seas. I was most shocked when I saw the ocean below him rose back into place. His abrupt stop above it must've caused the water to pressure down. There's no question about it, he's incredibly powerful.

The lightning man's eyes are fixed toward Androsia island, so my eyes followed to sight what he viewed. Right away I took notice of a silver shine speeding across the waters toward his direction.

"Brother, look there!" I pointed as my finger followed its rapid velocity.

"Are they going to battled?" brother asked.

"It appears so."

Several feet from the man of golden lightning, the steel creature abruptly stopped. While standing on water, it turned around and walked away. After a few steps, it leaped into the sky and formed wings from its steel back. It then swiftly jetted away from the man and flew back toward the island.

The man turned into nothing but lightning energy and zoomed after the creature's flee, leaving a residue to shadow his movements.

"I guess it wasn't a battle, brother. It looked like a game of 'catch me' since one's running away." I remarked.

"The steel creature that ran away almost looked like an Organism. Do you think that it was the K-Organism that the characters in your story encountered?"

"Possibly, and the man that was chasing after it-"

"-is a total mystery."

"A total mystery?" I questioned. "Wait, how *much* of the narrative did you miss?"

"Huh? This was in the story too?" brother questioned to my eyes. "I was listening, I promise. It's just... It's such a trip of the mind that I couldn't follow all of it at once and accidentally fell asleep," he genuinely displayed.

I laughed, shaking my head to his sudden pureness that he had at our beginning.

"You're now making me feel bad for not checking up on your awareness, what a twist," I reacted. "Brother, stories unwritten can hardly be repeated in the same. What do you recall? I'll try my best to summarize it."

"Okay, so this is what I remember. The lightning boy ran onto The Hour Bridge to reobtain the full capacity of his power. He needed it to help him win against some mutant kind of Organism because electricity wasn't enough. It was that same K- Organism we just saw," he pointed to where it was. "While on his way to his destination, the lightning boy encountered a lifeless body. The body was of another boy he seemed to recognize from a memory of being on the slicer. When I heard that, that's when I became dazed in thought, remembering that the body he'd found was mine."

"You're not dead or there, brother. Don't ever think like that!"

"I've lightened up from the roots of my shadowed beginning. Isn't to change, to die? It's hard to explain why I'm here and not there where I should be dead. Actually," he thought further back. "It's not hard to explain to you. Do you remember that time when we were in the tree watching the scene that fell from the sky, and I yearned to flashback?" he asked.

My heart stopped then raced by his sudden question. Is he aware of what he's subconsciously doing with me?

With fulfilled eyes, I smiled with all of myself and responded, "Yes, I remember, brother. I remember it clearly. Your consciousness vanished from my presence after you willed to look into the hourglass of the past. Your body then blazed into flames, and to the sky, you exploded into a short-lived sun. Ultimately, in my grief for you, I froze over my core to chase after you in death."

"I was never on the side you left me for. I ended up in a past scene not too far behind you, faded but alive. Eventually, we would've been present to each other again if you'd waited for me to catch back up with you. I ended up on the Slicer, and while inside, no other character could see me except for the lightning boy. I also couldn't touch any of them, but I never tried touching the lightning boy to see if we were real to one another. Objects were still solid to me, meaning that I could still be harmed. Now that I think about it, I should've hit the weapon out of Cole's hand instead of trying to push him down. Anyway, when the lightning boy looked into my eyes, it felt like two worlds had collided. Shortly afterward, the Slicer crashed, and I died. Within the sky, I reappeared then I fell again. Upon landing, I was severely injured and died in the arms of someone that came around before I was gone. Shortly after, I was standing on the bridge perfectly fine before an explosion in the sky took my attention. Something flying down hit the bridge, and I instantly ran to it with possible knowledge of what it was. When I reached it, it turned out to be me. I held myself in my arms and watched his life slip away, knowing that I was looped into becoming who you see now. The cycle ended at that moment, and I've been this shade ever since. Afterward, I saw a sunny reminder of me in the sky and remembered where I belonged. But in my lateness of returning to you, your hope had already extinguished, and you were freezing yourself. I should've quit viewing the entertainment and rushed straight back to you when I'd landed so that you wouldn't have had to suffer through that."

"You're right, you were pretty late. And you're also right that I lacked a bit of patience in my wait. But WOW, about everything else." I can only gaze at how much he's just expressed to me.

Is he truly not aware that he's exposed his belief in me again? He's as he once was before all of the stories and the confusions. He's being my brother again, but why? How?

"I know, it's a lot. You've got to think about it long enough to comprehend it. Even I glitch when I overthink it, and I'm the witnessing victim. Whether you believe me or not, I know that the body the lightning boy encountered was mine."

"No, no! I believe you. I'm just-" I grinned, too excited to talk straight. "You're suddenly acting as though you want for nothing more as you stand here before me. So, let me ask you again. Who am I to you?"

"Huh?" he knotted his brows, looking to the ground for answers. "Who you are to me?"

"Brother," I called for his attention, and there was no hesitation when his head rose to meet my eyes. I smiled at the truth that his feelings are indeed the same again. But why hasn't his mind come to an answer? "Who's Aiden to you?" I asked.

"Aiden's my brother," he smiled.

"Alright, now who am I?"

"You're-" he abruptly paused while looking at me.

His eyes began to go away, and suddenly he held his head with both hands.

He started to make a painful cry out, so I took his hand and said, "No, stop thinking," and he did.

He looked at me, showing the tears that were building in his eyes from his strain.

"You don't have to think about it if it brings you this much distress, okay?" I comforted.

"Okay," he replied, and I stepped away with developing thoughts about his peculiar behavior.

"You're unable to call me by my name and I wonder if it's because it's afflictive to your memory of watching me die. You react to my call of 'brother,' so I know your feelings for me believes that I am. I have a solution that will bring content to your vision and your heart alike. Why don't you choose a new name to call me?"

"Can I really do that?"

"A day ago, we had awoken underground knowing nothing, not even our names. We only knew that we had each other, so you named me, and I named you. We escaped that underground library together and have journeyed as one ever since then. Logic nor law can comprehend how we've lived so many lifetimes in so little time. Those loops that happened in a single day grew us up. If your feelings about me are still the same as yesterday, but your eyes can't see that, then call me as you see me today. Before the renewing Sun breaks the dawn, give me a beginning again and gift me a meaning to you."

"And that starts with a rename?" I nodded, and so he added, "Well, I guess I can't call you nothing at all, that'd make you hard to find." He laughed, and it brightens my heart to know that he's really himself. "Wait, nothing's actually a perfect call for you."

"No, it's not!" I refused. "I need to be called something real."

"No, no," he paused me with his laughter. "I'll call you Midnight."

"Midnight? Why that?"

"You said that you're the original Aiden in Aiden the fourth's body, right?"

"Yeah," I tried to follow.

"Well, if 'A' is equal to the first number and 'Zero' is equal to the first letter, then 'A' is equal to 'Zero' and 'B' is equal to 'one'. I simply took your four generations of A's and made them four zeroes. As the meaning of the first minute in a day, I'll name you The Core of Midnight. But I'll call you Midnight for short."

"Midnight, huh?" I humored at his explanation of me. "It's unexpected but I really like it, brother."

"Great. And how about you? What will you call me now?" he asked.

"I'll call you as you've always been to me," I looked into his eyes that didn't fully understand. "In terms you are and will always be my dearest brother, Seth."

"Alright, then I'll keep my name. It's probably better that way too. If both of us change our names, we might lose each other."

I laughed and said, "I can't afford that now we're equally seeing each other as brother again,"

"And neither can I." he smiled, then softened his reaction as a serious thought came to his mind. "What if I wanted your wings to go away, Midnight?" He asked. I angle my head to look at the crystals attached to my steel armor and instantly they burst apart into hundreds of pieces. With a swing of my arm, I casted those pieces into the ocean. Brother watched me as his smile abruptly returned. "And what about your armor? What if I wanted that gone too?" I liquified the steel on my body and then opened my palm and had it come together into its original pearl state. With a tight grip onto it, I tossed the steel pearl into the ocean without a second thought.

"Whew!" I took a breath while swinging back toward brother's direction. "What's next? This too?" I asked, pointing at the reflector on my wrist.

I ripped it off me and tossed it aside. It pinged a sound when it fell onto the bright.

"Anything else, brother?" I raised my arms to show him that I've laid to rest all materialized possessions. He shook his head and rushed to me, landing himself into my chest, and embracing me like he's never done before.

"You didn't have to throw away your arcana. I just wanted you to be able to feel me when I did this."

His embrace was a surprise, but I didn't hesitate to hold him back tightly. Now I understand why he asked me to set free all that had made me strong. I wouldn't have been able to feel his touch if I'd kept myself shielded.

Finally, during the dawn of our second day together, we've become whole to each again. Our embrace lasted only a moment, but it felt like a connection that will last forever.

"So, Midnight," brother separated himself from me and voiced in a curious tone. "I'm still a little lost about who that man was we just saw."

I laughed while turning away from brother and stepping toward the edge of the bridge. "This is your way of asking me to continue the narrative, isn't it?" I asked.

"Yup,"

"How bold of you," I said, as I turned back around to him. "But it works somehow," I easily gave in. "Where did you lose focus? I promise to summarize as best as I can."

He looked at me, excited to explain that "The lightning boy made it to his sealed power before the Organisms caught up to him. He saw that his power had become golden and encased in a lightning bubble but still he reached to reclaim it. However, the reverse happened, and his power sucked him into it, then everything became blank for me. I think that's when I fell asleep, so what happened after he got his power back?"

"Well," I laughed a bit. "I haven't made it that far yet, so you haven't missed much."

"Huh? Well, what were you talking about this whole time?"

"In an equation, there's the working before the answer. I was talking about the workings of the answer."

"Why not just talk about the answer?"

"Because then you'll never know why an answer is what it is without a question mark first."

"Tell me the answer since it's shorter and we're low on time," he requested.

"If you think you can catch on to what comes next, once more I will continue the narrative, and then we say goodbye to it. I've talked more than I've lived, and I'm bored of just imagining now. Let's go on a real adventure afterward, okay, brother?"

"Okay, Midnight. One more time, and we'll say goodbye to the narrative and leave it all behind forever."

"Alright, so, electricity danced around the lightning boy as he rushed toward where his was stripped from him. It took him but seconds to get there, as he's still got some sparks left in him. When he arrived at the lightning hovering in a bubble, he was taken by surprise. It no longer expressed the sapphire tinge he once knew. It now flashed bolts of a whirl of golden lightning through it. With the K-Organism closing in on him, he dismissed all concerns about the lightning's contrast and carelessly reached for its current state of appearance. Subsequently, upon touching it, it blasted into creation, a big bang that evolved him from a boy to a man."

Co6

Door 16: The Lightning Man in My World

Adam's (POV) -m-

A flaming light appeared at the center of the nothingness of all around, becoming the first something in existence that I can see. From that light, an appearance of sound rippled across the air, touching all senses of livelihood within me.

The flames were bright at first, but my perception quickly adjusted only to realize that I'm floating in the air.

"Synchronizing," the sound of an automation echoed into my ears. I looked to my wrist and noticed the strange material strapped to it, that appeared to be scanning me.

The sound of inaudible whisperings abruptly appeared in my ears. My attention abruptly focused on the ground below and my eyes widened in fright at the terrifying forms whose whisperings started to become clear. The creatures lined up on a bridge directly below me and staring up at me in wait for my fall as they repeatedly whispered, 'look at me,' as if they were all fighting for my attention. The scariest part is that their faces are beautiful, and their sounds are desperately humane, but the rest of their bodies displayed gruesomely mutated creatures.

Unexpectedly, the force that held me in the air let loose of its hold on to me and I fell. I didn't have time to react before my feet impacted the bridge. My landing stance made an incredible dent on the surface of the bridge instead of breaking my calf bone.

"Impossible!" My eyes shook to the ground then focused to my hands. "I should be injured from a fall that high," I then gasped, hearing the depths of my voice for the first time in my life.

The abrupt silence of the creatures' whispering rose my focus to where I last saw their crowd. Instantly, my eyes catch the menacing look of a Steel covered version of the creatures.

"Play with me?" It asked, in the innocent voice of a young boy.

I stepped away from them and their leader. While blinking quickly, I panicked and said "No! Stay away!" I hastily kept moving back while keeping an eye on them.

I looked back for a second and by the time my eyes looked forward, the steel creature had appeared a foot away from me with its arm stretched out for my body. "Look at me!" It screamed in my face.

My eyes widened as my life flashed before my eyes, revealing that it was lengthier than I'd thought. In a split second, dual lifetimes passed through me, denying what I thought was a short life. In truth, it provided an enlightened vision of the two lives that I was made from.

That instant evolution I'd felt, stimulated a sudden acceleration through the fibers of my being. Just as I'm to be grasped by the steel creature, it started to move in slow motion through my eyes. This allowed me to easily step away from it minutes before it will reach where I was.

Everything all around appeared to be completely still, the creatures, the sky, and even the sound of the ocean. This steel creature in front of me, however, is still pushing through the extensively fast speed that my body is moving at. It's slow motioned toward my former position made me wonder whether I'm genuinely moving at an impossible level of speed.

An intense chill came over me, so I quickly looked back at the Steel creature, and its eyes suddenly moved to view mine in real-time. Its stance suddenly normalized as its motion now moved in sync with my speed.

The sun is frozen in a painted rise, and the ocean's ceased its clash upon the shorelines, yet this steel creature can accelerate itself to equal my level? Is its speed even beyond mine? If so, why doesn't it immediately go beyond mine and kill me?

The figure's mouth separated, and in the childish voice of an innocent boy, it questioned, "Play with me?"

"That again? What kind of game?" I questioned, hearing the incredible depth of my voice again. I looked down at me and examined the broadness of my arms and the distance of my eyes from my feet. "How do I exist?" I asked myself.

"Look at me!" A begging scream came from the terrifying steel creature, and I immediately recalled what came after that. I raised my eyes up at its quick dash already seconds from grabbing me.

"No!" I shouted, raising my hands as a flash of magnificent lightning released from me toward the steel creature that kept coming.

After my sudden power surge couldn't stop it, I stepped back, but it was far enough to be a flick away.

Shocked by everything I'm learning about myself, I decided to run instead of fight. At a distance, I'm gone from where I was without a second thought.

I stopped myself at the beginning of the bridge then raised my hand to stretch the neck of my shirt immediately. I ripped the sleeves off my arms too as to make my breathing easier.

"My body feels amazing, but these clothes are a killing me. Why am I wearing clothes that are two small for me anyway? Did I really just come alive while wearing this?" I wondered. I looked around for answers and when I stared onto the bridge again, I voiced "The Hour Bridge?" and immediately became shocked by how I knew that out of nowhere.

An appearing flash of the steel creature crept up on me again. When I took notice of it, its hand was already in my face, so I impulsively dodged its grip.

It continuously struck at me which led me to grow from dodging, to abruptly blocking it with my uppermost force. That force sent the steel creature flying inland toward the jungle trees. It needled through one of the humongous trees and kept going for a period more.

"Whoa. How strong am I?" I couldn't comprehend.

Upon the sound of the creature stopping, it flew right back at me with a one-track mind. I quickly horizontally swung my hand at it, and a concentration of lightning energy released from me and sliced it in half.

Surprisingly, both halves of the Silver being began to reassemble themselves magnetically as if they were magnetically unifying.

"Regeneration? Are you that upset that I'm not playing this game with you?"

I look behind us, and my eyes zoomed across the bridge and saw that the other creatures were still frozen by how fast I'm still moving.

I looked back at the creature that wholesomely stood and muttered, "You're especially different from the others, aren't you? You're more persistent and impossible to get rid of. What do you want from me? If it doesn't lead to anyone's death, I'll do it so that you'll leave me alone," I tried to bargain.

It looked into my eyes and again repeated, "Play with me?"

"I think I get it now. A staring contest," I realized.

I quickly kept my focus on my gaze as I remembered what happened the last time I looked away.

"Synchronization complete. Host identity unknown. Welcome to the Arcana System." the mechanical voice echoed from upon my wrist.

"Arcana, huh? Thank you very much, I knew I didn't know myself. Regardless of who I am, I feel I know what I must do."

I kept my stare into its eyes, wondering if the first to blink determines the end. The steel creature suddenly bent all its joints in the opposite direction, broke its bones, and drained its blood. I kept my eyes connected to its own, though able to expand my vision to see its heinous transfigurations.

"Is this the game, watching you become what I would never want to imagine?" I questioned the steel creature.

The stomach of it sliced open on its own, and its guts came crawling out. Its expressionless face zigzagged into an atrocious smile as it altered itself.

"That's very nasty. My eyes are inflamed while watching your performance."

When I said that, tears of blood built into my eyes, and my pupils became slightly distracted by the red water.

I widened my eyes, brightening them with energy from within me. Lightning sizzled from my eyeballs and burned away the false liquid that clouded my vision.

"Either you're extremely hard to keep looking at, or you're intentionally trying to push me away. This has to end in a way where you don't come after me, so show me what that is," I demanded.

The steel creature's body suddenly began to heal itself and it reverted into its original form.

If it can go through such a traumatic change unphased, then stopping it will be no easy task.

The soreness in my eyes unexpectedly grew into one of desire when the creature began to transfigure itself. Its simplicity metamorphosed into an artistic display of the most beautiful life I've seen in my five minutes of being alive. My heart was easily taken by the false imagery of the creature's ethereal state even though my mind knew that internally its untrue.

What the steel creature had become was the completion of fulfillment that I never knew I longed for.

Furthermore, the daunting of its draw-in irresistibly began to demand my approach and I easily stepped forward with the thought of retiring my life to it.

For the death of me, I submitted to its intensions without question, and approached with fixated eyes of passion.

From pushing me away, to pulling me in, the steel creature's nature had altered drastically, and suddenly I saw an error within it.

Doubt surfaced within me, and I quit my steps toward it when I realized that its eyes are unchanged. I resisted the continued allure of the steel creature and even nearly looked away from it. Then remembered to look at it no matter what because looking away is what it wants me to do.

It's beginning to make sense now. It first became something frighteningly disgusting to try and force me to stop looking. Now it's become something of an impossibility to try to draw me in or to force me to stop looking.

"The eyes are the game and nothing else!" I voiced at it. I gazed into its pupil with absolute focus and assurance. "Every time any part of you would change, only your eyes would stay the same. If I focus on those, I'll be sure to get through to you. Perform as you must but I'm no longer observing anywhere beyond your sight," I told it.

The figure then altered to another form, I widely see, but my focus is on its pupil and that made everything else around blurry. Abruptly, its eyes began to tremble as tears of black liquid surfaced in them.

The steel creature's head looked away from me and its body unexpectedly sprinted in that same direction. I turned toward its fleeing escape along the shorelines, and without a thought, I hastened after it. I caught up to it quickly and reached for its neck. Unexpectedly, it offed onto the surface sea, surprisingly running on water. I froze for a moment, then leapt up in an arc out toward the ocean.

In my attempt to jump in front of the creature, I accidentally shot up from the ground with too much power and pushed pass the lower clouds in the sky.

When I'd stopped going up, the energy within me sparked a loud thundering sound all around. As I commenced in falling from the sky, darkened clouds began to form in the space of the atmosphere around me, and golden lightning flashed throughout all of them.

While thundering down the thunder clouds, the natural lightning within them struck at me, and infused me into being the full nature of its strike down.

Just as I'm to strike the salt water at a flashing speed down, I abruptly stopped right above the water, causing it to mesh out of place for many seconds. I hovered above the warping water using the power of the sky came with me.

My eyes intensely fixed onto the creature running out to me on the seas, and I shouted, "Stop!"

It looked into my eyes and immediately stopped running.

"Alpha Level – o1996," The arcana on my wrist voiced.

Although I wondered whether this device on my wrist was reading my power, my truest shock is seeing the steel creature stand on water for many seconds.

"Impossible," I reacted.

The steel creature evaded my eyes right away and gradually turned back toward the island. It then took three large steps and launched itself into the sky. From the vertebrates of its upper back, glorious steel wings took form and flapped to keep the creature in the sky.

I pushed after it, surprised by the various abilities it used to escape me. As I chased it across the air, a thought frustrated me when I was nearing it.

"Why did you play with me and then ran away before either of us could win? What was the game for?" I asked it, still not understanding the reason we played.

Its only reaction was to fly faster inland toward the island. As I arrived above the shores of the island, I paused my motion and wondered what I was doing.

"How foolish of me. I wanted this thing to leave me alone, and now that it has, I'm chasing after it? Am I confused or am I still playing the game?" I asked myself and observed it distancing my location by the second. "No, I'm neither!" I understood my reasoning as I threw my arm into the sky. For miles across the plane, the firmament darkened at my command. "There are too many of you to repeat this game with and get nowhere but annoyed. So, I'm using this first encounter to study you and learn the truth." I swung my arm down as my eyes targeted the shrinking creature fleeing in the distance. "Falling Lightning," I casted, and the sky clapped a thunderous sound before the brightest shine of lightning rushed down at the steel creature.

From every corner of every cloud, billions of joules combined and zapped it out of existence. When that area of the sky dimmed, nothing of the steel creature could be seen from where I hovered.

"I hope there's something left of it to find," I remarked. "I might've overdone it."

I looked up at the darkened clouds I'd casted above me and flew into them. Upon connecting with them, my body became one with the natural flow of lightning again, which allowed me to current to a distant location in a second.

I electric out from the clouds and instantly reshaped into myself while I hovered in the sky.

The first thing I noticed when I looked around was one of the biggest wonders I've ever seen. On the grounds of the island jungle, a crystal wall structured one huge circle over several acres of the land. Within that circle, the ground's flat and entirely frozen over, but the walls of it appear to be almost as tall as the areal trees.

When I took notice of the thousands of frozen statues standing within it, I began to wonder whether they were just that, or if this was an actual ice age existing in a tropical jungle.

The sudden sound of a whispering surfaced in my ear and brought my eyes to the direction of the steel creature's presence. The feeling of its nature appears to be coming from inside of the ice age below, so I zoomed down and landed into it myself.

Within here, the air is thin, and the wind is strong and cold. Ice particles dance through it, making me feel as though it was magically made. Now that I'm on the ground, the next thing I noticed was that every statue I saw was of a frozen creature that resembled the steel one.

"Someone powerful must've casted this ice upon these creatures to keep them provisionally dormant. Are they really that difficult to get rid of?" I wondered.

The sound of the whispering suddenly stopped, so I hastened in the direction I had heard it coming from. When I'd finally spotted it, it was surprisingly reabsorbing its scattered flesh at the central position of this crystal wall around the ice age. I quickly stepped toward it as it continued to regenerate its obliterated parts.

"Your survivability rate is quite a surprise. I didn't expect you to regenerate from absolutely nothing. It's like you're trying to tell me that you're supposed to exist."

As the steel creature fully recovered it cells, I raised my hand to it, and rooted up lightning cables from the ground at its feet. They strapped around the creature's ankles and wrists to hold it in place. The wrist cables pulled into the ground and laid the creature down on its back. Another cable shot up and wrapped around its forehead to bind its face in an upward fix.

I walked to the creature's side and knelt to view its eyes. Its body tugged to resist my lightning cables, but its vision kept a connection to mine that lacked resistant. It eyes are not forcing shut nor trying to look away, yet it continued to physically struggle to release itself.

"Why is your body still resisting when your soul isn't? Half of you wants to play, but the other half doesn't. What exactly are your eyes longing for?" I asked it while keeping my gaze.

The steel creature's eyes suddenly produced a line of black liquid that began to drain down the side of its face. Its mouth split open and snatched up at me, causing me to stand tall but keep my stare at it.

"If I remember correctly, those bloody eyes are a sign that you're losing."

The darkened liquid from its eyes pooled the ground it rests on and when it became a clear flow of true tears, its struggling body ceased in its attempt to free itself. When its tears came to a stop it took a lengthy blink to indicate the end of the game.

Upon opening its eyes, the darkened fluid on the floor crawled upon its steel. I stepped back while watching its sudden mergence with the liquid that came from its eyes. After it was completely consumed in it, it continued to lay there without struggling at all.

It looked directly up at me as I'm still over it and said, "You've won," in the tone of a young boy. "I've blinked my eyes, and now I must abide by a single request from the champion I will never play with again. Look into my eyes and state what you desire from me."

From the start this creature's voice has been the same. When it asked me to play with it and when it asked me to look at it, it never altered its tone. Its voice is unchanging so it must not be mimicking anyone but itself.

"This is great," I said while standing the creature up to its feet and releasing it from its bounds. "I'm excited that we're finally getting somewhere. If I'm being honest, the only thing I want from you is for you to leave me a--" I choked, developing a splitting headache and a collapsing voice that abruptly took my breath away.

"Aaaahhh!" I yelled out while dropping to my knees and pressing my palms into the snow, sensing an error pass through my entire core.

The pain stopped as quickly as it started, allowing me to naturally breathe again. I stood back to my feet and looked into the creature's eyes, tilting my head about the sudden epiphanic thought I've gained around it. It remained fixed in its position as it's now my turn to make a move, but this can't be the end. It still feels like something that I cannot trust.

I stepped back from it then turned away to not be direct in saying, "Just like that, you're at the beginning again but somehow now indebted to me? Forgive me for feeling like the game's still going on and that this is just another challenge. To be granted a wish from you is one thing, but to know exactly what to wish for is another. If I'd completed my statement just then, I wonder if you'd have left me alone or if you'd have left me feeling lonely. When your kind wins, you attack with the intention of annihilating. Now that I've won, should I then ask for your loyalty or for your suicide?" I sighed at the judgment I must make. "Being the crown of a mindless race will bring me no joy, and your death will bring me no answers. And so, I've decided," I turned around to it and addressed its eyes directly, "To the truth of my understanding, become that of which you were always meant to be. That is my single request."

The creature's body suddenly trembled as the black liquid that covered its steel armor began to drain off. As they separated, the steel body that remained, fell to the floor. When the dark liquid puddled onto the ground, I noticed a pair of eyes developing within the goo that remained. The liquid substance let off an ungodly shriek at me and darted my way. A knot in my brow followed a bolting strike from the heavens that melted to steam all residues of it.

"What was that thing? A parasite?" I questioned to myself, then look to the steel body left behind. "No way," I voiced watching his legs try to stand up. My motion to catch his impending fall was swift and I hugged him just in time to keep him standing. "Catch yourself. Are you truly a living person?" I looked down at the boy covered in steel armor. He gazed up to my eyes, and I immediately felt all sources of life from within them. "Wow, what a twist."

With stories of life watering in his sight, he humbly said, "Thank you so much for freeing me from the darkness that my nature had become."

"You're most welcome," I smiled at his politeness. "I thank you as well for teaching me something," I said, astounded to learn the potential nature these creatures can take on.

"Me?"

"Yes. Thanks to you, I now know that tolerance determines the victor of their game. I was curious about why you were and why you played, so I kept going. And now I know the truth."

Co7

Door 17&05: My Family and I Exit My World

Midnight's (POV) -o-

"C'mon, wake up!" I hear a distant shout as splashes of water invaded my nostrils and throat. "Midnight!" I was called.

My eyes opened, and I coughed out water, discovering myself held up in the ocean by my brother.

"W-What's happening?! Why are we out here?!" I asked him. I looked around wildly, spotting The Hour Bridge where we stood, far, far away from us.

I reduced his struggle of keeping me up by beginning my motion of staying above water.

"I had no choice," brother said, showing eyes of relief for my safety. "You were telling me about how the steel organism became a human after the man won the staring contest, and then you suddenly began trembling all over. Your eyes rolled behind to your sockets, and you were no longer respondent to me," he explained. "I quickly held you and forced us both over the bridge, hoping you'd come back to yourself after we impacted the salt water. You didn't, so I kept slapping your face and now you're here again. I'm so sorry that a current pulled us adrift before you came back to me, but I don't care. I'm just happy you're okay, Midnight."

"Don't worry yourself any further, brother. You did great," I commended. I looked to the direction we're flowing in and noted that, "This current is leading us to the end of this world, and the beginning of another. That vortex inside the darkened waters up ahead is the eye of The Tongue of the Ocean."

"Are we going to resist it's pull?"

"Of course not. It's our way to freedom. Aiden the Fourth has gone into it alone once before and he didn't make it through. I think that the only way to stop this loop, is if my bloodline and yours exit it together."

"So, either you and I, or your incarnation and I?" Brother asked and I nodded. "I was so caught up on missing you, I didn't care to even consider him. If your incarnation ever re-enters my life, I won't do anything less than loving him the same way you do." I smiled, feeling great that his heart is finally opening to more than just me.

"I'm proud to hear that. Are you ready, brother? We're getting closer."

"I'm not ready, but I trust you. You remember the thousands of times your incarnation lived through those loops, but I only remember one time. You've lived and learned way beyond me, so if you say not to fear it, I won't. I'll never doubt you again, Midnight. I promise."

I laughed saying, "Don't worry; I can feel you and I feel that truth coming from you. I'll never doubt you too, brother."

Brother's kept enthusiasm kindled a fire in me to make sure we get it right this time.

Together we're carried toward the vortex and as we drew near, a whirling spiral began to flush us down the ocean's nucleus. We kept a tight grip onto one another's arms as the flush ended along with the water that carried us.

Brother and I zoomed down a blank space in the ocean as our clothes dried from the pressure of our fall. We yelled our lungs out, knowing that impacting the ocean floor at this speed would kill us. However, the appearance of only darkness below led to the question of whether this fall to and soon or not.

"We're going to die!" brother freaked out in full agitation.

"No, we're not!" I held with both of my hands. It suddenly began to get darker and darker the longer we fell until there was nothing that could be seen.

A sudden twinkle in the darkness we're drawing toward made me quickly blink in remembrance of what comes next.

"Brother, we're falling, and it's terrifying, yes, but look around," I said to relax his heart.

As he observed around us, he gasped with lightening eyes as a galaxy of stars began brightening themselves all around. The ocean depth had become a void of space that we're now falling through.

Upon seeing this galaxy display, my eyes widened, remembering something crucial.

"Brother, we're about to lose our--" I choked and gasped at the emptiness I cannot breathe in. From the tips of my fingers and toes, I began to freeze over rapidly.

"What are you doing?! Breathe!" Brother demanded as his sound began to fade along with my vision. "Don't do this to me again!" he begged, but I've tossed away all the materials that had made me physically strong, and so I cannot save myself this time. Luckily, I'm the only one in danger while my brother still pledges his breath onto his life. I can now feel my conscience slip away, and I'm fading to begin again as I've done all times before.

A breath of life struck through my core and brought my awareness to light once again. My temperature heightened as I feel the ice that had consumed me begin to recede. Brother's holding me tightly with sorrowed eyes while blazing around us is the flames of a blue sun.

"Not this time. I won't let you die again while I'm here." His fire blazed the darkness away from us, becoming the greatest star around our fall.

"Wow," I reacted at his returned flames being so beautifully concentrated.

He looked to my eyes when he heard me and quivered, "You're.... you're okay!" He squeezed me tight, embracing me again. "Caring about you really does bring out potentials in me too, you know?"

"I guess it does," I laughed at his repeat of what I'd said earlier. "Your flames are providing oxygen and warmth for me to live through our spatial travel. I never thought I'd see you glowing again. Your flames were never a bother for me to be around. They make me happy."

"They do? The last time you saw it, you told me to turn it off."

I laugh at his reminder, "It was a different situation back then. As long as you're safe, I'll never ask you to put out your light. It's never burned me, and it's not doing so right now. They're actually quite beautiful through my eyes."

"So, you physically feel nothing from my flames?"

"I feel everything, but not as a threat, as a shield. It feels like you're keeping me safe," I explained.

His brows jumped, replying, "When you froze over in my arms, I thought it was because I didn't make it to you in time. But now I know that as long as you were still breathing, there was still time. Wow, if I knew then what I know now, maybe I could've saved-"

"-No!" I quit his thinking. "We don't know the extent of your flashback power, and when it's used, it changes too much. It creates a new future. Don't think about a second chance, brother. Don't you love who I am now?"

"Of course, I love you, Midnight."

"And I love you too, so don't ever think about changing what's past because that'll kill me. Let's just keep looking forward towards what's next for us, okay?"

Brother nodded, "Alright, no more thoughts of it. Let's leave that as history along with this world as we're about to leap over to a new one."

"That's the attitude to have," I praised. Abruptly, I began to check our surroundings. "Brother, keep up the flames while I figure out where we are."

"What's to look for? There's nothing but stars in a blank space all around us."

"Yes, but we're falling and that doesn't last forever," I informed, convincing myself to look down. I'm immediately astounded in my recognition of a familiar black hole below.

I pointed at it and said, "See, brother. There's a black void at the bottom of us, with a white halo ring around it."

"Oh wow," he's shocked to see. "Okay, that's scary. And we're going into that?"

"Yup. I bet you didn't see when it appeared. Watch when you see the blue Sun-" I pause, looking at brother with widened eyes.

"The blue sun?" He questioned. "You mean me?' he wondered, and I think he's correct.

"I—I don't know. I think this really is the same timeline as my previous incarnation. Brother, if that's true, we're going to have company soon," I worried, and right when I did, a shout came from above us.

"Get out of the way!" A voiced warned, and it caused us both to look up.

A golden light coming down reminded me of all I should have remembered to expect. My past self is on a collision course with us, and soon we will all be present again. I remember everything from his point of view, but all my actions right now are new. I must do this exactly like I remembered seeing it done.

"Midnight, I think someone's coming down with us."

"You're right, brother, and we have to push apart from one another."

"No, bad idea! You'll lose your breath and turn to ice without me. And even if you don't, we'll be permanently separated because we can't control our movements through this space."

"Listen to me; it'll only be for a second. That person falling toward us will cause us a great injury if we do not do this. We'll push apart at the right moment, avoiding collision while each of us grabs hold of his ankle. Once we make it, surround him with your fire, and it'll reach to me too."

"That's pretty precise! It could work but I don't think I'm ready!" he panicked.

"Don't worry, brother. Everything will work as it should. We're doing it now!" I shoved him away from me, and we both reach out to the gap between us. The speeding individual sonic through us as we each grabbed a hold of their ankle. Brother instantly casted his flames onto the person, and as predicted, it successfully reached across to me. The two of us are now increased in speeding toward the black point thanks to our newest third one, who's arrowing our flight down.

"I—I can't believe that worked. It all happened in the exact way you described it. How'd you know so confidently that we'd make it?"

Brother wondered as I looked to the figure that's a boy leading our way. His eyes are fixed on brother, who's eyes fix on me.

In this triangular sight of our triad flight, I knew for sure that, "It's because it's our destiny," is what I'm fated to say.

The boy's eyes turned to mine, and immediately I knew that through mysticism, I've transiently become omniscient in this moment of time.

"Midnight?" Brother called. I look to him, noticing that he'd questioned my name to the boy's eyes. "How-"

"-That's not me." I quickly corrected his thinking, fearing that brother may become confused and lose track of my identity again. "I'm right here. This is me, brother."

"Brother?" The leading boy questioned. "By any chance, are either one of you called Seth?"

"I am," brother responded. "And who exactly are you?" Tears filled the eyes of the boy as they guided their way to me.

"And you? He calls you brother, but Seth's brother is not called Midnight."

"I gave him a new name," brother spoke up. "How do you know this?" he asked the boy.

"Well, if you want to know," I began to explain. "You and I are Physically one in the same. However, our minds are not on the same level of knowledge. I'm from one loop in the future but I am not you. I am your father."

"What?" I questioned at how.

"Wait, this is your incarnation? This is your son?" Brother asked me and I smiled at him.

"Ours, yes." I corrected brother then turned my attention to the boy leading our flight. "In the future loop, my soul returned to life by entering your body after you gave up on living in circles. Brother and my memory of one another are in sync with our beginning. However, your knowledge of who we are is only in sync with the moment of your creation. You may see us as your parents, but he and I see each other as brothers forever."

"I—I have to process all of that," my son reacted, and I understood that anyone would be confused. "Wait, you said that you're from the future. That means that I'm the past version of you, so how are we both present?"

"I think that's how. The Present is the center of the Past and the Future. I think we can only be together right now but will have to separate soon."

"Oh, no!" brother reacted while looking beyond us and toward the vortex. "It looks like we'll have to postpone this topic. We're closing in sooner because of his speed!"

"I'm afraid there's no cutting this short. Only two of us are going to make it through," I shared the bad news.

"What do you mean 'only two'?" they both panicked.

"When we enter, brother and I will pass through, but you'll loop around again," I told my son. "I remember the memories of when you did this before, and that is what happened."

"What, No! Why?!"

"I wish there was a way to bring you along. As you are now, your mind is beautiful and pure. You feel extremely precious to existence, but I'm afraid that that's what's going to happen."

"I don't want to repeat this life, I want to come with you two. Is there a law that says I must not variate?" a hurtful expression built onto his face and his emotions casted onto us. "You're my fathers, aren't you? Save me, please!" he begged.

"I'm sorry, but I don't know how. Even if I did, I don't think I'm supposed to, or I will not be made, and my brother will not be saved."

"I—I don't understand," he shook his head and gazed at me with disappointed eyes.

"You'll understand why when you're saying the same words-"

I paused, instantly consumed by a traumatic reminder so deep that I began to feel like I more than just remember this, I've lived this. Why am I blindly following fate and repeating everything I remember hearing? I know within myself that I still don't understand why I abandoned him when he's me in so much pain.

"Forget everything I just said. You're my boy and you're crying out for my help so I will variate to save you. I'm a father now, and that means I'll always put you first."

His eyes were widened by my sudden change of heart. But I haven't changed. This is my break free to say what I've always felt.

I looked to my brother and with our eyes connected, he nodded his head.

Brother then looked to the boy leading our flight and said, "We'll always put you first." In that moment, brother and I gained a primary focus, and from that point on we became secondary to one another.

"What must I do to not loop around again?" our boy asked in haste.

"I'm not sure. I am thinking now about what makes you different from brother and me."

"Right, because the three of us enters one thing, but the same thing doesn't happen to all of us, and it makes no sense."

"Maybe it does," brother said with his focus locked onto our boy's wrist. "What if you loop around and never make it through with us because you're wearing that arcana?"

"This can't be the reason. This is supposed to give me my name," he hugged it and my eyes widened.

"Yes, brother's right." I thought about it. "Now it all makes sense. That's an object of this reality, and you're trying to bring it out of it. Trust me, if you love the name that the lightning man gave you, toss aside your Arcana and live as whom you are now. That's the only way you can come with us."

"Are you sure?" he questioned.

"Of course not, but this is our best lead to changing the usual outcome, so hurry!" I prompted him to decide.

Without hesitation, he removed the arcana and tosses it aside just as we impacted the void's momentum.

I've just made a major change at the end of this circle, and I won't care if it ceases me to exist. If it's in my control, I'll always keep a shield around my son's innocence and father him to face the world.

As we move through the void, my hold of my boy's ankle didn't vanish. At my side, a light from within my brother shined brightly through the void. Once again, he's casting a blue sun around the three of us.

It seems like there's darkness all around, if it's even appropriate to call it that. This primordial naught that consumes everywhere is a blank space which knows nothing and all of itself at once. It is a lightless void without shine that's making it exist and not exist at once.

'I wonder if…' I spoke, or I thought I spoke.

'Midnight!' I looked across to my brother as he waved a hand. 'Finally, you can hear me. Or—Or perceive me.' he corrected, as his words came through to my thoughts.

'I don't get it. Why is it impossible to make a sound?' I wondered.

'I'm not sure. It must be because of the part we've entered into,' brother gestured to all around.

'I don't get it. How are we all connected?' Brother and I looked to the face of our boy when he questioned us. 'Yes, I can hear both of you too.' he voiced to our minds again.

'It must be because of this blue sun that brother's casting out to give us light. This void consumed our sounds and sight of life, but his concentrated sun silently brought it all back. We can now see each other clearly and we're also able to communicate to coordinate.' I smiled.

'Sorry to bring it back around to me, but do you think that getting rid of the arcana will actually change my fate?' our boy wondered.

'It already has. This conversation we're having is unfamiliar to me, so I'm guessing that means you're here to stay.'

'You both quickly thought up an exit strategy to save me. I don't know how to thank you, but I'll try my best.' Our boy humbly expressed.

'We three are a family now, and that was just us showing care.' Brother said to him.

'He's right, you're family. You'll thank us by caring in return,' I made clear. 'If anything, I should be the one thankful to you. If I hadn't lived through your eyes, I would've never understood your pain of living through so many trials. You kept me pure because I was able to empathize with your emotions and that is a wonderful gift. I remember when I lived through your eyes you made a promise. You said that if you became me and had to choose between saving your son and not, you'd break fate and let your son through. Well now you've become me, and I'm fulfilling that promise by letting you through, my son."

'But Midnight, won't saving me cease your existence now since I won't loop around to the timeline which created you?' Our boy wondered.

'If that was the case, I'd already be gone. I think that two loops were merged at the end just now, the past and the future. Maybe I'm still here because we made a drastic change just as we left. I'm still here because we're not in that world anymore, but somewhere in between worlds. So, no world's law applies to any of us right now.'

'That's amazing. We're all finally able to choose our own fate.' Our boy smiled.

'Yeah, and I'm ready for it,' brother humored. 'But I'm still trying to wrap my head around understanding how you two are the same person but address each other as father and son. The two of you make me feel like I'm witnessing a twin paradox.'

I smiled widely at brother and thought to him, 'You and I are twins, brother.'

'I know, which confuses the situation even further because the three of us look alike.'

'Brother, he and I are only the same on a molecular level alone. We have our own individual thoughts, and our own names, so we are different.'

'Our own names?' brother questioned then turned his head to our boy. 'What do we call you?'

Knowing that he could potentially think of a fallen name, I reminded him to, 'Choose your identity wisely and live in what you know and not what you assume.'

'I understand,' he nodded to me, then sat his eyes onto my brother. 'My name is Andy Rose,' he shared, and I smiled at his choice.

With that arcana gone, our original identity, can finally rest in peace. Our new names are who we are now.

'Wow,' brother was astounded. 'You have two names?'

'It's actually three, but you can just call me Andy if you like.'

'Why are you so shocked, brother. Are you forgetting that I'm The Core of Midnight? That's four words and a sentence that you named me.'

'Oh, right.' We all kept our humor as we circled around each other's thoughts. 'Well, welcome to the family, Andy,' Brother greeted.

'We're very happy to have you join our journey,' I praised.

'First a name, and now a family. Throughout the eight thousand loops I've lived, this one is most fulfilling. I'm very happy to be here,' Andy expressed. 'My parents and I will exit this world together.'

'That's right,' I grinned as his acceptance made me whole.

After our greeting, the three of us continued through the black void and refused to look back at the reality we've left behind. As we travel through this great before, the world beyond and what's new to come is now our topmost thought.

'I see light,' Andy indicated to brother and me. 'Look ahead.'

When we both did, we spotted the light right away. My heart began pounding when I noticed it expanding.

"We're closing into it,' I noted.

'What do we do?' brother asked.

'We're going to impact that light no matter what, so we'll continue to hold onto Andy's ankle tightly.' I thought using both of my hands.

Brother followed my lead as the three of us prepared for another impact.

We flew down into the white light and instantly the nothingness of darkness has become the nothingness of light. The sudden brightness of its exposure forced my eyes shut to have visual peace.

'It hurts,' Andy cried through our thoughts.

'Keep your eyes shut,' I warned them both. 'There's a way to return from looking into darkness but no way to come back from being blinded by light. Let it subside, or we'll permanently damage our eyes.' I felt this to be true because even with my eyes shut, I can still see though my eyelids flesh and veins.

'Okay.'

'Alright,' they transmitted.

We kept a motion through this void of light for some time, robbed of another sense but still having a three-way mental connection.

Eventually, the brightness I viewed from through my eyelids calmed down, giving note to the receding light. That light abruptly vanished, casting only darkness into my closed eyes.

I opened my eyes to look around and before I could, oxygen from beyond my brother's sun invaded our shine. From the exposure of a new world, a breath of life entered my lungs.

Bo8

Door 18&01: To Begin Again in a New World

Goodbye to The Puzzle.

Midnight's POV (Cont'd) -p-

"Testing," I voiced, then smiled. "Yes, we can make sounds again!"

"Finally!" brother excitingly exhaled. "That mental cluster of ours was becoming harder and harder to compartmentalize the longer we went on."

"Wow, we're going upward now, and I didn't even notice," Andy stated.

"You're right. When we first entered the black void, we were being pulled down. How and why have we switched directions?" I asked for us to think.

I immediately thought to search for the light that we'd just passed through, and below us, I spotted it. A white circle with a black ring is emitting an outward force away from it. If the entrance is a black circle and the exit is a white circle, I guess this means there's truly no going back to that world.

"Check it out!" I hear Andy further react, and I looked up at him. "It's the sky above us," he pointed. Within another circular ring above us, clouds, stars, and a night sky are present. The ring appears to be expanding as we're flying up to it.

"Down became up, and day turned to night. A black hole absorbed us, and a white hole spat us out. There's no doubt about it; this is another world, Midnight." Brother stated.

As we neared the circle above, it became clear that it was another waterfall vortex in an ocean.

"Ready yourselves," Andy said.

We then passed through the waterfall, expelling ourselves from the depths of the ocean. We kept on rising higher and higher up to the sky. Before we rose into the clouds, I looked down and witnessed the sea pull itself together, eternally sealing away the evidence of our origins.

We rose high up into the atmosphere, at the peak of this world's gravitational reach. There, we encountered the edge of its magnetic slipstream and began to narrow along its curving motion.

From a distance so far, the circular shape of this world was revealed to us. It appears to be in utter darkness with no signs of light and no signs of life.

At the edge of this world, a sudden star peaked a light into our vision. It grew from a small shine to a bright galaxy Sun that's lighting half of the globe at a time.

"We've... finally made it, Midnight!" Brother expressed his excitement.

"Yes, we did. A whole new world," I joyously laughed.

My eyes immediately took notice of another global light that's closer than the Sun. It looked just like what brother, and I would call a Moon.

"This place is already beautiful to observe at a distance. I'm a little anxious about landing on this planet, Midnight." Brother confessed his feelings "What if we stand out to the residence already on that world?"

"If there are people here before us, then the only way we'll stand out is by showing how differently we think. We're from another reality and sharing anything of what we think could categorize us as crazy or crown us as kings."

"I'm not going to be anyone but myself," Brother carelessly outspoke.

I humored and said to "Be yourself, yes. But before recklessly doing that, we must learn their general opinions first, brother." I looked ahead and asked, "Isn't that right, Andy?"

Andy didn't look back, so I squeezed his ankle, wondering if "You're okay, my boy?"

He looked around at me, and with an utterly brand-new expression, he asked, "Who are you?" He looked to my brother and asked, "Two identical boys? What are we all doing here?"

I looked at my brother, and his expression is the same as mine. Before either of us could react, Andy suddenly dropped from leading the flight. From pulling us across the atmosphere to dangling behind us, brother and I kept a tight grip on Andy's ankle and forced him along.

"Why have you suddenly stopped flying, Andy?" Brother asked as Andy's weight increased by the second, making it difficult for us to keep him up.

"Gravity's pulling you down. Hurry up and remember how to fly, or you'll slip out of our hands," I said to Andy's eyes.

"I—I don't know enough to remember something like that. It looks like there's not enough time for you to tell me either. You're beginning to struggle to keep me up. Quickly take a hold of each other's hand before you lose your grip on me."

"No!" brother fought. "We're not letting you go. Our journey as a family is just beginning."

"Eventually, this pull-down will take me away from you. Therefore, you must not lose each other in the sky, as I'm about to lose you both on my way down."

"Listen to Andy, brother." I reached out as he looked at me. He reached back, and we connected to make a closed triangle of us. While looking back to Andy's eyes, I asked, "Do you honestly not remember anything about anything?"

"I only know what I know right now. Since you both seem to know me, tell me in short, who am I?" My eyes widened then my brows knot as I thought it impossible to detail or even simplify a short answer since his life is a web.

"You are the world to us because you're our son," brother replied to Andy, and I looked at him quickly with smiling eyes. He's so committed now he immediately understood that it wasn't a general question.

"And who may you two be?" Andy asked and I looked to him with an immediate answer.

"We're the brackets that created your appearance in this life. We're your parents, and we're a family."

"Thank you for making me feel this way before I depart," he wholeheartedly expressed.

The weight of him continued to increase, causing brother's and my arm to strain and Andy's ankle to bruise. Without warning, he twisted around and kicked himself loose from my grip. Brother managed to hold onto his wiggle, but now he's alone in doing it.

"What are you doing?!" I shouted.

"I mean a lot to you two, so I won't let you let me go. I'll let go of myself to leave you unburdened. Farewell, my family."

Andy forced himself from my brother's hold on him and fell with a relaxed look in his eyes.

Brother cried out as we continued in our journey without him. We watched Andy ablaze into a celestial body on his way toward the new world. Brother and I were already arcing around the other side when Andy finally landed. Even so, we knew he did because the impact was the brightest and most incredible light I've seen from a collision.

"Midnight,"

"Yes, brother." I look to my brother's eyes that are focused on the world below us.

"Do you think he fell because we brought him with us?"

"Well, he was supposed to stay in the other world for one loop longer, but that world has no effect on us now. I don't think he fell because he's miraculously here. I think he had no choice because it was the will of this new world we're fixed to. If that's the case, it may be a foreshadow to what will happen to us too."

"I expected us to go somewhere other than around and around for life. I don't care if it's down there as long as we don't have to separate to do it."

"I know. If we are to fall, I hope we fall together too, brother."

Arm in arm, brother and I traveled above the world as its motion led us around a continuous cycle.

After two cycles, I started to feel like this was going to happen for a very long time.

"Are you feeling for food, brother?" I wondered. He shook his head, and I said, "Me neither; nor do I feel for a drink."

"Maybe we don't need them. I haven't discharged my flames since we exit the void, yet we're freely traveling along the highest point above the world, and still, we're alive. We've gone through so much in the last day that I'm not even sure what the limitation of life is anymore."

"New world, new rules, and new possibilities. I can only speculate, but do you remember when I first died, and I left my heart behind for you?"

"Yeah, the tesseract cube that represented the other world you'd created for me."

"Uh-huh. Well, I think that this world resides outside of the one we came from but somehow, they're still connected.

"I saw that the ocean closed up after we passed through it. Maybe that means that passages from world to world are only in one direction.

"I'd assume so as well. The first world was connected to my imagination, but this second one feels foreign to me. I am certain that this is the work of a greater architect who's extensively beyond my capabilities."

"How can you be so sure, Midnight?" Brother wondered.

"You and I both know of the characters in the world that I've created, but before them, who's created us, brother? I think whoever made us, created all of this as well," I gestured to the vastness of the space around this world that we currently circle.

"Speaking of your characters; it was so vivid to see them in action," Brother expressed.

"Yeah, the narrative was unexpected too. I first told it from afar, and then it got too close to us. Eventually, I had no choice but to tell it from within because we lived alongside it. That world we left behind is dangerous, brother. Even if we could, we should never venture back into it."

"What about the characters you've created and left inside of it? Will they die, or will you continue to tell their stories?"

"They'll live, and their stories will grow to a balance on its own without any further divine interventions by you and I."

"So, that's it? It's a bit anticlimactic, Midnight."

"How so? All the topics we questioned were covered. While in my world, we witnessed the creation of its primordial man. I have a strong feeling that his strength will cleanse all the Organisms from their poisoned state. He will eradicate them all from that world without destroying a single cell all because his soul is strong."

"I thought the lightning man's Alpha abilities were impressive, but to be able to bring someone back to themself by just staring into their eyes was pretty astounding. His all-around strength will make him a hero of Androsia. I wonder what the village that the other three characters were transporting him to is like."

"Careful, brother. That world is now dead to us so we won't wonder upon new information that may develop within it. However, through deductive reasoning we should be able to connect the points of all that will possibly happen next. The lightning man's name is Adam, and he'll become more than a hero. He'll become the initiation of humankind, a legend itself."

"You're right. His actions will involve everyone. Once he saves the Organisms, all of their reanimated lives will continue to grow in a safe new world."

"Exactly, brother. It's a happy ending to that story. The end is the beginning of change for that world. After the change, everyone will be alive at once for one generation only, issuing in a new age. In the time after that, history will come along with the creation and continuation of their developing generations. In their future, all that would be left for them to do is to develop a system to live as one."

"That's so interesting to think about. They'll have civil wars and huge fights, forming hierarchies and independent regions. With the Organisms no longer being a threat to the Alphas, their powers will evolve, and it'll be them versus themselves."

"That's right. Settling on who'll gain command over an island doesn't seem like it'll be a simple task. But that's years into the future, brother, a whole other story."

"Well, I love it now. It's not so underwhelming after you've shared the points of what may come next."

"You really enjoyed it?" I asked.

"Yeah, of course! Your story was beyond what I'd ever expected. When I asked you for it a day ago, I never thought it would come to this. I never thought it would come true, let alone lead us a world away from our starting point. It truly was an exceptional narration to listen to."

I significantly smiled, expressing that, "I'm thrilled you enjoyed it that much, brother."

"I did, and I want to remember it since it's over now. Are you going to give the story a name? I bet you'll call it Alphas."

"Hmm," I thought for a second. A name would help us to separate them from us, but I feel it's inappropriate to give one to characters that exist with freewill. We've interacted with them, so we can no longer see them as mere figures of our imaginations alone. They're real now, brother."

"Alright, them don't name them as a story, Midnight. Name them as a world."

"That's a pretty good idea," I complimented brother's alternative solution. After giving it a thought, I issued that, "For its natural beauty, its pending paradise, and its population to come, I've decided to call their world, Eden; to begin."

"Eden, huh? That sounds pretty good on its own," brother appreciated.

It was a great name to close that chapter of our life and put it all behind us.

We've crossed onto another plane, and in this new world, our concerns are only on what's present. This world we alternate around and around is our next mystery we need to solve.

A sudden golden radiance flashed up from the planet below at a quick speed, leveling its shine to our lining flight.

"Midnight!"

"I see it," I confirmed at my brother's alarm. It flashed back down as quickly as it came right back up. In the face of us, the light reappeared and motioned along with our flight.

A voice, matured but incomprehensible to my ear, spoke from this golden radiance in an exotic tongue.

"Did you get any of that?"

"Yeah, but I doubt that I can properly repeat any of it. It was... Shlama allawk-something," brother tried to mimic.

The golden radiance intensely brightened and as it dimmed; two small spheres separated from it. The spheres came over to us and hovered in our face, showing the same radiance as the big one. I looked to my brother, and he nodded while reaching to take a hold of one. I followed his lead right away and upon the slightest touch of this small radiant sphere, all of me is consumed by an abrupt surge of infinity.

"S—So much life!" brother reacted with an unbelievable expression in his eyes.

He's right to respond in that way because I feel it too. It feels like I've just been granted an endless amount of time. I can't even correctly comprehend the immense current that flowed into me. After seeing through the eyes of all my incarnations, I thought I'd learned the meaning of supremacy above all that's created. But this new force now bestowed upon me has eradicated all former beliefs of such understanding. I know nothing compared to this feeling of eternity I'm filled with right now.

"Tell me, young ones, can you understand me now?"

My eyes widened as I looked to the glow, hearing Him from within myself.

With a hand placed onto my heart I said, "Clearly,"

"Me too," brother expressed, feeling his chest as I am.

"Wonderful. The boundary that divided us is no more, and we're now in complete comprehension," He replied. **"How is it that the two you still haven't grown up, when I've been gone for so long?"**

"Radiant Sun, you speak as though you know our faces," Brother voiced.

"Radiant Sun? Can you not see me beyond that?"

"We can't. You're simply a voice from a radiance that's leading our flight right now," I indicated to our continued motion.

"It's apparent that I've transcended beyond my physical form. My body is now long gone, and soon my soul will move on as well. May I ask you how long it's been since your travel around this world began?"

"I'm not sure. Everything looks similar around and around, but we've only gone around a couple of times," I answered.

"It's been three cycles," my brother said, surprising me with his knowledge of accuracy from afar. "When you showed up, we were finishing the third and is now on our fourth."

"Just three cycles? That would then mean that every cycle up here is equivalent to eleven years below. Time's undoubtedly moving slower up here than it is down there," The Radiant Sun voiced, nudging our thoughts to the world below us.

"How can you be so sure it's been exactly eleven years?" I wondered, then my eyes widened thinking, "You were here at the start of our flight, weren't you? Are you Andy Rose?"

Brother quickly looked at me then looked at the Radiant Sun as we both waited for an answer.

"I am not. I must choose my identity wisely and live in what I know, and that is not the name I've lived knowing." He said, and I knew that he'd indirectly confirmed what's true. **"I thought it was just a dream, falling from the stars and being born from a vestal young woman. No one should know anything before life, but somehow, I believed I did. And now, after seeing you two, I know it for sure that I was right to believe in the beyond."**

"I have so much to ask you," Brother teared up while looking at the Radiant Sun.

"I do not have long, so I'll only outline to you what's crucial for your survival. From the moment your eyes laid upon me, a restart to your cycle began in order to level you with the new timeline I've initiated. This fourth cycle we're going around is now the first one again. You must continue to count the cycles so that when it's your turn to fall, you'll know when and where you'll land in the world below."

"I knew it. Midnight and I are fated to fall just like you had, aren't we?"

"I'm afraid so."

"You just came from that planet, so you should know. Is it a world that brother and I can be ourselves in?"

"The Adamah is still quite young in the development of its reality. However, I assure you that it will grow and evolve into a place of generalize acceptance. I'm uncertain of when you'll fall, but when it happens, you'll know who you must become to survive the era that chooses you."

"The Adamah, huh? Is there any way that we can skip venturing into there and just move on to elsewhere?" I wondered

"You must explore this life before you can move onto a new one. It's a necessary trial that you cannot evade because there are two ending paths after it: the correct one and the incorrect one. The incorrect way will bring about an eternal repeat, and the correct way will bring about everlasting peace. There's no way around this life, fore you still cling onto what you should no longer have to become as I am, beyond this world."

"So, it's a test of our hearts?" Brother asked.

"Yes."

"I don't get it. What are we clinging onto that we must lose in order to follow after you?" I wondered.

"Your bodies. Your physical forms must be left behind for the Adamah's cultivation as a thank you for your trial lives upon Her. When your souls ascend, you'll come to know the infinite time of yourselves. Sentient, formless, and genderless, you'll transcend as I have, pushing beyond all boundaries of universal connectivity. You'll then rise to an eternal place where the love of trillions of past lives assembles. Together, all chosen hearts in existence will singularly unify with each other and become the meaning of forever itself."

"Whoa!"

"But for that to happen, we must first live in this world?" I reminded, then thought to ask. "After you fell from us and entered your life on the Adamah, whom did you become? What was the name of your mortal body?"

"Continue with your cycle count, and it will one day add up to my origins on that world. Upon your discovery of my identity, I ask that neither of you take on the persona of me. A name is a period that should only happen once. Therefore, the exact name will bring about a similar repeat of its history. Avoid this at all costs or you could be sacrificed as well. Be yourself, and if desired, become my kindness to achieve an indistinguishable likeness to me. Your purpose, however, is to be thankful while living caring and fulfilling lives."

"Once Midnight and I are alive at once, we could have nothing in that world, and I would be happy."

"Just to exist alongside you would bring me joy too, brother."

"The strength of your bond is immense. However, there's no guarantee that you'll both descend at once. The world will call on you when it needs you so there's no choice in when you want to live. Only once you're alive and aware on the Adamah will free will be bestowed on you."

That confirmed information made brother and I look at one another with worried eyes. I'm dreaded to think about the nightmare that just sounded by hearing that feeling lost in life is a possibility.

"No," I refused to accept it. "There has to be a way to secure both of our lives into one timeline! I can't live a whole lifetime feeling like someone that won't exist while I'm alive is missing. There must be a way that you can't help brother and me fall together."

"There is none. However, I've presented each of you with two percent of my primordial spirit. Leaving that part of me in you could act as a Vesica Piscis for your inevitable meeting if you do fall in the same generation. If you both live at once but don't fall at once, you're assured to meet at least once in your lifetime. One half of my soul will try to find the other, and that'll bring you together. Any connections after that will be up to how you see one another in life. Forget not, if possible, that all your memories will be taken before your trial life begins. You could meet once and remain strangers forever."

My eyes widened, not only for learning the fact that our memories will be lost but also for the fact that He's only bestowed us a total of four percent of His spirit. When it was first issued into me, it felt endless, and I can still feel the limitlessness of His existence within me. If this is only two percent of Him each within us, then at Ninety-six percent He must feel like...

"I think I understand what you are now," I voiced to the Radiant Sun.

"Before I descended onto the Adamah, I learned of you two as being my fathers. But now that I've existed the earliest, restarted time and forged a new path of reality, my motion is now fixed into the world you're fated to enter. I've become the Father of time, and because a part of my vitality is inside of you, you two are directly my sons. All those that doctrine to my time will be your brothers and sisters. Teach them and treat them with absolute love and kindness."

"Oh, wow," I reacted, taken by surprise and bewildered in trying to understand how our thinking can change in the snap of a finger. "And just like that, we're not orphans anymore," I laughed to brother, whose reaction shows high signs of obfuscation, puzzled in trying to connect the dots.

"S—Sons?"

"Don't overthink it, brother," I said, bringing his focus to me. "Do you remember why you renamed me? Changes happen, and this might be one of them we have no choice but to adapt to. While we're journeying through everything, we must apply ourselves to these alterations, or nostalgia will break us into stagnant thinking. Thinking is theoretical while knowing is practical. Let's keep knowing, okay, brother?"

He nodded and said, "Alright, Midnight," easily giving in to my suggestion. "Since we'll believe in this together, adapting to it should come easy for me." Brother turned his focus to the Radiant Sun and asked, "What do we do now, Father?" our perspective permanently changed.

"Be ready."

"How many cycles apart is too far apart for Midnight and me to meet in the life below?"

"Seven, depending on whether you die an elder or not. To guide you, I'll manifest three stars that'll each define 700 years," Brother and I looked around and spotted three bright stars developing across the galaxy. Brightly they circled each other in a faraway shine. They look like one big star if I blur my vision while keeping my stare. **"Every 700 years, a star will fade away. When all three stars have faded, you both will have lived and died, allowing me to return to the Adamah at one hundred percent of my power."**

"Wait, you're going back to that world?"

"I am."

"And we won't be alive to see that happen?"

"As the keys that will unlock my return, you will not."

"In the time after we live in that world, will we ever meet you again?"

"A needle of a chance, fore you may become as substantial as I am now. The state of your afterlives could allow you the potential to explore all the planes of endlessness."

"Amazing!" My heart filled with knowing how much more there is to explore. "Then, how about we linger in this universe and wait for you after we die?" I suggested.

"Yeah. Once you're done with your future mission for this world, you can journey to other places along with us," brother added.

"Thank you, boys. A very generous offer, but I cannot come along. I've promised a dominion above and below to the residence of this galaxy. Assurance of such is one of eternity, fore a crown is forever. Journey as you must, but always know that my gates are open when you want to settle down and come home to this universe." The Radiant Sun suddenly began to speed off toward a further reach.

"Wait, you're leaving?"

"It appears so. The new first cycle is coming to an end. And as no one, I cannot be seen after one. From here on, I'll leave you both be with apart of me."

"Where exactly are you going?"

"The world to come is one in which the eyes can see, but the flesh can never touch. It is the representation of everything and nothing all at once and the foundation of the primordial thought of creation. It is where I will build my Empyrean before my return to save all that is good." He responded within us. **"I'm going into the red giant."**

The Radian Sun of Father kept furthering in distance and its trajectory is toward nonother than the greatest light in our present space, the Sun.

"I've said all that I could. This is my farewell," He distant.

"At least leave us with a title to remember you by," brother reacted.

"To those who believe in me like you two do, I'm your Father. Once I collide with the great light, that'll remain lightly true forever more."

The Radiant Sun voiced His final statement within us from such a great distance then struck into the outer shell of the Sun. It caused an intensifying shine and an immeasurable amount of warmth to let us know that He's always present.

When the full spectrum light normalized several seconds later, both the sight and sound of father was gone but a percent of his presence remained in us. Where the rest of Him resides now is within the flaming body of the one true Sun.

The new first cycle officially ended, leaving my brother and me to travel together alone by the new second cycle.

Henceforth, our journey continued slightly adjusted due to an immortal spirit tethering itself to us and our ladder up to life.

Soon after, the new third cycle had passed. For the time, brother and I moved onto the fourth cycle.

.... Eleventh, Twelfth, Thirteenth, Fourteen, brother would exhale when we'd reached a new point in our repeated cycle.

.... Thirty-Fifth, Thirty-Sixth, Thirty-Seventh, Thirty-Eighth, I noticed him becoming wiser and more specific with every cycle he counted.

.... Fifty-Nineth, Sixtieth, Sixty-First, Sixty-Second, he's now able to coordinate and measure our position from above as it is below.

.... Seventy-Third, Seventy-Fourth, Seventy-Fifth, Seventy-Sixth, he's now dividing our positions into future points labeled to compartmentalize within one another. Brother called their separations, 'the months and the days.'

The months are supposedly 10 largely separated positions of time, and the days count 35, 36, or 37 steps within each month to add up to one complete circle.

.... Eighty-Seventh, Eighty-Eighth, Eighty-Nineth, Ninetieth, brother's managed to divide every point distinctly. He explained to me in the order of one to ten how;

(37, 35, 37, 36, 37, 36, 37, 37, 36, and 37 days in the ten months add up to 365 days in one circle. He labeled that complete circle of a cycle, a year.

Brother then went on to say that there is an even smaller time within the days and that came as the biggest surprise to me.

He's somehow broke into deciphering real-time calculations upon the Adamah before we've even landed on it.

He's preconceived the actual motion of the living beings below into two clocks.

The first clock was called the decayotton reality. It followed a 9-simplex pattern that dismantled a day into 72 seconds a minute, and 60 minutes an hour to make 20 hours equal a day.

"And so, ten hundred hours would be considered midday, while twenty hundred hours would be equal to midnight," brother explained.

"Amazing. I can't believe you've taught yourself all of this already," I expressed my shock in watching him rapidly evolve before my eyes. "What about the second clock?" I wondered.

"Well, the second clock I'll call the dodecayotton," he labeled. "It's an 11-simplex pattern that cycles a day as 60 seconds a minute, and 60 minutes an hour to make 24 hours equal a day. And so, twelve hundred hours would be considered midday, and twenty-four hundred hours would be equal to midnight."

Brother's ability to understand and give repetitive roles to motion using numbers grew to almost beyond my ability to follow along.

It's now the Ninety-First cycle, and brother has gone into smaller dimensions within even the littlest, convincing me of his detailing capability. With his accuracy, he has the potential to tell stories even beyond what I've told him. He's consistently growing toward an unmatched cleverness, but I must pull him up for some air. Sometimes when we're quiet for too long, I could feel him slipping deep into his head, and I refuse to lose him while he's right next to me.

"Hey, brother," I called him away from his complex thoughts that's vibrating a paradoxical sleep through his wakened eyes. He blinked to return to normality and looked at me with focused eyes.

"What's up, Midnight?" he asked.

"It's been Ninety-one cycles already. If eleven years on the Adamah is equal to one cycle up here, how much years has it been since the Radiant sun left?"

"That's easy. It's been exactly ten hundred one years on that world," He smiled, gazing down at it. Brother's attention shifted toward the galaxy of space, and he pointed to indicate that "One out of the three stars left for us has completely faded to nonexistence, while another is halfway through its fade. Only one more star is still filled with light. In one hundred cycles also known as eleven hundred years,

Father will return. Since we'll descend before He does again, our time is almost here, Midnight."

When he said that, it immediately triggered a concern that has long bothered me. "Brother, if I'm to descend now and you to descend eight cycles from now, we'll never know each other and live our lives in two different times. I fear spending my whole life searching for a bond who doesn't exist yet. And after I'm gone, you'll live a similar life, searching for a bond who no longer exists."

"I've thought about it too, Midnight," brother related. "If I'm to descend at all before you, I would carve my existence into that world and leave every piece of me on every part of it. I would ensure your finding of me, even if by then I'm nothing but history. Nevertheless, if you were to fall before me, well, I don't know what I'd do then."

"You'd wait to hear from me. I'd tattoo myself in history for you to find me and have a peace of mind as well. Once you discover me, dead or alive, you'll be fulfilled, never having to worry about not knowing. You can live looking forward from then on, brother, but ultimately I'd never want us to suffer a trial of separation," I voiced my feelings.

"Me neither, Midnight. This is why I remain faithful and rarely think about it. I know we'll get through this together." I smiled and nodded in total agreement. "And also," brother laughed after thinking for a second. "I'm glad you recognized eight cycles as being the average length of life on the Adamah. After our Father shared a percentage of his power with us, he revealed that every cycle above is equal to eleven years below. Since He'd only lived three cycles, I first assumed that it was the maximum amount of time an individual could live, but now I'm positive that it's untrue."

"Father's voice was matured but far from frail. He might've been a man, yes, but I don't think He lived to be an elderly one."

"Which is why I'm thinking on it so hard now. If He had much more life to live, what could've possibly caused His death so soon? This is something that only Father can answer, and we've waited too late to ask Him."

"Now that you've thought up the question, brother, I'm now curious as well to find out what could put a stop to eternity before eternity decides to end naturally."

"Eternity? Midnight, if that's your consideration of Father, then only He can put an end to Himself."

"This is true. Whatever death He'd faced must've been by choice. From the sound of His voice, His heart seemed far from fragile for self-infliction to be a consideration."

"No one chooses to die for nothing, cause even relieving pain is a reason. Maybe Father loved someone, and His sacrifice was to keep them alive."

"That someone must've been a major body since time itself restarted after His death. For something as extraordinary as that to take root, the love He died for was likely everyone and everything."

"The entire world?"

"Yes. The speculation is imposing, I know, but not beyond possibility. We'll most likely find out the truth when we descend, brother. Even if Father didn't leave behind a story of Himself, I'm sure many others will have written stories to teach future eras about him. If father's forever carrying along their reality, He's timeless or time itself. Proving such legendary capabilities would ultimately construct Him to being factual of a single term, The Absolute."

"Midnight, you've called Him so many names that I sometimes wonder if we're still talking about Father. That time He shared a total of four percent of his power with us, you said to Him, 'I think I understand what you are now,' What exactly did you figure out at that moment?"

"I've figured out the same thing that you did. I simply can't come to a fixed explanation because He is no one thing, but many things at once. Which is why I call Him many names or the first one to pop up into my head."

"I know you have it in you to explain it better than that. You're great with words.

"I don't need to explain it any better. I'm sure you know what I mean, brother. Just think about what it felt like as Father's golden radiance flowed into us. My vision cleared and broadened my feelings and understandings of a perspective that I didn't think could exist. I thought that if the two percent was only a sample of Him, then all of Him deserved to be called nothing less than totality itself. What I meant when I called Father, The Absolute was that he's The Unconditioned Ultimate Reality, The Wholly Other, The Supreme Being, and many other names. He's the Anthropomorphic Form, Being, Entity, Power, Law, and so on that possesses Maximal Otherworldly Status, Existential Ranking, Existential Greatness, or Existentialism. Concisely, the Absolute is the one that is, in one way or another, The Greatest, Truest, or Most Real Being that could ever be."

"That was a great explanation," brother's eyes sparkled at me. "I loved your explanation a lot and can highly relate to what you just said. You were always so good in your etymology, Midnight."

"Thank you, brother, and it looks like you've found your calling in horology, with your mathematical development."

He laughed, saying, "I guess so. Hearing you describe Father just now reminded me so much of the narrative you told me when we were in Eden. It feels like a lifetime ago since we've left that world behind."

"I know, I miss telling you stories too. But you also know why I haven't begun a new one yet."

"Yeah, I know. You don't know how telling a new story will react to us on this new plane. Just like in Eden, any world you think up has the potential to drag us in, specifically me. I'm the one keeping track of our time and missing even one cycle is dangerous to our alignment."

"Right, you must stay focus for just a little longer, okay? Once we're alive and together on the Adamah, any kind of story you want to hear, I will make real for you, brother. Until then, teach me a little more about this intricate axis you have cycling around your head. And please don't go so hard on me with the numbers this time. I don't understand them the way that you do."

"Alright, Midnight, I won't. I guess it's my turn to tell you a narrative." he smiled then engaged. "In shapes, the most difficult one to calculate into creation is a sphere. What if I told you that I've thought up a pattern to creating this perfect circle using not only numbers but the repositioning of a story itself?" He hypothetically questioned.

I abruptly engaged myself into listening to brother's furthering knowledge of numerical discoveries.

The night brother and I first woke up, we began to label the sun, the moon, and the meaning of day as it happened. We didn't get to continue because we learned that our biggest problem then wasn't the length of time. It was the Organisms that began attacking us when the sun sat. Luckily, by the sunrise on the following day, brother and I had left Eden behind. Now we're here, zooming around the Adamah's atmosphere while waiting on our time of descension.

.... One Thirty-Sixth, One Thirty-Seventh, One Thirty-Eighth, One Thirty-Nineth, and we're well over our hundredth cycle. I'm presently and utterly convinced that my brother's deranged or simply a genius. He believes that he can collectively determine an approximate sum of those presently alive on the Adamah. There's half a billion, but is he right? At this stage, I'm wondering if the number of years below is accumulating into him. It'd require lifetimes to easily learn this much knowledge, not just One Hundred Forty Cycles.

In our continued travel, we're not at all quiet with each other as curiosity around his brain always brought a question out of me. Eventually, we'd talked so much that we'd ran out of new content and simply enjoyed the company of traveling alone together. When any new content surfaced, ninety percent of it was about how the world down below started to display more and more noticeable changes as we went around it. The side of the world that was primarily dark began to show more and more signs of life with every passing cycle.

By the One Seventy-fourth cycle, a glow began to come from the Adamah that was different from any fire that used to shine bright from it. It was like, a new light. Abruptly, that light began to rapidly spread twinkles across the land wherever there was darkness.

An inch of a cycle after, structures of mass height began to rise into place and hastily expanded. I wondered why the world abruptly began to move so quickly and brother answered that with a census.

By the One Seventy-Fifth cycle, there were Two billion living souls on the Adamah, providing many hands and many minds. It was unbelievable to think that it only took them four hundred years to increase by so much.

Their growth is now moving nearly as fast as our travel. In nine more cycles also known as ninety-nine years on the Adamah, they could increase to almost ten billion.

There were many explosions on the surface of the Adamah before and after the One Seventy-Sixth Cycle. But during this time, innovation presented itself when flying objects developed by its inhabitants who'd began to soar the skies below us. Their advancements showed precedence in their developments and a multitude of growth.

The most astonishing thing brother and I had seen, was the metal objects shooting to the stars as the Adamah's inhabitants attempted to reach a point in space. On the One Seventy-Ninth cycle, there was written success of a landing on the moon, and the world below experienced an expansion level event because of it.

Now permanently orbiting below brother and I, are many metal objects that seem to observe information on the space upon and around the Adamah. Just like the moon, they were manmade satellites.

Upon reaching our One Eighty-First cycle, brother didn't voice our positioned count as he usually does. We're less than One cycle away from two thousand years passing since we've seen our Father, and all three of the stars He'd created are all but gone. Once we reach the One Eighty-Second cycle, it'll be less than one hundred years on the Adamah before Father's return. If brother and I are still going to descend before His second coming, then it's going to happen soon.

Since brother didn't voice our current cycle like he usually does, he must be deep in his calculation. To break the silence and get a woke reaction out of him, I decided to voice a disturbing thought to bring him out of his thoughts.

"What if we die up here, taking an eternity to conclude with this wandering flight? From flesh to bones and from bones to dust, our cells could forever zoom around this globe in a fixed circulation." His vision instantly petrified showing widened eyes.

"Whoa! I'm sorry. Don't be scared. I really frightened you with that thought, didn't I?" His facial response wasn't a reaction to me but to the world below.

His outlook on it instantly sparked a curious awe in his eyes, a fresh reaction that's equal to the time we first woke and saw each other in Eden.

"Is something wrong, brother?" I asked him right away. "Your atmosphere feels refreshed."

"Brother? Is that who you are to me?" He asked, and my eyes shook right away, wondering if his time has come.

"Please tell me that this is just for a laugh. You truly know me, right?" I asked, wanting him to look at me with knowing eyes again, but he simply shook his head.

"I'm sorry, I don't. I actually don't know myself or why I'm here if that makes you feel any better," he said, and it shattered my heart to know that I might have to say goodbye.

"It doesn't. Nice try though," I tried to keep from getting emotional.

The intensity of gravity suddenly weighed down on my brother, and aware that I shouldn't hold on, I refused to let him go until my limit was maxed.

"What's happening?!"

"You're—" I tightened my grip and added my second hand, still struggling to refuse fate. "You're slipping! Try to come back up to me," I wrongfully asked of him.

"I—I can't! It feels like it's out of my control. Am I going to perish?!"

"No, you won't, you'll be alright. I figured that you couldn't stop this. That was just me being selfish and hoping that our journey could avoid this gap. I wish we didn't have to risk falling lifetimes apart and fall at once, but the choice really isn't ours." I grunted as his aggressive weight increased and placed pressure on my joints.

"Stop this! Neither of us are budging. Why continue to strain yourself? You're in pain by keeping me up, and it's burning my heart to watch. Let me go. If I knew you before, I don't know you now."

"You've forgotten me? How ridiculous of you to say when your heart is retorting to showing me how blind it isn't. Look around, brother, we're all we've got. Even before we shared equal halves of the same soul, you've always meant-" I paused, immediately thinking about the golden radiance in me and its capabilities.

I placed around my will the desire to grant him half of me. And instantly, my energy began to transfer into him. As it happened, his weight lightened up the tension from my joints. I've just started a process that will buy us a little more time together. Hopefully, by the time I'm done, my turn to fall will be here too.

"What is this feeling?" Brother wondered.

"We've each inherited two percent of a Radiant Sun. I'm giving you half of what is mine, so now you'll be at three percent, and I'll keep the last one."

"Why?"

"In magnetism, two equal forces on the same side are likely to repel one another. But two equal forces on opposite sides are likely to attract at their center point, which isn't always good. So, to avoid using half of our lives before we come face to face in a Vesica Piscis, I've given you more. Making us a larger to a smaller force will draw me into you sooner, brother. You just have to recognize me when I come."

"One percent is still smaller than the eyeball; it's the pupil. What if you encounter me and my shortsightedness of you causes an omission?"

"Then I'll wait until you're far away and wave to you," I took a breath as I finished the release of energy into him. "I'm sure you'll see my point then. But it shouldn't come to that because our paths are now even more intertwined. If you embrace me as you've done before, we will untwine and become two for two again, circling each other's world from then." Brother's weight began to gradually increase again as my diversion away from the situation came to an end. "I'm—I'm going to let you go now."

"Wait," he halted my release of him. "What do I call you?" brother asked.

I smiled, thinking about the complexity behind such a simple question. My safest response is to tell him who I presently am and explain nothing of who I used to be called.

"You named me 'The Core of Midnight', but you call me Midnight for short."

"I—I named you?" he slipped from me after questioning.

"No!" I shouted, reaching for him who's already lost to me. "Don't forget, okay?! I'll land somewhere in your future!"

"I won't, I promise!" Brother's figure distantly drew toward the planet.

Ablaze of blue sun awakened around brother as his speed toward the earth burned a shine of his way down. He's gone, and now it's my turn to keep up the cycle count.

On the 181st cycle, brother lost his memories, and gravity began to take him down. I was able to hold him up for a half cycle longer than he was supposed to travel before I had no other option but to let him go.

It started with the three of us so long ago, and now it's just me all alone. It's amusing when I think about my pending fall. I'll be the only one of us to accurately fall without any intervention or delay since I can't keep myself up when my time comes. The time I land into that world will be the exact time I'm meant to live.

The feeling of my identity began to fade when I realized that I don't remember where I came from. More of myself vanished when all I remember is zooming across the space with my brother. What were we doing before that?

I suddenly don't know my name and all I remember is being here. Right here and now is not a memory, so in short, I've become a blank slate. Who will I become now?

Ao9

Door 19&02: To End Again in a New World

Romer's (POV) -s-

I gasped, blinking quickly and wildly swinging my hands to try to hold onto something. I instantly came to a pause with the quick realization that all around me there was nothing. There's not even ground.

"Space? How am I in space? This must be a dream. How else am I able to breathe?" I completely calmed myself with this thought as I began to admire the beauty of Earth from an atmospheric height that I never thought I'd see it from.

A blue star impacted the Earth and caught my eyes right away. It was an astonishing sight to witness, but before I could adequately react, air from below my level rushed up my nostrils. From outer space, the Earth's gravity started to pull me toward it for no reason. "No, no! Stop!" I frantically tried to keep myself up. I became ablaze, and the wind around me increased, but it feels transparent, so I know it's a dream.

This motion down kept quickening with every passing second. My heart nearly lost its beat at the sight of the ocean coming up to me, and I panicked all the way down. Upon impact, I shut my eyes and held my breath. After a few seconds of feeling as though I'd impacted nothing, I opened my eyes and saw that I was being pulled deep down into the depths of the ocean. It made me gasped even further, terrified, wondering where this is leading me.

"Wait, I can still scream and talk? This can't be real, bei." I voiced.

As I dusked toward the ocean ground, I found that I was suddenly intangible to touch. I kept my comfort in my belief as I reached the ocean floor. Through it, I passed, and into the planet's mass, I continued down.

My vision was blinded for most of my travel down, sometimes encountering open spaces in the Earth filled with molten lava or diamond crystals. After a lengthy while of traveling down, I came to identify a small sphere occupying its own space in the path of my fall. I impacted it, and as expected, there's no touch, just a simple pass-through.

Unexpectedly, while inside of it, I came to an unusually slow and then a sudden stop. It's very dark in here, but as I had that thought, a twinkle began the lighting of many glowing dots around me. Directly in front of me, a group of those twinkles gathered and attached to one another. They took on a human shape and form, specifically curving like woman's body. When its body fully developed, it sparkled into the brightest twinkle around itself.

It floated in front of me in silence, and I asked it, "Who are you?" to see if it was sentient.

"Most inhabitants land on the surface of us, hardly within. An anomaly such as yourself enters our core once in a miracle. Welcome to the Adamah. We are The Malkuth," it said with a multitude of soft voices, probably comprised of the number of twinkles it took to create its body.

The remaining twinkles that are floating around suddenly pushed away and landed on the inner shell of the sphere around us. They began to shape into the continents and the ocean separation. In a matter of seconds, I'm viewing the Earth's geographical mapping from within the core of it.

"Wait, the Adamah is what I call planet Earth?" I deduced while gazing at the being whose sounds appear to be harmoniously unified and elegant. Understanding that I could be talking to what I don't comprehend, I asked, "Why have you brought me here?"

"You made it here on your own. You're here for the reason of who you are. You're about to live on the Adamah as the human who means The Ides of Four Thousand Years. As the figure who's the center of the four major directions, your position above all is fixed. You get to choose anywhere you want to land since you're in the core of the world."

The Malkuth tried to explain, but I'm not quite understanding. How can I land on anything if I'm in an intangible state of mind? I know this is a dream that I'm lucidly traveling along, so won't waking up be the answer of landing? If that's the case, I'll use my present awareness to find the whereabouts of the blue star before I wake up. Dreams usually don't happen the same twice, and I don't want to be left wondering how this one ends.

"So, you're capable of instant transportation?" I wondered for clarity.

"From this position, we both are. But for reasons, we never leave," The Malkuth voiced.

"Alright. Then show me the way to the landing mark of the blue star I saw. If this whole world is your residence, then you should recall the impact of the object I mean."

"Of course, I know. It left a mark that's impossible to forget. I'll direct you toward the Catalyst you seek. When you land and rise into your identity, do not remain fixed. Roam across the lands of your nation and wisely age up to a great man, learning all that you can. Then when you're ready, roam around the world. Your strength and weakness both reside within your singularity. Your rarity can potentially cause you to be unheard of or greatly renowned," It advised.

The twinkling hands of The Malkuth lifted to touch my cheek and my heartfelt the billions of emotions it carries within it. I couldn't feel any touch at all on my entire journey down to here, and now suddenly, I'm feeling broadly compassionate.

"As a Keter to us, happiness is ultimately all we want for you," The Malkuth added while moving its hand down to my chest. Suddenly, it shoved me away as its unified voice said, "Go now, and make your own fate."

I'm turned around at an increasing speed outward to darkness. The speed grew into sort of an absorption vortex toward a sudden appearance of a small white light.

There's no specific location in my head as I could be headed toward anywhere on the surface of the Earth. Since I'm traveling up from the core, the surface must be that growing light I'm rushing toward. I wonder if I'll see the blue star when I arrive at the top or if I'll just wake up after I rise.

The Malkuth spoke to me as though I didn't exist yet, leaving me with some unanswered questions of why. I'm already alive with a name and a family, so why am I weirdly dreaming of another story?

As I traveled further and further, the bright light gradually grew until my sight was consumed by a blank brightness.

A strong miniature cry exited from my breath as my first sounds cannot form words. While alone in my thoughts, I realized I'm at my birth and being hugged into comfort under my mother, who brought me into this life as her final son.

DOB: ***(o1999-o1o-o1st.)***

Nineteen Years Later

(o2o18-o4-o2nd)

I opened my eyes, naturally breathing as I'm fully reminded of my rolling situation. I looked out the window and noticed that we're only on Baillou Hill Road.

"We're eleven minutes away if you're wondering," she said, and I looked to her focus on the road.

"How long was I asleep, sis?" I asked her.

"About nine minutes."

"In nine minutes? No way!"

"You surprised me. I didn't even notice when you fell asleep. You sure you ready for your class this evening?" She asked.

"I'm not tired at all, just in my thoughts, I think. I don't understand what it was, but-..."

"Don't stop now," she's interested as usual. "But what?"

"I don't know if I understand it enough to try to explain it yet."

"Two heads are better than one. Tell me what you dreamt, Corey?" she insisted.

I already let it slip a little, so I might as well keep on talking.

As best I could, I told her about the blue star I saw while in orbit and then about the celestial body I encountered in the core of the earth and everything it told me. By the time I caught her up, we were almost at the intersection near Marathon Mall."

"-And the last thing I remember was a white light and a baby crying before I woke up in this car. Well, I was the baby crying."

"That's a crazy deep story. You dreamt that last night?"

"No, bei, just now."

"In only a few minutes? No way!" She's shocked.

"That's what I said too, remember? So why do you think I had it?"

"You're asking me? That whole dream was on drugs, and it had a lot going on in it. The quickness of it was more like a premonition than a dream. It seemed like it was leading you toward finding out one thing,"

"What the blue star was," I said.

"Right, but remember you said it was called the Catalyst last, so that's most likely what it is."

"Wait, what's a Catalyst?" I realized I didn't know.

"It's... It's hard to explain. Bring up the English dictionary on your phone."

When I found the app, I searched and learn that "A Catalyst is a substance that increases the rate of a chemical reaction without itself undergoing any permanent chemical change. It's a spur, stimulus, or impetus existing to prompt cellular and mechanical growth.

"From that meaning, I understood that a catalyst could be an object or a person. Since you asked, in your dream, to be sent to the landing point of the catalyst and woke up here after, maybe it's me. Aww, you love your big sister that much?" she mocked.

I laughed and said, "Whatever. And I didn't wake up here first. I woke up when I was—" I paused, thinking about how my witty remark could be the answer. "I woke up when I was born at the Princess Margaret Hospital."

"Oh, wow. If the catalyst is a person, you have most of our present population to look through. There's almost four hundred thousand of us so I don't envy you."

"Maybe I don't have to look through all of them."

"What's on your mind?"

"In my dream, the catalyst was foreshadowed from before my birth. Since I just dreamt about it a couple minutes ago, maybe today is the day I'm going encounter it."

"Maybe," she considered.

I couldn't further elaborate to her because we were already at the gates of the college after just turning onto Old Trail Road. I took out my student identification and showed the security to easily gain entrance.

"When do you finish?" Sis asked as she stopped her vehicle to let me out.

"I'll call you," I said, as I exit.

"I can't promise that I'll be free all night."

"I only have one class this evening. Sometimes it ends at nine and sometimes sooner. It depends on, Mr. Culmer."

"Alright, then I'll keep 9 p.m. in mind. See you later and keep safe," she said, then left the grounds of the college.

I turned to the school and gazed at a sign that held the college's crest. Learn, Grow, and Achieve is the motto I read for BTVI.

It's about 6 p.m., and the Sun has begun to set as night came over the island. I entered the campus, and while on my way to my major, I started to realize that my usual focus is now clouded by wonder. I placed a dampener on my thoughts and vowed that I'll think more on the Catalyst after class.

When I approached the classroom, I entered the practical workshop and then opened another door to enter the theoretical classroom. I stood at the entrance, at the rear corner of the class, and a multiple of heads looked my way. I immediately saw that it was more crowded in here than usual. I recognized my classmates, but there's a few others scattered about that are somewhat strangers I've only seen around campus. From what I can gather, it looks like a mix-up, or a crossover has happened.

"Take a seat, Romer."

"Yes, sir," I replied, looking for one.

"There's a vacancy here," I heard a voice come from the front right of the room.

The tables in here are long and pearl white, capable of holding five persons in a stretch and their bags too. There's usually two to three of us at a table but this evening there are five and six. I spotted the empty chair located second to last at the first table. When I sat down and someone else entered, I realized that we have the capacity to fit many, but we just lack the seating.

"Wait there for a moment, more chairs are on the way," Culmer told the man. "Since most of you have arrived, I'll let y'all know what happened and why. As y'all know, I lecture two levels of Heating Ventilation and Air Conditioning twice a week: HVAC One & HVAC Two. Well, instead of properly scheduling One to come on Monday and Two to come on Tuesday, there was a printing error that placed both classes on today's Monday evening. After tonight, I'll see HVAC One students again on Wednesday and HVAC II students on Thursday. The following week we'll continue on the regular schedule.

"How'd this happen, Teach?"

"This error was printed out on your syllabus since January, and I think no one noticed because it showed dates and not days of the week. We're living the reality of what would have happened if no one caught it in time. All of my students in one class at once."

"I thought April fools was yesterday, Culmer."

"You and me both, Ellis." Culmer chuckled as he sat behind his desk. "I have some separate work on my laptop for y'all. While I put it together, do whatever."

There's always someone loud and attention-grabbing to start everything off with a story that's so highly exaggerated you'd wish it happened. He started talking, and that was it for some of their attention.

"Bei!" a rough call for our attentions came from the entrance of the class.

The person was resting down a load of chairs he'd just brought inside. His gaze is fixed in my direction as he marched over.

"You mussy ain want ya life, king. Why you in my seat, Supervalue?" he asked, and I knew then that he wasn't talking to me.

"You really have to shout like that?" A young man in a hoodie voiced as he's approached by the man who just brought the chairs. I recognized his tone as being the one who called me over to this empty spot.

"'Do whatever' doesn't mean you get to spill blood in my classroom. Do you see how white in here is?"

"Then I'll do it outside, Culmer." The man slammed his palm on the desk. "Get up!"

"No killing on the campus. I'm pretty sure the janitors would hate you until you graduate."

"Ugh!" the man raged.

"I like this spot, and my life too. Why you trying to make me choose one?" the young man slid off the hoodie, appearing to look close to my age.

This man in front of us appears to be at least a couple of years beyond us.

"How about I do your math homework for you," the young man recommended.

"Make it Electrical too."

"Are you kidding me?"

"Do you see a smile?"

"Fine, alright? Now can you cool it, bei?" The man stood up from pressing his hand on the desk and then cracked a smile.

"You must really like that spot. I don't really care that you took it, Moore," the man said then looked at me. "But it was a light move to not even keep your old spot vacant for me," he scoffed, then walked off.

I looked at the young mand right away, and he sighed, "Can we pretend you didn't hear that?"

"I don't get it," I shook my head at him.

"What don't you get? I came from there and sat here then when you entered the classroom, I called you over to sit there."

"So, you used me?"

"No, of course not. Didn't you see that I just took all the heat?"

"That spot wasn't all you wanted, though. I can see the animosity you have for that man. I bet I'm also here because you didn't want him next to you."

"All he does is copy my work anyway, so intuitively, you're right. But aside from that, I'm doing a pair of homework now so I wouldn't call that using you."

He's right, which makes me wonder, "Why'd you trust a stranger to go along with your plan?"

"A stranger?" he laughed. "You don't recognize me, bei? I mean, we've never officially met, but we take a subject together. I've seen your character in a classroom setting, and I knew I'd be cool next to you."

"Workforce Prep," I remembered him, and then further remembered that we even bucked each other by the vending machine once.

"Yeah, that's the class. I'm Moore," he greeted.

"Call me, Romer," I introduced.

"Nice to officially meet you," Moore said, then went back to his prior work.

After a minute of feeling like something wasn't right, I remembered what he was called elsewhere and it wasn't Moore, it was Romeo. Which one of his names is the right one?

We began the topic for the day after several minutes of idling. Culmer had sent an email to the lab for some documents to be printed, and a student volunteered to collect them. Upon their return, Culmer stapled a load of paper together and passed them out.

"The sheets I'm sending around will be handled by a pair of students who'll share one grade. An HVAC I and an HVAC II student will make up each pair."

"Wait a minute, Culmer. This ain't no test, right? I mean, it can't be."

"It is absolutely a test; an open book one consisting of questions from both levels of HVAC."

"How is that Fair? We second year students know way more than the first years, so they'll be of no help to us," a student complained.

"Speak for yourself. I study ahead of time," a student argued against.

"They'll help you remember some of the things you may have forgotten, and that's a lot," Culmer explained. "Questions that'll be a test for the first-year students will be a review for the second-year students. Vice Versa, questions that'll be a test for the second-year students will be a learning experience for the first. I need y'all to prove to me that the predecessors and the successors can cooperate to make an A."

"I still don't like this idea," A student opposed.

"Well, I'm supposed to have y'all for three and half hours, but not this evening. Once you're done with this quiz, you can leave," Culmer added.

"Yo, you for real, teach? Okay, say no more then," a student said and got started right away. Many followed his lead, striving for a short evening in here.

Culmer sat back at his desk, as we began our only lesson for the day.

A test paper slid into the view of my eyes with Moore pointing his finger at the heading.

"Write your name, Romer," he indicated, and I took up my pen and wrote my full name. I passed it back to him and he wrote his as well then opened the test. As he wrote, my eyes were on his hand because it's rare of me to meet a lefty.

I guess he and I are doing this together through convenience. Moore's in a corner seat and an HVAC II student and I'm an HVAC I student right next to him.

"I wish this were a pop quiz and not an opened book test." Moore grunted while flipping through the pages.

"Why would you wish that?" I wondered.

"Because we'd be out of here even quicker. Pop quizzes ask questions from your memory, knowledge, and history of experiencing the answers. These open-book tests could ask any questions around the subject, even for answers we don't yet know. This is fair because we're permitted to search for it and searching is what'll rob us of our time."

"Sounds like 'Blueprint Reading', bei," I thought

"That class is a prime example. I hate those tests," he laughed.

Moore flipped back to the first page, and we began our work. Shortly after beginning, we bucked elbows once or twice when we tried to simultaneously write down an answer on our separate sheets. Since we had to work together, distancing wasn't an option, so we switched seats. He's left-handed and now at my left, while I'm right-handed and now at his right. We can write in sync from here without disruption.

After being into the test for a while, I see that Moore was right about the length of time increasing due to us having to search. Some of the questions had us paused for minutes at a time, unexpectedly. The web search engine failed to bring up accurate top answers for some of our questions through millions of results. For that reason, our first- and second-year textbooks came in handy.

We also managed to speed things up by finding the synonyms of keywords in questions and asking them in a new light. That method sped us through search engines a little quicker than we were going at the start.

It took us about an hour and forty minutes to finish up; more time than some, less time than most.

Moore packed his bag before me and took the test up to Culmer. As he gave in our results, I thought about his name again and picked up on the anagram I didn't notice at first. Moore and Romeo are the same name rearranged. But which one is his real name?

After Moore gave in our results, he left the classroom.

I stood up from my seat then walked to Mr. Culmer's desk and said, "I can't remember if I wrote down my name or not."

"Yeah, you did," He replied while showing me the front of our test paper.

After seeing my name and Moore's, I said, "Okay. Thank you, sir."

I left the classroom and after two steps outside I heard Moore ask, "So, what's next for you, Romer?"

I turned around and saw Moore putting his jacket in his pack. He placed it on his back then walked up to me.

"Nothing much, bei. My ride's coming in about an hour. I'm thinking of heading over to the bleachers and calling her here sooner. How about you?" I asked.

"I soon head home as well."

"I bet. I know it's tiring to be working and studying."

"Working?" he questioned, and I indicated down at his shirt. "Oh, right, no. I mean, yeah, it was tiring, but I quit Supervalue a year ago. I only wear this shirt now for assignment excuses."

"Really, bei?" I laughed. "Is nothing straight forward about you?"

"Nothing opinionated. Just ask me directly. Hey, since we're headed the same way you wanna walk with me?"

"Let's move," I agreed, and we got started. As we walked toward the bleachers, I noticed a tattoo on his right wrist and voiced, "A dragon?" trying to keep up with it swinging back and forward. He raised it up to the light and properly showed it to me. "Oh, it's a wolf," I recognized.

"Yeah, a wolf head," he confirmed, looking at it himself. "I'm glad a dog wasn't your first guess."

"It almost was," I shrugged. "It looks clean though."

"Ha-ha, thanks. I got it four months ago from this place downtown for about a hundred dollars."

"Inks are expensive."

"I thought the same thing, that's why I was going to back out on my first tattoo until later. But the artist agreed to add the diamonds on the upper left and right of my chest with no price change. I got three tattoos for the price of one."

"Sick deal."

"I know. I can direct you to there if you want one too."

"Nah, I was just admiring the art itself. You'd probably lose me with your directions anyway."

"Why? You're not familiar with the city island?"

"Nah, not much. I'm Exuman. I was born here in Nassau, but I was raised there."

"Interesting," he reacted.

"I'm only up here for school. Afterward, I'll probably head back home, rest up, and figure out what's next for me from there. Is it obvious that I'm not from here?"

"Yeah, kind of."

"Well, I can easily tell that you're not from here either."

"And you're right about that. I was born here in Nassau too, but I grew up on a family island just like you. I'm Androsian." he wildly smiled, then expressed that, "What a coincidence that I'm meeting an Exuman so soon after thinking up a theory around your island."

"What kind of theory?" I wondered.

"Well, as you know, we praise Andros Island as being the largest in our nation, but that's only one in seven hundred. What about the other six hundred ninety-nine islands and cays? In my search for the second largest island, I unearthed a contradiction when I added up the bits and pieces of the Exuma's Island and Cays to three hundred sixty-five total."

"What does that mean to you?"

"If half of seven hundred islands is three hundred fifty, and Exuma has three hundred sixty-five islands and cays, then it should be considered the largest too. Am I right?"

"Interesting concept, but how can Exuma and Andros both hold the title of the largest to you? One must be larger since nothing is exactly equal in this world."

"I'm glad you said that because just like us, when lands are born, even if they're twins, one comes first. When it comes to quality, Andros is seen as the largest island in our country. But when it comes to quantity, The Exuma Islands and Cays are counted as the largest of all."

"Now you got me thinking. So, if our islands were twins, Andros would be seen as the largest, while Exuma is the actual largest."

"Basically."

"Well, now I'm wondering what makes you think that Quantity trumps Mass.

"Let's play a game to find out," Moore suggested. "Let's imagine that each of our seven hundred islands and cays were a day."

"Alright," I nodded.

"How long's a year?" he suddenly asked.

"Three hundred sixty-five days," I easily answered.

"That's the same number of Islands and Cays in Exuma, right?" I blinked at never thinking of it that way before. "Exuma is the only one that's a year on its own. Now tell me, what do you call three hundred sixty-six days?"

"A leap year," I easily answered again.

"Right, but the three hundred sixty-sixth day could also be called 'the first day after the first year.' Andros and Exuma are not merged, so they cannot be seen as a leap year. Hence, Andros, is either a day before a year or a day after a year. Exuma is the center of either position so that's why I believe that it's the Largest."

"Well, I'll still have to side with Andros as being the largest," I opposed. "Exuma can fit inside Andros's mass more than three times and there would still be space."

"Heh, you're right." He laughed. "It's very contradicting which is why both lands are kingdoms to me. It doesn't matter which one holds the first or the second king, you know?"

"Nicely put."

"Thanks, it was an abrupt thought. Anyhow, since tonight was a mix up, we may not meet like this again. Why exactly are you returning to your island to find a resolution? Don't you have a place you can stay here and figure it out?"

"Yeah, I have older siblings around, and I'm a loved nephew too. But it's mostly by choice that I don't want to remain in Nassau after I graduate."

"I feel you on that. When I graduate, my big brother wants me to come to the Abaco Islands to play a part in another one of his entrepreneurial ideas. He's started an operation to becoming the number one roofing and security business on that island. My elder sister, on the other hand, offered to help me get a job at where she works. She's the manager of food & beverage in a section of Baha Mar. She sprinted up to that ranking dead fast, bei. I wouldn't be surprised if she levels up to general manager in no time. And finally, my mum. My mum back at home founded a South Androsian tourism business where she tours the island's natural blue holes with foreigners. That business is supposed to grow soon with the upcoming reopening of our main hotel, Emerald Palms. But since it was sold, it'll most likely be renamed by its new owners. Mum wants to train me to take over for her when that happens. This way she can rest after decades of doing it but keep it going with me."

"You have so many directions to choose from."

"I know, and yet I haven't decided on any of them. I'm 22 in a month, and I don't know what I want to become. I just want to be happy and explore. I want to leave this time pocket of a country and travel beyond to at least learn something about the outside world. Only then can I know what reason there is to settle in my own."

"Wait, you've never left our nation before?"

"Four years ago, I visited the Floridians, and I was back in eight hours. My sister went on a shopping spree and needed someone to help bring back her luggage. I spent most of that trip in this grassy mall place, so I didn't see much of the outside world. I traveled there again in January, three months ago, but I met a few hiccups on my way there that nearly caused me to miss my flight. See, after the immigration officers saw that I booked my ticket last minute and that I only left my country for eight hours the last time, they stamped my passport. I had to return four days after I left to 'build trust' or something."

"Wow, they carried you hard, bei. And those are the only times you've left our country?"

"Yup."

"I can see why you think about the outside world so much. I've traveled a bit with my family, so I know a little more than you but not everything. The biggest thing I've learned is that you need currency for everything out there."

"I think that's why I was left behind so much. I'm the last born of seven, and my older siblings traveled there many times. But I came nineteen years after my oldest sibling, and the funds were dried up by then, I guess."

"That could be it. I have a lot of siblings too, but not as much as you. I'm the fifth of six."

"It's great having siblings, isn't it?"

"Yeah, they grow us further and more out of our comfort zones. There's always a challenge when you're not an only child, and I think it's fun."

"Me too," Moore agreed.

"Trust me, even though they make me mad sometimes, I love them to death, bei."

"I can relate."

We finally reached the bleachers and when we got here, I realized how fast time could move when you're in deep conversation.

Moore sat down and rest his bag beside him and asked me, "Is HVAC your favorite thing to do, Romer?"

"Nah, that'd have to be art and sometimes craft. Your ink caught my eyes because of its design."

"You draw?! That's lit. You have any samples on you?"

I thought about it for a moment and realized that "I do."

I sat beside him and opened my bag to take out the folder that held my art. I handed it to him, and he flipped through it, staring quite astonished.

"You're talented with the coloring pencils, no lie. Your blend is nice, and for an observation artist, you're pleasantly capturing the correct details from reality into your art."

"You're an artist too?" I assumed.

"How'd you guess?" He closed my folder and handed it back to me.

"Observation art is a technical term, and so was the rest of your description."

"Quite smart that you picked up on that so quickly. I took the BJC and the BGCSE for the subject. The skills I've learned in school has stuck with me, so I still do random pieces here and there."

"It was in school for me as well. I learned that I loved creating images with my hands from my eyes or my imagination. My interpretations are inspired by my soul, so drawing is just me being me."

"It's great to find meaning in something you love that can help you both financially and emotionally. I can tell that you'll make a fortune from your art. Although, it'd be great if more of them told a story."

"What do you mean?" I wondered.

"Out of all those pieces I saw, my favorite has to be your portrait of yourself. Not because it was drawn the best when there were others drawn better, but because it told a story to be solved. In the art, there's a crown on your head and a chain around your neck that's cut off because the drawing doesn't show below the neck. This would make some believe that the chain is plain, while others would think that there's more to it."

I felt my neck and remembered that I'm wearing the chain right now but its inside of my shirt.

"You're wearing it, right?" he asked.

"Yeah."

"Well then I presently have the opportunity of learning the answer behind the art."

I lifted the chain from out of my shirt and let it hang in the front of my chest.

"Amen," he reacted to the cross near my heart. "What a surprise and a great ending to a mystery."

"Yeah, that was deep. Now you've got me wondering how many strangers thought it was a plain chain too."

"Don't worry about that. Art that holds heavy meaning to you will always have a higher value than something done for the mere attention of strangers in the world."

"I know, I create my art from my emotions and make great use of them," I rested my bag aside and pulled my phone from my pocket. I opened the SoundCloud application and showed him my display photo of his favorite art by me.

"CoreyOB?" he questioned. "Wait, this app is for music. Don't tell me you're a singing artist too?"

"C'mon, bui. I'm showing you the photo, and you're looking everywhere else," I pulled my phone back to myself.

"No, no, I saw the selfie portrait you drew as your display photo. It was just hard to miss everything else around it. But since I saw what I saw, I've gotta ask. What does OB mean?"

"October's Best."

"That's a bold claim. I know I won't forget it. You're gonna let me hear a sample of your music, right?"

"Bei, it's just a hobby that helps me to further express my emotions. Beside my visual art, this one is a personal vocal journal displaying my passion toward everything that means something to me."

"If it's that personal, isn't it the best time to let me listen? We're still in our meeting phase, so no story in your songs will involve me or my complete understanding of them."

"You're trying to make me sound shy, but I'm not. I'm straightforward, and you're quite smart so I wouldn't put anything passed you. All you want to hear is how I sound singing, right?"

"Pretty much," he nodded.

To get beyond this, I opened my phone and said, "Okay, I'll only play one for you right now, and possibly send you some links later."

"Deal."

"Aight," I said while opening my tracks. "It's a choice between 'Far Away' and 'Where I'm From.'"

"'Where I'm From', sounds like the beginning of you. Let's start with that one."

I played the song from the phone's speaker and we both listened. About twenty-five seconds into it, more started talking and saying how he likes it already. I paused the track and asked him to hear it all first.

"You're right. Silence, my bad. I'll listen fully and then make comments after, okay? Continue."

"How about I run it back to the start?" I replayed the track and began it once more.

OB-
Yeah, Yeah, uhh, Yeah
Yeah, Yeah, Yeah-- Hey.

I feel like the most slept on where I'm from.
People they don't get along where I'm from.
Feel like it's so hard to get put on where I'm from.
Two-Four-Two where I was born where I'm from.
and I ain't ashamed of it.

I took all my struggles in the young and made a name from it.
Yeah, everybody saying I'mma prosper, know that day's coming.
I can't wait for it.
Yeah, yeah, I can't wait for it.
And if I ever make it,
I'mma make a way,
so all the kids,
they can make a name.
Ain't no leaders in the system trying to make a change,
Selling everybody dreams but it's still the same,
It may never change,
let's be innovate.
And all this talking I been doing,
hope it's not in vain.
I got nothing to lose and everything to gain.
Can you stand the reign?
Can you stand it, yeah?

And I'm the most slept on where I'm from.
People they don't really get along where I'm from.
Feel like it's so hard to get put on where I'm from.
Two-Four-Two, where I was born, where I'm from.
I just hope they miss me when I'm gone where I'm from,
Nineteen Ninety-Nine, a king was born where I'm from.
Hope everybody sings my song where I'm from.
Two-Four-Two, where I was born, where I'm from.

FYF-
Yeah, we got it popping, yo.
The young legend from the kingdom he rose.
A lot of obstacles and dangers on the path that he chose.
When the reality show, it's all a part of the growth.
If I don't make it, I just hope that they still proud of me, though.
You see, I grew up in a place that you can't live off a lot.
Even on the end clines, still no going up.
Put all I trust place beneath in Jehovah I trust.
Cause everything, I do for humans, it ain't never enough.
You see I got down on my knees, and He spoke to me,
I can't let these fake people get too close to me,
Living in this life of sin, ain't how it supposed to be,
And I refuse to let these frustr- get over me, nooooo.
I just can't lose hope.
Holding on the edge, but I can't let go.
I'm thankful to the people who then told it, and they know.
Cause every time I win, I remember ya for sho.

OB-
And I'm the most slept on where I'm from.
People they don't get along where I'm from.
Feel like it's so hard to get put on where I'm from.
Two-Four-Two where I was born where I'm from.
I just hope they miss me when I'm gone where I'm from.
Nineteen Ninety-Nine a king was born where I'm from.
Hope everybody play my song where I'm from.
Two-Four-Two where I was born where I'm from.
And I ain't ashamed of it, no.

Moore expressed his excitement at the end of it by saying, "That was very patriotic. Where I'm from was a great song. I hear a star in you, Romer,"

"You think so?"

"I felt so."

"Many people hear it and claim that I'm going places, but no elite has invested in my sound yet. You identified two voices on the track, right?"

"Yeah, I did. I could hear which one was you."

"Well, the other is a long-time friend from home, FYF Aaron. 'Where I'm From' is my creation, he's simply a featuring artist on it."

"His addition was spot-on, and he synced nicely with your sound. Trust me; you two are talented, and it's only going to get better from here. You have the voice already, Romer. You only need an instrumental artist, a studio, and an outstanding debut for you to be shining."

"Thanks for swelling my head, bei. It means a lot."

"I'm just spitting facts. You know you got it. Your lyrics are powerful too. Your lyrics represented our country and that's admirable. Keep it up, and eventually you'll be seen by all. Once you're a topnotch social influencing Bahamian and your voice holds power, your compassion will model in the new ages you sing for."

"Bui, when you speak, you place my thoughts on such a grand scale. How do you do that?" I'm surprised by how motivated I'm feeling.

"I'm just being me and seeing the end goal as usual."

"Well, fame isn't my end goal. Fortune to care for my loved ones is what I aspire for."

"Which is a great focus, but logically that comes with prominence. People hardly get away with being wealthy and completely anonymous."

"I expected as much. I've had many future thoughts on how to get there without changing or sacrificing who I am. For me, art is the safest route, and it's been my passion from forever to now. My love for it developed in my touch before my voice. For some reason, when I sketch an image, I'm proud to give back to the world, my interpretation of it."

"I think that sketching or singing are both capable of giving you a strong recognition. The choice is ultimately up to what you feel you want."

"Profiting from any of my art is not only up to me but up to our nation as well. If I'm not selling their taste, then I'll only flop out."

"Tell me about it," he reacted as though he related to it. "I'm glad you understand that, so you know what you have to do. Another smart thing would be to sell your art as your album covers."

"I've thought about that too," I shared.

"Then do it. Believe that we'll all eventually see you, and someday we will. I mean, that's how I think. From my perspective, you have everything you need to mark yourself into history. Whether it's within our country or in the lands beyond, the world is your canvas to have fun with. The best thing you could do for yourself is to make your signature matter. You can then paint a dot that will sell for a lot because it'll have your name beside it."

"Interesting," I reacted.

"Why are you wasting your time in this place?" He abruptly asked. "You seem very talented."

"At BTVI?" I wondered.

"Not the college itself but the subject you've chosen in it. You could've majored in one of your dominant talents."

"My dad is skilled in HVAC, and the curiosity in it rubbed off on me, I guess. Plus, it's business. Income is essential to survival in this world. My talents would do me more justice away from here than within it. Here, all we have to make ends meet is general labor. Besides, without my father's impact on my life, I doubt I'd even be at this school right now."

"It doesn't matter. I bet we'd still meet. You are who you are, and in any reality, I bet I would take to your character because I am who I am."

"You think so?" I grinned, realizing that we're super deep into conversation. "Yeah, you're pretty cool yourself. Not many people I can talk to who understand the creative struggle, you know?"

"I feel you there. It's always good to have a trade, and it's great if that trade is your dream. But if it's not, then I suggest using it to survive until you succeed in what'll fulfill you in life. You can be anything in the world, Romer, just never settle until you've lived."

"I won't do that for sure," My brows twitched, realizing that "You know you haven't talked about your art at all? Are you gonna show me anything, Moore? It's only fair."

"Dang, my turn already? I was just getting into your world but alright, let's focus on me for a bit." Moore took up his backpack and rested it at his feet between his legs. He reached into it and took out a thin laptop then said, "You'll have to take in a lot of information to understand. Time is what's needed to appreciate my work,"

"I don't think I have that much time," I thought, knowing that it's almost 9 p.m. "But whatever it is, I'll try to be quick with it,"

"W-Wow. I'm a little nervous," he hesitated in opening the laptop. "My talents are up and down along with my confidence. Sometimes I feel like I'm the best at what I do, and then other times, I feel like I'm not good enough. By the time my confidence rises again, I'd be slightly altered from the direction I wanted to carry my skills in. This is sometimes a blessing because it comes with a new light of ideas and information. Most times, it's a curse because it feels like I'm repeatedly beginning. You'll go further than me in life because you complete your creations, and I alternate from mine after a time."

"Nah, don't downgrade yourself like that. It sounds like you're just going in circles with minimal growth. If that's the case, take advantage of it. When you finish with a scene in your life, you should try connecting it to past events in hopes that it all comes back around to connecting to sense. If you can piece together your rise and falls, I think you'll realize that those shifting scenes will have created the appearance of one big scene. You'll then begin to understand the shaded past and the present light. One side will be known, and the other side would be-"

"-Midnight!" he exclaimed. I looked at him, wanting to laugh, but his deepened expression brought a further question. "Are you trying to tell me that Midnight's in my presence right now?"

"We still got a couple of hours before then," I said, seeing him still paused on me. "Listen, I don't know where you got midnight from, but you did say the answer at the end of your last question. One side will be known, and the other side would be now."

He laughed and said, "I mistook 'known' as in knowing, for 'noon' as in midday. Since we were talking about my talents going up and down, I started thinking about night and day."

"Oh, I can see why your mind arrived at that analogy."

"Don't worry, I understand you now." He at last opened his laptop and began searching for his work. "Just like you, I'm more than one kind of artist. One of my talents consists of capturing realized art and making it a reference image to your eyes. The other, however, is a put together that can be viewed in sound or silence. Silence has the highest compatibility to it since it's a compilation of many parts that can only be silently understood," he turned the work to me after opening it up. "Sound has the potential to bring confusion in this story if your eyes don't view the words themselves."

"CASTERS Book One (Chapter 12: True-Twins.)" I read.

"Wait, what?" He turns the laptop back to him and smiled saying, "Oh, I see. It's the right story but a previous title."

"That looks like a novel. So, you're an artist of the mind is what you're implying?"

"Yup," he handed the laptop to me, showing the title he just typed.

"'The Puzzle of a Twin Paradox,' inspired by ***Ein.S and Watts,"*** I read. "There's no written by or created by on it."

"It's an anonymous creation."

"And you're the anonymous author of it, Moore?"

"In the flesh."

"Bei, I've never met an author whose work I've read. Is this why you asked about the length of my time? You wanted me to read it all?" I asked, pointing out the issue that, "Time might not be on our side. How long's the story?"

"Too long, and it's uncompleted. No one's viewed it yet to tell me how long it takes to get through the incompletion."

"Oh, well, then I'll read it when it's done."

"It's been paused for a while, but I promise you, its limited completion is enjoyable. The center of the puzzle is thought provoking."

"Wait, awhile? If the story is that epic, then what's taking you so long to finish it?"

"I haven't experienced it yet, the ending. I started the story in our reality then took it into fiction, and to end it, I'll need to bring it back to reality."

"I'm not quite following, Moore."

"Um, alright. There are supposed to be nineteen chapters that that I label as Doors. The first two doors begin in the real world, and the last two doors end in the real world. The thing is, I've only written eighteen chapters so far. Why? Because The Puzzle of a Twin Paradox is told from the point of view of two similar boys. I've already written the beginning from through my eyes, now I must find him to complete the end from through his."

"Oh, that clarifies it. So, if you've done all you can and require an individual to complete what you can't, what are you doing to find them?"

"I—" he paused a bit, "I'm willing to show you right now," he pointed to the laptop on my lap.

"You're kidding, right? Pray this person is looking for you too, or this method of approaching the four hundred thousand of us one by one will take you forever. Showing your story individually to find that one is also risky; your work could get stolen."

"They'd bring it right back because the whole thing is just one big identity that you can't miss, ours, whoever he is," he emphasized.

"Okay, so it copyrights itself, good. But was it written to reach across other languages? Your person could also exist outside of our region, you know."

"If you have a better suggestion, I'm all ears, Romer."

"Publish it, bui. I believe if you do, whoever you're searching for will personally find you. Once united, you can put a close to your story and republish it. A remastered piece is just as cherished as its masterpiece since it clarifies without change, the notable original."

"A good idea, but still impossible."

"Because you think you need more than you, right? What if you don't? Right now, you're stuck in a loop because you need someone to finish the story for you. But you're also using that incomplete story to try to find that someone you need. That's a pending stagnant and an overall paradox to begin with."

"Let me guess. You have another suggestion?"

"Find an actor. Let him play the role of who you're looking for, and you can publish it with one real and the other a character."

"Brilliant! I didn't think of it like that. And then if I want, I can put at the start that I'm myself and my main character is an actor of someone else."

"Why not leave that out of the intro? If you do that, the one whom the message is for will receive it, while all others will receive nothing more than a puzzle."

"Hehe," he laughed. "I see what you did there. Alright, I'll try that, Romer."

I looked at the laptop, a little curious about the story after hearing how complex it could be. "The Puzzle of A Twin Paradox, huh?" I questioned, beginning to read, *"My eyes bring into vision a boy longing for happiness and fulfillment in his sight.,"* I read, thinking, "Wow, that's a deep beginning."

"C'mon, at least read it all first," he said, quoting me.

"You're right, silence," I laughed, catching on.

I looked to the laptop and began to read the beginning again, but then my phone abruptly rang. I looked at who was calling and told Moore that I had to answer.

"Yeah, what's up, Sis?"

"What's up? You never called."

I looked at the time on the laptop and said, "It's only 8:47 p.m...."

"And it's dark! I'm coming for now!" She alerted to me, then hung up.

"Your ride?"

"Yeah,"

"You have to go?"

"I'm afraid so," I closed down his laptop, showing that, "How unfortunate, bei. I wish it were earlier in the day so I could read enough to at least get into it."

"It's all good, OB." He took the laptop from my hand. Maybe it's just the wrong time to show you. Everything happens for a reason, you know. Come to think of it, I should text my sister Dassah and beg her to come and get me," he pulled out his cell and dove into his task. "She's probably tired as hell from work so I might have to bribe her best friend Desha this time. Ugh, I should've done this sooner." I laughed at his self-commentary, and he looked at me while knotting his brows. "Thought you were leaving,"

"Not yet, bei. She sounded like she was just on her way. I've got a little time to spare, I bet."

"What're you going to do with it?"

"Continue to wait. That's what I've been doing here while talking with you."

"Well, you can't read anymore, and I don't have a 'House on the Block' with me," he said, and I showed a lost expression. "Oh, right, it's my very first story and it's a short story. I wrote it when I was seventeen for a passing grade in English to graduate high school. Unexpectedly, I got an A."

"What's it about?"

"It's a supernatural/thriller about two kids breaking into a witch's house. It interested my former teacher Ms. Evans so much that she made me a short-lived celebrity among the seniors by reading it to each class. I must've liked how it felt because here I am, writing more stories today. Although, this newest one is very personal to me."

"It sounds like that moment changed your life. You've found your calling because of it."

"I think it did, you know. I must say goodbye to a couple of my teachers before I leave, if I could even find them. They're always being transferred around, ya know?"

"You're adamant about leaving our nation, huh?"

"Yeah, sometime this summer or fall."

"Are you ever coming back?"

"That depends on what I find out there. I'm on a mission, remember?"

"To find this person that your actor will portray, I know. Do you know how he looks?"

"I—" he paused and then scratched his head. "I don't know yet, but I'll know eventually. I dreamt that he gave me an extraordinary amount of ambitious power, and I've been looking for him ever since to give it back if possible."

"Wait, wait, so... you're looking for a dream boy that you're not even sure is real? And when you wanted me to read it earlier, you thought it could be me?"

"No, we were sharing our talents, remember? Don't get it twisted, I'm only saying that I know he's real. It's just not easy for you to believe."

I shook my head with a smile and said, "I'm open to an extent. But Moore, think about it. Isn't it reckless to leave where you know, possibly broke and literally on a dream?"

"Yeah, but everything I've learned about our modern world makes mundane sense. If I don't seek adventurous and possible truths beyond comprehension, I'll die of boredom before I die of old age."

"You're a daredevil, I'll give you that. In any event, you're casting hooks further than many who live here dare to. That's quite inspiring. I wish you luck, bei. I'd say to write a book about it, but you've already beaten me to it," we both laughed. "I'm curious about something else. Why'd you rename the title of the story from being CASTERS, was it?"

"How do I put this? CASTERS is a story of magic, science, and alchemy. I've published six chapters of it on the writing website called Wattpad, but I've eleven chapters in total. While I was writing 'CASTERS (Chapter 12: True-Twins.)', I accidentally took it beyond as far as I should've gone."

"Can you try to describe what happened inside of the chapter?"

"Well, while The Pyro Caster hovered in mid-air unconscious, another unconscious individual was blown across the air and ended up crashing into him.

When the two fell, the competition around recognized the other individual as being The X Caster, wearing his infamous mask. With both now unconscious, someone decided to remove his mask, and it was learned that the two Casters were, in fact, identical. Shortly after their reveal, their arm tattoos glowed and a unison spell casted from them. They were encased within a sapphire crystal shell and shielded by fire. In chapter twelve I was supposed to dive into the shell and tell a short story of two boys waking up in an unfamiliar world. I took it too far."

"Something unexpected happened inside of the crystal shell, didn't it?"

"Yup. The boys woke up and found themselves in an underground library, having no clue of who each other were, only that they were there. They worked together to get to the surface and as they did, they learned of their similarities. They sounded and acted in similar ways, so to avoid confusion, they decided to take turns naming each other so that there'd be more of a difference. After getting to the surface, they rose into a jungle, quiet, lifeless, and void of any living creatures. There were huge trees and ancient buildings under a midday Sun. They searched until it was nearly dark and found nothing more than the island's edge to edge surrounded by an ocean. Out of boredom, one identical asked the other to tell him a story. At the end of their first day, that terrifying story began to come true. They were nearly destroyed by what was created from imagination and trapped inside countless amounts of endless cycles. They eventually found a way to escape through a vortex in the ocean on day two. It then led them out into another world instead of breaking them back into the CASTERS story. And it turns out that all of that had to happen because those two boys ended up in the real world, and one of them created CASTERS. Me."

"Wow, that's insane. I see why you renamed the chapter to 'The Puzzle of A Twin Paradox' and made it its own story. So, what are you going to do now for your next attempt at chapter twelve?"

"There will be no next attempt."

"What?! Why? You can't just quit a series you've posted. Your fans won't like that."

"I didn't say I was quitting, but I am starting over. I'll begin the next part of CASTERS on chapter thirteen. I'll start in the past with a baby's birth on the same day as the two main characters who were trapped in the crystal. I'll begin CASTERS again with a fresh character, who'll be bestowed the mantle of protagonist of the series."

"If you're going to do that, then you're acknowledging that A Twin Paradox is still chapter twelve of CASTERS."

"I guess I am," he scratched his head. "I've always been an over-thinker, so I wasn't too surprised when I became an over-explainer. I'm no different from you. You're just better at telling shorter stories than me. A Song is to an Album as a Chapter is to a Book. I'm wondering, Romer, which one's your favorite song you've performed; Where I'm From or Far away?"

"Neither. My favorite song is written but still unperformed. It's called 'Dollar & A Dream.'"

"Unrecorded too?" I nodded. "Does it feature anyone?" he further asked

"Nah, it's just me."

"Perfect. I don't mind hearing the acoustic version before your studio recording."

"I see what you did there, but I might sound lil rusty, bei," I cleared my throat a bit. "I wasn't prepared to sing, but let's give it a shot," I closed my eyes while starting to remember the feeling and tone I felt while writing it. To the air I voiced, *"How I'm supposed to feel?"*

I've Been exposed to so much fake,
don't even know what's real.
Got some scars on my heart,
I'm still tryin' to heal.
So I just talk to God,
I don't know how to deal.
Emotions bottled up,
I keep 'em all concealed.

Save Me...
Save Me.

Cause I ain't been feeling like myself lately.
So much going on and it's crazy.
Got me concerned about my safety.
Try to focus on the highs and not the lows.
Life is unpredictable.
That's just the way it goes.
I just keep it pushing,
can't be stagnant on this road.
People tellin' me I could go places with these flows, yeah.

And I try to be open-minded,
but this world could be so cold.
I'm constantly reminded,
contract for my soul.
And I'll be damned if I ever signed it.
We were forced to stand the reign,

well I'm tryin to change the climate.
I'm talkin Rolex and diamonds,
I'm talkin all the finest.
I'm talk-in'

I ain't gotta worry,
cause I know I got it.
Living in the struggle in this life be tragic.
That's why I keep a couple hundred in the mattress.

That's what I call a Dollar & a Dream.
Always been the type to have a trick inside my sleeve.
Lay up on the mic and put my soul in melodies.
I put my heart and soul inside these melodies, make sure they're hearing me," I ended.

Just as I did, I stood up remembering that "My ride could be here at any minute, Moore." I placed my bag across me and stepped forward saying, "I've got to get to the gate."

"Wait a minute, Romer!" he paused me. I looked back to him as he stood from the bleachers and began to walk to me.

"It was nice to meet you, bei. But I've really gotta get going."

"Can I ask you a bold-ass question before you skip out?" He asked, holding a bewildered expression.

"How bold are we talking?"

"On the lines of you meaning something to me even though we just met," he said with an unmistaken seriousness.

"What's the question?" I wondered.

"Will you become my protagonist in 'The Puzzle of A Twin Paradox?'"

"You want to make me your main character? Why do you think I'm worthy of being the actor of this dream guy you're looking for?"

"You came up with that idea that I should use an actor, and it has willed me to publish much sooner. It only makes sense for me to ask you first, with no other person in mind. I truly appreciate you sharing your art with me today, and I see it clearly, your natural talents. If you agree, Romer, I can write a scenario where you did get to read 'The Puzzle of A Twin Paradox.' I can use that scenario as the prologue to the story, and the interaction we're having right now as the epilogue to the story, a scene where you didn't get to read The Puzzle."

"That's smart. In that way, you can place The Puzzle of A Twin Paradox at the center of the prologue and the epilogue."

"Right. But I can only achieve this through your agreement to collaborate with me. So how about it, Romer? Will you join me in an adventurous story that has the possibility to circle the ages for eternity?"

"That's a mouthful. You're basically asking me, a stranger, to become immortal in remembrance with you. You're right, a bold request indeed. It could end up being a great success for me or a great downfall to leave my name in your hands."

"Bei, I promise to write respect beside your name forever, as you're deserving of it. Many blazing stars had powerful sparks initiating them because in truth no star grows without a supporting name. Aladdin was to a Genie, as Arthur was to a Wizard, and *Mundi* was to *Da Vinci*, as *Keter* was to *Da'at*. If-"

"-Keter?" I questioned, remembering that "I've heard that name before."

"It means *The Regal Crown*. And Da'at means *Knowledge*. So, what do you say, Romer? Would you like to utilize my knowledge as a part of your rise to regal? You'll be helping me, as I'll be helping you."

When he said those words, I instantly remembered the dream I had before class. If I didn't voice it to my sis, I would have forgotten it completely by now.

When it suddenly came back to me, I looked straight into Moore's eyes wondering if he could be the Catalyst of the blue star.

"Hmmm," I thought to test him. "Let's supposed that I was this person, what would your reaction be to finding me?"

"What you're asking me to do is bolder than me just asking you to let me use your name."

"My name is as close to you asking me to be him, and now you can't do to me, what you would do to him? If you think it'll be that disrespectful to me, then I can't agree to play the role of your main character."

"Fine," Moore stepped to me with no hesitation and embraced me with a hug. "You win."

I wasn't aware that it happened until it was happening. A daunting force began to flow into my emotions and caused the reaction in me. The longer he held me the more my confidence rose.

"This is what I would do," he confirmed. "Then I'd say, thank you so much for existing and proving me sane. It's great to see that you're happy, healthy, and alive with a family that loves you wholeheartedly, brother. You've fulfilled my life by setting me free from the shackles of living in a theoretical possibility alone. For this, you're my bond forever, Midnight."

A radiant energy overflowed me just as he removed himself, and now I suddenly feel like I can do anything.

Moore's eyes widened, looking at my paused expression as I'm still trying to process all that's happening in me.

"You're not upset, right?" He wondered.

"No," I could barely speak.

"Your face says otherwise." Somehow, I managed to get a grasp of myself and regain control over my emotions.

"Midnight?" I asked. "Is that the name of the protagonist you're looking for?" I needed clarification.

"When I saw him in the dream I had before I fell into this world, that's what it was. I believe he'll know it's me because he gave me so much power and told me to embrace him as I've done once before. He said we'd become equal again, and I'm guessing that means I'd give his power back to him. It's just a theory, and I'm not entirely sure how it all works. I guess I'm just waiting for someone to say that they felt a reaction from me when I do it."

I kept my reaction within, but I'm shocked that everything has just been confirmed. Moore's dream and my dream match.

"Encounters change your life, and most times it's the course of it, Moore," I responded to him. "If I was the dream person you were looking for, what would change in your life right now?" I asked to further test his actions.

"Well, Romer, I wouldn't need to publish anymore. I'd just give the book to you since the whole thing is to find you and give you what is yours. Heck, I wouldn't need to leave for Canada this fall anymore either, cause the search for Midnight would end right now. I'd feel fulfilled to know that my dream was true and happy to not be alone in believing in it. Believing in something intangible together is longer lasting than believing in it alone." He explained. "Be honest with me, Romer. Are you asking me all of this because you felt something just now?"

"Nah, just your warmth," I untruthfully replied and diminished the hope he had in his eyes. "I'm sorry."

"For being honest, Romer? Don't be."

"I'll be your protagonist, Moore. You can publish using me, aight?"

"For real?"

"Yeah, bei."

"Thanks, yo. I appreciate this opportunity."

"I appreciate it too. Grab your things and walk with me. I want to ask you something else, bei."

Moore closed his backpack and collected it. He made his way back to me and we began to walk to the gate.

"What is it?" He wondered.

"When you leave for Canada, when are you coming back?"

"I honestly don't know."

"Do you think it's right to ask me to act as someone so close to you and then leave the country forever? At least set an alarm for when to return home. Don't get lost searching for ghosts in the first world."

"An alarm, huh? Okay, I'll give myself about three and a half years. If I haven't found who I'm looking for by then, I'll return."

"Three and half years from now?"

"No, from the beginning of this year, Twenty Eighteen. So, I'll come home at the center of Twenty-Twenty-One."

"Make that a promise."

He laughed and said, "I promise, bei."

When we stopped at the gate's exit, I thought to ask about something I'm still unsure of. "Since we're getting to know each other, what's your real name?"

"Dimonlee Moore," he answered, and I knew it was true. It was the same name I read on the test paper we handed in this evening. "My family call me Dimon for short." If I hadn't seen the spelling of it earlier, I'd think he was referencing the gemstone.

"Nice to fully meet you, Moore. My name is Corey Romer."

"I kind of figured. CoreyOB, remember?"

"So, why call yourself, Romeo?"

"Victor Romeo was an alias I came up with, just to be myself in the disguise of someone more confident in college. Romeo is just the rearrangement of my last name, Moore. However, Victor is the name of my grandfather, so because it's in my line, I used it."

"Your given name is unique and unforgettable. I think you should keep using, Dimon. I was a little suspicious before, but I'm glad you never tried to hide your real name from me."

"Don't worry, Romer. I'll play characters but, in the end, I'll always be myself, especially to someone real like you."

A vehicle pulled in through the entrance of the gate and as it came around to the exit, I saw that it was my sister.

"Let's go, Corey," she braked the car while sounding pissed.

"Take my number," I said to Moore, since I have no time to add nothing more. He pulled out his phone to type in the seven digits as I walked to the passenger side of the car. "Message me, and I'll save you," I opened the door and sat inside. "I'll see you later, bro, or in three and a half years."

My sister gassed the vehicle out of the college quickly, and we were gone from there in less than a minute.

My mind gradually moved onto the matter of how mad she probably is, but I'm also wondering why.

"Don't ever try that with me again, Corey, or you'll walk home."

"Okay, what? It's 9 p.m. and we agreed on 9 p.m."

"Who agreed? I called you when it was barely noon today, and you said that you'd call me later, when you were ready. How much later were you going to wait?"

"Wait, at noon?" I questioned. "You must be mistaken, Sis. You dropped me off at the college at 6 p.m., only three hours ago. I had an evening class, remember?"

"No, it was this morning. You had a morning class."

"Someone has to be wrong, and I'm not fighting you on this. If you want to think that I messed up, then okay, you're right." I let that die.

My phone vibrated, and a message came through with a link to a song.

'Yo, it's Moore. I was going to let you read my story to some of the epic orchestral music I listen to while I write them, but we missed the opportunity. Instead, here's the song that opens the story and ends it as well. Hope you find enjoyment in hearing it. Safe travel home and goodnight, Romer.'

'I will listen to it now." I replied. *'Get home safely as well. Goodnight, Moore.'*

I plugged in my headphones and clicked the link, and it took me to a song called *'Dreams'* by *Nuages*. It started to play right away and opened with a quote.

'Let's suppose that you were able, every night, to dream any dream you wanted to dream.

And you would, naturally as you began on this adventure of dreams, you would fulfill all your wishes.

You would have EVERY kind of pleasure that you could conceive. And after several nights, you would say, "Well, that was pretty great." But now let's um-- let's have a surprise.

Let's have a dream which isn't under control. Where something is gonna happen to me that I don't know what it's going to be.

Then you would get more and more adventurous, and you would make further and further out gambles as to what you would dream.

And finally, you would dream, where you are now.'

A serene beat came on after the quote and drifted my thoughts to beyond the cosmos.

"So, did you find it?" My sister asked, pulling me back to reality. I paused the song and unplugged one of my earphones.

"Find what?" I asked.

"The Catalyst, of course. We talked about it this morning," sis clarified.

Although it was three hours ago that we talked, I knew what she meant. It's so weird that we both remember having the same conversation but two different times in today. If I really was there from this morning, what would I have done all day?

"Oh, you mean the blue star," I smiled shaking my head. "Yeah, I think I found him, and oddly enough he was looking for me too."

"Wait, him? So, the Catalyst was a person after all?"

"Yup, and he had a dream just like mine, of seeing me before his birth."

"You're messing with me, right?" she doubted.

"I'm not."

"You want me to believe that a shared dream literally came true? That's unbelievable." She's shocked.

"I'm not forcing you to believe it."

"How did he react when you told him that he was the Catalyst?"

"I couldn't tell him that."

"Why? You want us to go back? I'm not even upset anymore. This is very interesting."

"I can't tell him right now. I'm presently too much of an intervention for him. He'd give up on publishing what he wrote and even traveling away to learn something more if I spoke up now. I can't say anything that'll rob him of these future experiences. He seems careless, reckless, and like he moves with his heart. He's willing to give up everything for this dream to be true, but in reality, we need to eat, and we need to thrive. I'll let him go for now. He'll return home eventually, and before that happens, I'll be to him as who he'll think I'm acting as."

"And who does he want you to act as?"

"His brother."

I placed the earpiece back in, and I think she got the picture because I managed to continue playing the track without further interruption.

I'm sorry for being dishonest and refusing your feelings today, Moore. What I felt was not imagined, and so I do acknowledge you. But you must live this last adventure before I tell you the truth, brother. When you finally come back and publish *'The Puzzle of A Twin Paradox'*, we'll rise together inside of a legend of The Bahamas.

'If you awaken from this illusion and you understand that

Black implies white.

Self implies other.

Life implies death.

You can feel yourself, not as a stranger in the world.

Not as something here on probation.

Not as something that has arrived here by fluke.

But you can begin to feel your own existence as absolutely fundamental.

What you are basically,

Deep, deep down.

Far, far in.

Is simply the fabric and structure of Existence Itself.' -Watts.

:oo1)

Printed in the United States
by Baker & Taylor Publisher Services